LINE OF GLORY

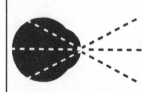

This Large Print Book carries the
Seal of Approval of N.A.V.H.

LINE OF GLORY

A NOVEL OF THE ALAMO

THOMAS D. CLAGETT

THORNDIKE PRESS
A part of Gale, a Cengage Company

GALE
A Cengage Company

Farmington Hills, Mich • San Francisco • New York • Waterville, Maine
Meriden, Conn • Mason, Ohio • Chicago

Thorndike Press® Large Print Western.
The text of this Large Print edition is unabridged.
Other aspects of the book may vary from the original edition.
Set in 16 pt. Plantin.

LIBRARY OF CONGRESS CIP DATA ON FILE.
CATALOGUING IN PUBLICATION FOR THIS BOOK
IS AVAILABLE FROM THE LIBRARY OF CONGRESS

ISBN-13: 978-1-4328-6136-0 (hardcover)

Published in 2019 by arrangement with Thomas D. Clagett

Printed in Mexico
1 2 3 4 5 6 7 23 22 21 20 19

For Chester and Donna Clagett,
my brother and his wife

"The cause of Philanthropy, of Humanity, of Liberty and human happiness throughout the world, called loudly on every man who can to aid Texas . . ."
—Daniel Cloud, letter to his wife, December 26, 1835

"Do not be uneasy about me, I am with my friends."
—David Crockett, letter to his family, January 9, 1836

"We will rather die in these ditches than give it up to the enemy."
—Colonel James Bowie, letter to Governor Henry Smith, February 2, 1836

"To the People of Texas and all Americans in the world—I am besieged by a thousand or more of the Mexicans under Santa Anna. I have sustained a

continual bombardment & cannonade for 24 hours and have not lost a man. The enemy has demanded a surrender at discretion, otherwise, the garrison are to be put to the sword, if the fort is taken. I have answered the demand with a cannon shot, and our flag still waves proudly from our walls. I shall never surrender or retreat. . . . VICTORY or DEATH."
—Colonel William Barrett Travis, letter, February 24, 1836

"A horrible carnage took place."
—Lieutenant José Enrique de la Peña, diary entry regarding the battle of the Alamo

"It was but a small affair."
—General Antonio López de Santa Anna, after the battle, March 6, 1836

CHAPTER ONE

Stepping through the open oak doors of the old Alamo chapel, Susannah Dickinson raised her hand to shield her eyes, not so much from the brightness of the sun lowering in the sky, but from that awful red flag. There in the distance, peeking over the edge of the west wall, it fluttered atop the church tower in San Antonio de Béxar. That ugly flag had flown there for the last twelve trying days.

Across the way, the men gathered at the south end of the main courtyard, their rifles and muskets in hand. Word had spread quickly that Colonel Travis had something he wanted to tell them.

Nestled in the crook of her arm, Susannah held her baby daughter, Angelina, wrapped in a soft Mexican blanket. She felt Angelina's tiny hand tug at the cameo brooch pinned at the throat of the high collar of her dark-blue cotton dress. Glancing down, she noticed a few strands of her own brown hair had come loose from the bun she'd tied it into and tucked them back behind her ear. She was neither frail nor stout but somewhere in between. She always thought herself plain of face, though her husband still said she was the most beautiful woman he'd ever seen.

Inside the chapel, her husband gave a shout. "Let's move along, men."

Almeron Dickinson, who commanded the three cannons at the top of the rough earth and timber ramp at the back of the chapel, walked outside with his nine gunners. That rascally firebrand, Lieutenant James Bonham, had been assigned to Almeron's battery on his return to the fort. Only two days before he had ridden through the Mexican lines, bringing a letter from Major Robert Williamson telling Travis that help was on the way. But Almeron had told Susannah that Bonham had been decent enough to offer Travis the truth — that Williamson was still organizing a troop — and that, in his opinion, Williamson's letter was, at best, only a gesture of hope. As Bonham passed by, he smiled and addressed her by name. She had to admit he was a very handsome man with his piercing brown eyes and a charming smile. It was a pity that his ears stuck out so.

Hurrying to catch up with Bonham and the others was a private by the name of Tylee who had a lazy eye and hailed from New York, and his friend, Anthony Wolf, a gangly fellow with big hands from San Felipe on the Brazos River. Wolf had two tow-headed boys, twelve-year-old Nathan and Aleck, eleven. She'd seen them earlier inside the chapel looking for "anything iron" they'd said, but she had no idea where they were now. Gregorio Esparza passed her, removing his sombrero, saying, *"Con su permiso."* She nodded and said, "Of course." They always exchanged these pleasantries whenever he walked by her. After five years living in Mexican Texas, she had come to appreciate the proud manners of the Mexicans born here. *Tejanos* they were called. As Gregorio and the others headed to join the rest of the defenders in the big courtyard, Susannah felt Almeron pat her on the fanny, followed by a reassuring wink. That always made her smile. It was one of the few things that lightened her worries.

A moment later, she saw Travis appear before the men, ramrod straight, dressed in his fine blue coat with a red sash tied around his waist and a sword at his side, along with black boots, black bow tie, and

11

tall silk hat. Susannah was certain each item was no doubt freshly shined and cleaned and brushed by his Negro slave, Joe.

Colonel William Barrett Travis. Almeron spoke highly of Travis, saying that he'd managed to keep the garrison together in spite of Colonel Fannin's failure to arrive with his promised four hundred troops. Susannah could not stand Travis. She thought him rude, abrupt, and very full of himself. At twenty-six he was only four years older than her. Some women were impressed by the fact he was a lawyer, and manly in appearance with wavy, red hair, but not Susannah. It was bad enough he acted as though he was better than everybody else, but what galled Susannah was that he had left his wife and two children and a pack of debts back in Alabama. As if that weren't shameful enough, the man made no secret of his consorting with whores since coming to Texas. To her mind, Travis was not an honorable man.

A cool breeze made Susannah draw the blanket over Angelina's head, covering her light-colored hair. Susannah wished she'd put on her shawl but didn't feel like going back inside the chapel to retrieve it.

"Come on, boys! We don't want them waiting on us," David Crockett said in his

Tennessee drawl.

"We're coming!" one of his men said.

"Mrs. Dickinson," Crockett said as he went by, tipping his coonskin cap to her. His men hurried past, greeting her, some nodding, others tipping their hats, as well.

Susannah was so glad that Crockett and his Tennesseans were here. Well, most of them were from Tennessee, anyway. It was always good to hear friendly voices from back home.

She noticed four or five men remained behind at the palisade. She recognized them as some of the regular soldiers who had come with Travis to the Alamo. He had assigned most of his crack shots to defend the wooden palisade, it being the weakest spot of the fort. Those sharpshooters included these regulars, and Crockett and his men. Travis must have told those regulars to stay there, she decided. As much as she hated allowing Travis credit for anything, leaving the walls unattended might otherwise give Santa Anna and his Mexican soldiers the wrong idea.

Looking at the palisade was disheartening. Almeron had told her that most of the Alamo walls were two to three feet thick and nine feet high or better and made out of adobe bricks. The walls of the chapel were nearer to four feet thick and sturdy, built out of stone blocks. Franciscan monks had seen to its construction. "They intended it to last," Almeron had said. But the palisade was nothing but a row of timbers sunk into the ground, standing a little taller than a man and lashed tight together. It stretched over a hundred feet from the chapel to the low barracks that made up part of the south wall, along with the main gate and the small house that Colonel Bowie took as his quarters.

Outside the palisade lay a tangle of cut down cypress trees, maybe fifteen or so, she guessed. Captain Jameson had seen to it that the branches had been sharpened to deadly points and set facing out. "Those fancy-dressed Mexican soldiers'll catch hell if they try getting through them," Captain Jameson had said. When was that? Susannah wondered. Ten days ago? Eleven? She could not recall. But ever since then, each day, Susannah had seen more and more Mexican soldiers, some wearing blue coats and white trousers, some in red coats with black trousers, and others dressed in all white. And every one of them surrounded the Alamo. Like a noose drawing tighter.

A young boy gave her a nod from the edge of the group in the main courtyard. Galba

14

Fuqua was his name. She returned his gesture with a brief smile. He and about thirty others had ridden in a few nights ago. The good Lord had been watching over them, for they made it through the Mexican lines with nary a scratch. They were friends and neighbors of her and Almeron from the town of Gonzales, about seventy miles east on the San Carlos River.

Susannah still could not understand why, with all the messages that Travis had sent out pleading for aid, Galba Fuqua and those other thirty friends were the only ones in all of Texas to come to the Alamo to help with the fight.

The creak of one of the chapel's heavy, oak doors made Susannah look over her shoulder. She saw Gregorio Esparza's wife, Ana, bringing her four children outside. At eight, Enrique was the oldest. His little brothers, Manuel and Francisco, held onto his mother's skirt, and Ana held the hand of her four-year-old daughter, Maria. Ana adjusted the *rebozo* she wore, pulling it closer about her shoulders. That *rebozo* was nearly as black as her hair. Susannah turned back toward the gathering men, tucking Angelina in closer to her chest.

"What do you think Colonel Travis is going to tell them?" Susannah asked.

"I can tell you what he won't say. He will not surrender, not that one," Ana said.

"No," Susannah said. "He won't do that." She saw several men headed for Jim Bowie's quarters next to the main gate. "When do you think the attack will come?" she asked.

"Very soon," Ana said quietly. "I don't think the saints who watch over the chapel can protect us much longer."

Susannah knew she was referring to the stone statues of the four saints standing in the alcoves of the chapel façade, two each on either side of the main doors. Since the siege began, she'd seen Anna and her children come out at least two times a day, get down on their knees, and pray to them by name: Francis, Dominic, Ferdinand, and Anthony. These Mexican Catholics sure put a lot of store in these dead folks, always asking them for help. God was good enough for Susannah.

"This morning," Ana continued, "my husband told me he counted over four thousand *soldados* and at least three hundred lancers. They fire their cannonballs at us and play the 'Degüello' for twelve days and nights. And suddenly, a few hours ago, they stop. Santa Anna, he has a reason." She spat on the ground. *"Hijo de puta."*

Susannah smiled. Mexican cussing was

16

one of the other things that made her feel better. Not that she approved of swearing and taking the Lord's name in vain, but Ana had just called General Santa Anna the son of a whore. And though Susannah agreed with the sentiment, they were not words she would use, but somehow Mexican curses had a lilt to them. She found that appealing. Seemed all the Americans who came to Texas figured out the meaning of those Mexican cuss words right quick, too.

Ana, children in tow, moved up next to Susannah and said, "I believe the soldiers will be coming soon. *Sí, muy pronto.* I am surprised Santa Anna has waited this long."

Twelve days, Susannah thought. Had it only been twelve days? It seemed much longer. Much longer . . . And before that, a lifetime . . .

Did we make a mistake, Almeron and me? She wondered. Was this my fault? Is this our punishment?

A shout of "Make way!" drew her out of those dark thoughts.

She saw six men carrying Colonel Jim Bowie out of his quarters on his wooden cot. Only a few weeks ago, he had been elected by the men to command instead of Travis — who didn't seem too happy about it. But what did he expect? Bowie had brought over a hundred volunteers to the Alamo before Travis rode in like he was Jesus Christ himself with his thirty soldiers. And when Santa Anna and his army showed up, he and Travis patched up their differences and agreed to both be in command, evident as it was to Susannah that these two got along about as amiably as a badger and a bear. Not to mention that Bowie liked his liquor and Travis didn't approve, as he never touched a drop. But it was strange and disheartening that the very next day, Bowie fell so ill he dropped face down in the courtyard. Doc Pollard couldn't say what it was, only that the malady was of a peculiar nature and affected his lungs. Whatever Bowie had contracted, he was now lying flat on his bed, with a man hoisting each corner and one on each side. She could see a blanket covered his legs, but, he being a tall man, his boots stuck out over the edge of the bed. The crowd parted, and he was set down at the front of the assembly. As he sat up, a coughing fit overtook him.

Susannah heard Enrique ask his mother something in Spanish.

"No," Ana replied, "*Papá* will not send us away. I told him, if he stays, we all stay."

Susannah glanced over and saw the determination in Ana's dark eyes and wished she

had even a little of her iron will. The sound
of Bowie's voice made Susannah turn.

Chapter Two

James Taylor rested the butt of his long rifle on the hard clay ground, cupped his hands over the muzzle, and waited. It occurred to him right then that he'd turned twenty-two the previous week. With work details and guard duties and the whole damn Mexican Army camped outside the walls, it had slipped his mind.

To his right stood his brother Edward, two years older, and on his left was his kid brother, George, though he'd always been called Georgie. James decided there was no point in mentioning his birthday now. But they'd have a real celebration later, after this business with Santa Anna was settled.

"At least the damn Mexes ain't playing that damn stinking tune of theirs," Edward said. "Sounded like they's killing a hog."

"I get the chance," James said, "I'm going to stick one of them bugles up Santa Anna's ass."

"Be proud to hold him down for you," Georgie said and wiped his nose on the sleeve of his blanket coat.

James saw the weariness on their faces. Hell, it was on everybody's face. But there was tension in the air, too. He could feel it, and he didn't like it. An attack was certain to come and soon, and every man inside the Alamo knew it. Only yesterday the damn Mexican soldiers were building scaling ladders, lashing them together with rope right out in the open so everybody could see them doing it. Of course, they were careful to stay back better than two hundred yards so they would be out of range of both musket and rifle. The bastards.

"Maybe Fannin's coming. Think that might be it?" Georgie whispered anxiously.

"That would be good news," James said as he scratched his dark side-whiskers.

Edward hung his head and closed his eyes. "I got an idea."

"What?" Georgie asked.

"Keep quiet."

Georgie frowned at Edward and shot a look at James.

"We'll find out soon enough, Georgie," James said.

As far as James could tell, aside from the sentries manning the walls keeping watch in case of any Mexican advance, nearly every man in the garrison had assembled.

"You notice anything?" Edward asked. "It's all Travis's men on the walls."

Glancing about, James quickly realized his brother was right. Travis's regulars manned posts up on the north wall and along the east and west walls. Looking behind him at the low barracks, he saw a couple of men on the main gate and also a big man and a fellow with a pipe in his mouth standing watch at the eighteen-pounder cannon at the southwest corner. Glancing toward the chapel, he caught sight of a few boys at the wooden palisade, and at least one more on top of the chapel.

"Guess whatever he wants to say is just for us volunteers," James said.

Georgie nudged him, pointing his chin toward the hospital. Doc Pollard was helping to bring out the sick who could walk to join the group. The hospital was just a few yards away. It and the chapel were the tallest buildings in the fort.

Movement on the hospital roof drew James's attention where a couple more of Travis's regulars stood watch. One was near the flagpole. Hanging from it was a white banner with a big blue star in the middle. Some Latin words were written on the flag.

Travis had run up three different flags over the last twelve days. He kept a flag flying day and night, he said, to let Santa Anna know they were still here. One was the flag of a bunch of volunteers calling themselves the New Orleans Greys. Some rich businessman in Texas or Louisiana, James couldn't remember which he'd heard it was, had outfitted them with muskets and some old grey uniform waistcoats and sealskin hunting caps. They had planned to join up with Colonel Fannin once they reached Texas, but in all the celebrating and drinking they did in New Orleans that night, only about half the company managed to board the ship before it sailed the next morning, leaving the other half behind. They were the ones with the flag. Once most of them managed to sober up, they got passage on another ship. After they landed in Texas, they went looking for Fannin, wherever the hell he was, and ended up in San Antonio de Béxar, the day before the Mexican army did. Those Greys high-tailed it into the Alamo, along with Travis and Bowie and James, his brothers, and all the others fighting for Texas. Figuring this fight would be as good as any, the Greys handed Travis their flag. It was blue with a gold fringe and an eagle in the center. Bold lettering read

23

"First Company of Texas Volunteers from New Orleans."

Another flag Travis flew had red and white stripes and a whole mess of writing on it. James couldn't recall the words or where it had come from, or this one with the blue star and Latin words. He and his brothers didn't know any Latin either, but Bill Garnett, a Baptist preacher who hailed from Virginia, said he did. He told them that the words on the flag, *"Ubi, libertas habitat, ibe nostra patria est"* meant "Where liberty dwells, there is my country." James had wondered why they didn't put the English words on the flag, but as he hadn't been there when it was being sewn, he decided there was no point in worrying about it.

Bowie coughed that terrible cough, and James saw he had propped himself up on his cot. He was so pale and sweaty, holding a blood stained, wadded up bandana tight in his fist over his mouth. Like Ma had done in the weeks before she died.

Travis waited. He appeared more anxious than James had seen him before, pacing back and forth. That slave of his, Joe, stood off behind him. He held Travis's double-barreled shotgun in his hands.

"Speak your peace, Colonel," Bowie said and wiped his mouth.

James adjusted his hat. Beside him, Edward leaned on his rifle.

Travis raised his arm and pointed toward the red flag beyond the west wall of the Alamo.

"Santa Ana's blood-red banner waves from atop the church tower there declaring no quarter," Travis said. "It threatens not only us but also dares to make all of Texas a wasteland. And yet, here we have stood, rebellious and defiant."

James saw Georgie glance over at him, a spirited smile on his face.

"Each of us has our reasons for coming to Texas," Travis continued, raising his voice so all the men were certain to hear him. "A new start for many of us, the promise of a fresh beginning. It is my belief that the fate of that promise might well be in our hands. We have held the enemy though our numbers are few. We have not lost a single man, but we have cost the enemy many. We have heard their drums and bugles and have withstood their bombardments."

Travis paused, and James could swear he was gauging the spirit of each man before he continued.

"The enemy will attack and soon, that" — Travis halted and cleared his throat, like the words had gotten caught in there — "that is

25

certain. And while my hopes for aid and reinforcements ebb, my desire to fight to the last remains firm.

"By holding Santa Anna here, by protecting our country, our families, and our friends from those who would savage liberty to maintain tyranny, you have purchased twelve precious days for General Houston, his army, and the life of Texas. I could not ask for better, or braver men than I see before me." A proud smile crossed his face.

"I remain here with my command. We shall make our stand and sell our lives dearly." There was steely resolve in his voice. "Dearly." He paused, looking from one end of the group to the other.

"And now," he continued, "I ask each of you to make your own choice, to stay or to go."

He took his sword and drew a line in the dirt before him.

"Let there be no doubt," he said. "Any who choose to stay, step forward across this line. Whatever your decision, you are all honorable men."

A moment passed, and James blew out a hearty breath. He and his brothers had come to the Alamo for a new chance, a new life. They each had plans once this fight was over. James placed his hand on the tomahawk he kept hanging from his belt. He'd found it out on the prairie a few years back inside an old chest that had likely fallen off of a settler's wagon. The weathered condition of the chest led James to believe it had been lost for some time. And it was a good tomahawk.

James glanced at his brothers and said, "Like Pa always said, 'Bend your knee to no man.' "

"All together," Georgie said.

James saw the hesitation on Edward's face. "Something wrong?"

Edward sniggered. "Not a thing."

James and his brothers started across the short distance to the line and Travis, but a lanky fellow from Ohio named Holland, carrying a Brown Bess musket and wearing a beegum hat, was already on the other side of the line, a satisfied grin on his face.

Crossing the line, James turned and faced other defenders coming across the line. There was Crockett, carrying "Betsy," the name he gave his long rifle, and his Tennessee boys. Captain Jameson and Preacher Garnett and Cleland Fleet and Hardin Bishop and others assigned to the north wall, where James and his brothers were also stationed, came over. James was glad to see them all, though he heard Edward make a dissatisfied grunt when the five Tejanos who were also posted with them on the north wall came walking toward them. There were a couple of other Tejanos in the fort. One was assigned to the eighteen-pounder at the southeast corner. The other was on the battery on top of the chapel. Most had come in with Captain Juan Seguín. But Seguín had been sent out to find Houston and bring back reinforcements. He had not returned. These Tejanos didn't talk much to the *"americanos,"* leastways as far as James could tell. But they despised Santa Anna more than the *"americanos"* did. "Would you kiss the hand that beats you? Or lick the boot that kicks you?" James had heard one of them say. And they were fighting their own people, too, their own blood in some cases. Like the stories James remembered Pa telling about families that split over siding with the British back during the Revolution. Well, these Tejano boys were surely taking a big chance, which earned them James's respect.

The five Tejanos from the north wall followed a big, nasty-faced sergeant named Juan Abamillo. He held a long rifle in his hands and was a crack shot. He also carried something that looked a lot like a tomahawk in his belt, except instead of an iron blade tied onto the end of the stick, like the one James carried, it held a sharpened triangle-shaped stone. A vicious looking thing. When James had asked about it, Abamillo told him it was a war hawk club that he'd taken from a Comanche warrior. "Was he already dead when you took it?" James had asked. "No," Abamillo had said. "After."

More men came over the line. Those Gonzales boys. And the Greys from New Orleans, too. A pudgy fellow from Denmark with butter-colored hair, Lieutenant Zanco, crossed, and that was good since he saw to keeping all the cannons and other firearms in working order. Well, him and Major Evans, the chief ordnance officer. James saw Evans cross, too. And Sergeant Johnnie McGregor stepped over. James enjoyed it when that Scotsman played a tune on his bagpipes to drown out the Mexican horn blowing and drum banging. Sometimes Crockett broke out his fiddle and joined the beefy sergeant. But they hadn't done that for a while now.

"We're with you, Colonel," one of the sick men from the hospital said as he helped a friend over the line.

Captain Dickinson and his men came over, taking a spot near James and his brothers. James saw Dickinson look toward his wife, who was standing in front of the chapel holding their baby girl. James couldn't see Dickinson's face, but he did spy hers, and he knew a worried look when he saw one.

Bowie weakly called out, "Boys, carry me over that line, for I intend to die fighting."

James figured there were close to a hundred men still standing across the way, and it appeared that every one of them followed Bowie as he was brought across. And James could swear he saw Bowie nod at Travis, and damned if Travis didn't stand a little straighter, a little taller than he had been.

James was standing taller, for that matter. Made a difference, too. Edward was actually smiling for the first time that James had seen in over a week. And Georgie was grinning, as well, but his attention was on Bowie's quarters, the small house to the right of the main gate, where his two caretakers were watching from the window. Juana Alsbury and her younger sister, Gertrudis Navarro, were the stepsisters of Bowie's wife, who had passed away some years before. Juana was married to some doctor fellow. Gertrudis looked like she was near about seventeen and real pretty. She tilted her head down, raised her eyes, and gave Georgie a little smile, and that's when her sister pulled her away from the window. Georgie was mighty sweet on Gertrudis. Had been from the moment he set eyes on her. Twelve days ago. James had told him pursuing that gal might not be a good idea. But Georgie didn't want to listen. Hell, he was only a kid.

Then James caught sight of old Moses Rose standing across the way. All by himself.

Like James and brothers, Moses was assigned to the north wall. He was a Frenchman and told stories about being in Napoleon's army over in Europe — a grenadier he said he was — and James and Georgie liked hearing those tales. It was hard not to like Moses. His first name was actually Louis, but everybody called him Moses on account of he had so much white hair, and being fifty-five or fifty-six. Maybe fifty-seven. Moses said he didn't know for sure. But it was certain he was one of the oldest men in the Alamo.

It was hard to miss Moses, and not because he was standing over there all alone. Moses was stout with a raw, leathery face. Some believed he could pass for Mexican if it weren't for the thick graying moustache he wore because, unlike Mexicans, he kept the ends twirled out straight by using any kind of grease, though he preferred lard when he could find it. He wore it that way, he said, because the Emperor Napoleon had ordered all the grenadiers to have long moustaches, and that was why he swore he'd never shave his off. He also stood over six feet tall, one of the tallest men James had ever seen. Him and Colonel Bowie. Come to think of it, Abamillo was nearly as tall as them, too.

"Come on over here with us, Mose," Bowie growled, waving his hand. "We'll give Santa Anna and his men a fight they'll always remember."

Moses shook his head.

Crockett spoke up. "I don't much care to be hemmed up, but I wouldn't want them catching me out there, either. Stay with us."

"Je suis désolé, mes amis," Moses said, holding up his hand. "I cannot do it."

James was about to speak up when Travis stepped forward.

"Mr. Rose has made his choice," Travis said, "and we shall respect that."

"Merci, Colonel," Moses said.

"Wait until after nightfall," Travis said. "Darkness will be your only friend out there."

Travis dismissed the men.

"Less than two hundred of us, and he's running out," Edward grumbled as they

32

headed back to the north wall.

"I sure hate to see him go," Georgie said.

James figured he'd try talking to Mose shortly. After the old soldier had time to think things over, he'd see how important it was to stay.

CHAPTER THREE

Susannah carried Angelina inside the chapel to the sacristy room that Travis had given them as quarters. There was a wooden table and a wobbly chair, as well as an overturned barrel to sit on. The sagging rope bed, only big enough for one, served as Angelina's berth. Almeron had told Susannah to take it and sleep with Angelina, but Susannah said no, that she would sleep next to him. Almeron had gotten some hay from the horse corral by the east wall and placed it on the floor for their bedding. It was a far cry from the big cabin he had built for her near the riverbank on their land back in Gonzales. The cabin also had a comfortable featherbed she had gotten very used to over the years. Maybe it was all still there, unless it had been burned. As far as Susannah knew now, the only possessions she and Almeron owned were his flintlock pistol and rifle and the clothes on their backs.

Angelina had fallen asleep in Susannah's arms, and she placed the child gently on the rope bed. It was covered with an old blanket with an oniony smell that, despite Susannah's efforts, she had been unable to wash out.

A chill came over her as the terrible thought returned. Jezebel! The old accusation had plagued her for some time, but in the last few weeks, the word struck like a hot knife thrust into her soul. She could still see the faces of those harpies back in Hardeman County in Tennessee. Some of them had been her friends.

Susannah straightened up and touched the cameo brooch fastened at her collar. It was not her fault she had fallen in love. She could not help it. That was what she had told herself when cousin Daniel had brought a friend with him to Christmas supper at Mama's house back in Tennessee. He wore the dashing blue uniform of the United States army. His name was Almeron Dickinson, and he was a lieutenant of artillery. Susannah had never seen such a handsome man before, and from the way Almeron kept stealing glances her way, she knew he must fancy her, as well. He was leaving the army in a couple of months. He said he had already made arrangements to take over the blacksmith shop in town, and he would come courting. He was twenty-seven. She was fifteen.

True to his word, Almeron came calling, and, after a few afternoons together, Susannah's heart leapt when he presented her with a small cameo brooch. It was made out of some kind of seashell, but he couldn't recall the name. A stiff, lacey band of gold filigree surrounded it. It had been his mother's, he said. Untying the knotted scarf from around her neck, Susannah then overlapped it so Almeron could pin the brooch where the scarf crossed at her neck. Susannah's mama made a low noise in her throat when she saw the brooch.

Three weeks later Almeron asked Susannah to marry him. When she told her mother, Susannah was heartbroken. Mama didn't approve. Asking her why, Mama said she'd done some asking in town and found out that Almeron Dickinson hailed from Bledsoe County. "Nothing good ever come out of Bledsoe County," Mama declared.

The next day, a tearful Susannah, fingering the brooch pinned at the collar of her dress, told Almeron she could not marry him. When he asked why, she said it was because her mama refused to allow it. He told her she was being foolish, and if she loved him that was all that mattered. Susannah dropped her hand from the brooch, said she wasn't a fool, and he shouldn't call her one. He said he didn't say she was a fool. She planted her fists on her hips and insisted she'd heard him, plain as day. He told her she was being foolish again. Susannah pulled off the brooch and shoved it into his hand. Next thing she knew, Almeron had turned and walked away, muttering. A week went by, and then another. Almeron had not come calling.

Him leaving her was bad enough; calling her foolish had only sharpened the blow. She told her friends they'd had an argument, and it was his fault. A month later, Susannah's good friend, Delphi Elwood, told her that Almeron Dickinson had been coming around and that she believed he'd taken a fancy to her. Susannah said she no longer had feelings for Almeron, and if her friend was happy, then she was happy for her. That night, Susannah cried herself to sleep. Her mama told her she needed to take her mind off of Almeron, and the best way to do that was by keeping busy. She instructed Susannah to start taking in laundry. Susannah cried herself to sleep again that night.

Late in the spring, Delphi Elwood's father

announced the betrothal of his daughter to Almeron. When Delphi asked Susannah to be one of her bridesmaids, she said yes, but only because Delphi had asked nearly all of Susannah's other friends, and they'd accepted. In the past months, Susannah had been careful to avoid Almeron's blacksmith shop.

The day before the wedding, Susannah walked to town to deliver some clean aprons and towels to Lyle Bromley's tavern. Stepping through the doorway, she stopped abruptly upon seeing Almeron inside, enjoying a jug of whiskey with his friends. She hoped to slip away unnoticed, but Lyle tapped his knuckles on the bar, alerting Almeron. His smile was still as sweet as she remembered. Without a word, she delivered the linens and left. She walked quickly for home, but Almeron caught up with her and asked if he might walk with her a bit. Trying not to let her fluster show, she nodded. Within the half hour they were talking like old friends. Soon they were kissing by a tree near her home, and Almeron pulled something from his pocket and held it out to her. It was the cameo brooch.

That night, they eloped to neighboring McNairy County and were married. Justice of the Peace McKeon added an extra dollar to the marriage fee on account of he and his wife being awakened at such a late hour. Susannah wore the brooch on her dress. She promised Almeron she would wear it every day.

Susannah was overjoyed. Her mama and her friends were not. Soon, though, her mama accepted her daughter's marriage and was glad for her happiness. But the name calling started within days. *Jezebel! Harlot! Man-stealer!*

A lot of folks stopped bringing their clothes to Susannah to wash. Another blacksmith set up shop at the other end of town. When her mama died a month later, Susannah was beside herself with grief. And then Almeron told her of an opportunity he'd heard about. A chance to start fresh. A windy fellow by the name of Green DeWitt was calling for three to four hundred people to join with him down to Texas. Each settler would receive a full league of land. Susannah didn't know what that meant. Almeron told her it was four thousand-four-hundred-twenty-eight acres. Susannah could not imagine that much land! All they had to do was become Mexican citizens and abide by Mexican laws. Susannah started packing. Texas sounded like a tonic to her troubles.

Like Susannah and her husband, many of

the DeWitt settlers were from Tennessee, others from Missouri. When they saw the lands DeWitt had been granted by the Mexican government, Susannah decided Texas wasn't the Promised Land, but there was promise to it. Corn, cotton, and fruit trees were planted right away. Everybody pitched in and built the town of Gonzales up from nothing. Inside of a couple of years they had two general stores, a livery stable, a millinery shop, a barber, and a busy tavern. Almeron had his blacksmith shop and was part owner of a hat factory. Susannah gave birth to Angelina, and Almeron announced to everyone within earshot that Texas was now that much more civilized.

In spite of all this good life, Susannah harbored uneasy feelings, sharing none of them with her husband.

And then Santa Anna decided the *"norteamericanos,"* as he called them, who'd come to Texas were acting much too independent. At least that was how Susannah understood it. He ordered a bunch of his soldiers, a company of dragoons Almeron said, to Gonzales to haul away the six-pounder cannon the town had. DeWitt had gotten the cannon earlier for protection from wild Comanches. It was next to useless really, a thin cannon barrel fixed to the back of a cotton wagon. Best it could do was belch smoke and make a loud noise, but it did scare off the Indians.

But Almeron and the others gave those Mexican dragoons a good spanking when they showed up. Not a single Gonzales man was so much as nicked. After that ruckus, a lot of other Texians joined in, and together they ran every Mexican soldier between Gonzales and the Rio Bravo out of Texas, tails between their legs. "Don't come back," they hollered at them.

That had been last fall. Seemed like a lifetime ago. And now, Susannah was fretting, waiting for Almeron. She had to tell him.

The sound of boots on the flagstones of the chapel floor made Susannah clutch the brooch. She saw the gunners walk past the sacristy opening and trudge up the ramp to the guns when Almeron came in looking for her.

"You heard everything?" he asked.

She nodded sharply.

"I know this isn't what I promised you when we came to Texas," he said, coming around the bed to face her. "But there's still a chance for you and Angelina. Santa Anna won't kill a woman and her child. We can make a white flag and —"

"No," she said, cutting him off. A tear welled up in her eye, and she quickly wiped it away.

"I know how hard this has been for you, Sue."

"No, Almeron, you don't." She held back more tears.

He moved toward her. "What's wrong? Tell me."

"Please," she said, taking a step back. "This . . . all of this . . . it's my fault."

She saw the confused look on his face.

"I don't understand," he said.

She turned away, nervously biting her lower lip. *All my fault,* she thought. There was a whisper and the sound of shuffling feet outside the sacristy entryway. She saw Ana Esparza and her husband ushering their children past the sacristy doorway. They stayed in the monk's quarters, next to the sacristy. When they had entered the Alamo, Travis had told them to take that room, the old chapel being the strongest part of the fort. Ana caught Susannah's eye with a look that said they were going out to give them privacy.

"Tell me what's troubling you," Almeron said.

Susannah took a deep breath. What she

had to say needed saying all at once. She hoped she could. "I have loved you from the moment I set eyes on you. When we ran away to get married, that was the happiest day of my life. We could hardly wait to take our vows. And I did not have one thought about Delphi Elwood and her feelings."

"But I —"

"Let me finish. She was my best friend, and I lost her friendship. I lost all my friends. They told me I ought to be ashamed."

"And that was cruel and uncalled for, but they —"

"Don't you see? Maybe they were right. None of this would be happening if it wasn't for —"

"Sue —"

"No, listen to me. It's because of my selfishness. I'm to blame. My friends knew it. The town knew it. That's why they drove us out."

"They did not."

"They did! And we ran, all the way down here to Texas. You got our land, your smithy business. Things were good, all right. Too good."

"Yes, and then we had Angelina. Was that wrong?"

"No. That's not what I'm saying. We are

being punished because of me."

"No, honey."

"It's true." Her face flushed hot, the blood rushing to her cheeks, and she closed her eyes. "We got run out of our home in Tennessee because of me. A Jezebel. We run here and now that black-hearted Santa Anna wants to run us out. It's like running is all we do." She opened her eyes. "And it's all my fault. I brought us to this. If I hadn't married you, we wouldn't be in this fix. I look out over the walls, and . . ." She let the words trail off and glanced down at Angelina, then looked back at Almeron. "Is dying here how we purchase back our honor?"

She held back her tears and felt Almeron's hands on her shoulders.

"Look at me, Sue. I always loved you. I didn't want Delphi Elwood. Her pa wanted the marriage. I wanted you, and I kept hoping you'd show up somewhere in town, walking past my shop or someplace, so I could bump into you. Talk to you. And when Lyle told me you were doing laundry for him," he went on, "I was in his place every day for better than a week before the wedding day, praying you'd come in. You cut it close, too. But asking you to marry me? That was my idea."

"But —"

"Hold on," he said gently. "Nobody run us out of Tennessee. Coming to Texas was my idea, too."

"I know," she said, feeling the panic rise as she ran her finger over the brooch at her neck. "But then Santa Anna and things were moving so fast and . . . and I couldn't catch my breath, and now the whole Mexican army is sitting out there. We've lost everything, Almeron. All our belongings —"

"Sue —"

"My mother's ring, our . . . our china all the way from Philadelphia. We don't even know if our home is still standing."

"Sue!"

"This is our punishment for what I did!"

She put her hands over her face, afraid she might burst into tears, and then the familiar closeness of Almeron's strong arms around her, his hand gently stroking her hair.

"I'm so scared," she whispered.

"If I was them Mexican soldiers out there, I'd be the one scared."

She tilted her head up at him. "What do you mean?"

"I mean you got more gumption than anybody I know."

She gave him a puzzled look.

"It was about a week after your mama

45

passed; you were coming into town bringing me my supper. You'd put it in a basket you had in one hand, and in the other you were carrying a live chicken. It was for Mr. Barlow. Payment for goods we owed him from his store. You recall that?"

Susannah did, though she didn't know what this had to do with anything.

"I can still see it, clear as day. Delphi Elwood leaving Barlow's Dry Goods Store. I believe she was carrying a bolt of blue cloth rolled up in her hands, probably for a new dress. A couple of friends were with her."

Susannah remembered them. "Mealymouth little brats who wouldn't know what to do unless Delphi told them."

"And Delphi marched right up to you in the middle of the street and called you a dirty name, loud enough for the whole town to hear. I started up the street to tell her to go on home, and there you stood, facing her. You didn't say a word, just looked her square in the eye. Folks stopped on the street, watching. You'd been taking her insults a long time."

"But she never said them to my face," Susannah said. "Until that day."

Almeron nodded. "She and her friends were always calling you shameful names

after you passed by. But that day was different. She called your mama that same dirty
name. That's when I saw it."

"Saw what?"

"That look on your face. I'd seen it a time
or two before when something really riled
you. You dropped the basket and went after
Delphi, swinging that chicken like it was an
ax. She let out a scream, that roll of cloth
fell in the dirt, and she ran for home, her
friends hurrying after her. She kept her
distance after that, and I couldn't have been
prouder of you."

"But I don't —"

"We're not being punished on account of
anything you did. And there's no need to
buy back our honor. We never lost it in the
first place."

Susannah calmed down considerably.

"No one ran us out of anywhere, neither,"
Almeron continued. "All that was other
folks trying to make us feel bad, like Delphi
calling you names, pushing you around like
you was less than kitchen help. Just like
Santa Anna's doing. And we're showing him
there's things worth living for, and worth
dying for. That's the whole reason we're in
this place."

She heard the conviction in her husband's
voice and saw it in his eyes, those eyes that

had never lied to her.

A voice said, "Beg pardon, Captain. Officers' call."

Susannah glanced over and saw the skinny messenger at the doorway, his head down, looking anywhere but at her and her husband standing in the middle of the room in each other's arms.

"Feel better?" Almeron asked.

She nodded and gave him a quick smile. He kissed her and left, joining Lieutenant Bonham, who appeared outside the doorway.

Susannah made up her mind she'd not fret nor wallow in worry. Some of the men would be coming by to pick up the clothes they'd asked her to wash and mend. Something told her that would not be enough, though. She didn't know why. A feeling swept over her. Keep busy. Mama, rest her soul, used to tell her not to squander time, for life was too precious.

CHAPTER FOUR

"It is as I said, James. I cannot stay." Moses Rose bent down and took a stiff-looking piece of red cloth from behind a weathered cupboard. It stood near the low doorway of the flat-roofed stone room at the northeast corner of the north wall. It was where he had slept most nights since coming into the fort, he and his young friend James Taylor, his two brothers, and a few others.

"But in here anyway you're with us," James said. "Hell, these Mexicans can't hit nothing. Except this wall." He jutted his chin at the far wall.

Moses stepped over and ran his hand over it as he did almost daily since coming into the Alamo. Some limestone and some rough brick. There were so many cracks crisscrossing everywhere. At least the holes big as a fist had been plugged up. And he knew the other side of the north wall was in even worse shape because that was the one the

Mexicans had battered every day and night with two eight-pound cannons. Dozens of cannonballs lay scattered about on the ground outside the wall. Every man inside the Alamo was aware of the damage. The Mexicans, too. From what Moses could tell, all the hours he and *Monsieur* Taylor and the others assigned to the north wall had spent shoring it up with standing timber braces outside and shoveling dirt building an embankment inside hadn't amounted to much more than a bandage on a belly wound. It might stop the bleeding for a while, but the belly was still torn up.

Moses shook his head wearily. "She will not hold much longer."

"All the more reason we need you to stay," James Taylor said.

Moses carefully unfolded the cloth he held and blew bits of dirt from the item inside.

"Do you know what this is?" he asked, extending his hand, showing him a medal. It was a white, five-pointed cross. A wreath of oak leaves and green laurel surrounded it. The center of the cross held a gold piece engraved with the profile of Napoleon with an inscription.

"No. It's kind of pretty, though."

Moses smiled proudly. "*Légion d'honneur.* The Legion of Honor. The emperor presented it to me after his victory at the battle of Borodino."

"Looks like one of those words on it says Napoleon," James said, studying the gold centerpiece.

"Ah, *oui*. Very good." Moses pointed to the rest of the inscription. "This says *Empereur des Français*. It means 'Emperor of the French.' "

"How did you get it?"

Moses wished he hadn't let him see it now. "It is of no importance."

"Hold on. You told us a lot of stories about fighting over there in France and Europe but nothing about any medal. You earned that. Means something."

"It was a long time ago. Thirty years. *Mon Dieu*. You were not even born," Moses said as he wrapped the medal in the cloth and slipped it inside the pocket of his buckskin shirt.

"Well, you don't want to say, that's your affair. But I sure wish you'd stay. We're all in this."

Moses considered his friend James, standing across from him. He had a slight build, but there was fierceness in his eyes. Since they had taken refuge in the Alamo nearly two weeks ago, almost daily this rebel Texian had climbed the north wall and shouted profane insults at Santa Anna and his army. "Your mothers are all whores!" "What's that smell? Did Santa Anna shit his pants again?" "If you don't want to come fight, give your rifles to your womenfolk. They're probably better men anyhow!" Moses was certain this lad would have fit well in the *Grande Armée*. Quite well.

"Tell me something," James said. "Why'd you join that French army anyway?"

"There was no choice. Every Frenchman had to join."

"That's pretty much what we got here. We fight or we let that son-of-a-bitch, Santa Anna, piss all over us and tell us to like it. You've been a fighting man, Mose. You understand."

Moses looked out the doorway at the Alamo courtyard. Yes, he understood. At the battle of Ulm the *Grande Armée* cut the Austrian lines in half and sent the curs running. On the hills of Somosierra they scattered the Spanish army, then marched victorious into Madrid. At Austerlitz they routed the cursed Imperial Russian Army. Battlefields stretched across miles. So did the blood. And the Alamo was a little piece of ground, barely three acres. Farmers and shopkeepers and bankers defended the walls, along with a few soldiers. How much blood had they seen? How much slaughter? As much as he had waded through? Had any of these men held their bleeding, dying friends in their arms, listening to their pitiful cries, their last words? Moses could still see faces of comrades, their only comfort a kiss he placed on their foreheads before they died.

"Well, all right, I tried," he heard James say, heading for the door. "You keep a keen eye peeled, Mose."

"It was in Russia at a little village called Borodino," Moses began, still staring out into the courtyard. "The emperor gave the order for us to attack the Russian earthworks along the Kolocha River. We were the elite of the line infantry, the grenadiers. Napoleon himself decreed only the most fearsome men would serve in the grenadiers. As always, we were sent into the teeth of the battle."

Moses drew in a heavy breath.

"My good friend was beside me. We had been boyhood friends in Marseilles. Orphans. We drank together, whored together, fought many battles together. Our regiment charged the Russian earthworks, shouting our war cry, bayonets forward. We would crush these mongrel peasants."

He looked his young friend in the eye.

"They fired, volley after volley. Our friends, our fellow grenadiers, fell dead, the wounded screamed in pain, but the regiment advanced. Nothing could stop us. I saw smoke and fire from their cannons, but I did not hear their roar. We were shouting for glory, for the emperor. A moment later, my friend was gone." Moses spread his hands apart. "*Pas plus.* No more. A Russian cannonball had severed his head from his shoulders. Before the battle he'd raised his voice to our company and said, 'I've been wounded twenty-two times. God will not allow me to die.' " Moses shrugged. "God has a debauched sense of humor. *Oui?*"

James gave him a nervous, lopsided grin. "What did you do?"

"Continued the attack, of course. We broke the Russian line. I and a few others captured one of their eighteen-pounder guns. We turned it on the *bâtards.* I wished we'd killed them all." He grunted disapprovingly.

"When the emperor presented us with our medals, he said we had made France proud." Moses shook his head. "All I could think about was my friend who was dead. Before Borodino, fighting was like a game for me and my friend. But on that day, everything changed."

Outside in the Alamo courtyard, he saw long shadows and men busying themselves with chores: filling their powder horns, building cooking fires, brushing their coats clean, anything to keep themselves from thinking about what was coming. Moses understood that well. "I believe I was about your age," he whispered almost to himself. "War was all I knew."

"What was that, Mose? I didn't hear you."

He waved his hand. "It was nothing."

"Well, I'm real sorry about your friend. Real sorry," James said. "But we'll lose Texas and a lot more if we don't fight. We're going to win this war, I promise you. And I will personally make Santa Anna regret the night his mama ever spread her legs."

Moses clapped James on the shoulder. He was going to miss him, and his profane curses.

"You are a brave man," Moses said. "*Colonel* Travis and *Monsieur* Crockett and *Capitaine* Jameson. Every man here. There is only one difference between all of you and me."

"What's that?"

"I am not ready to die. That is all." He took his rifle that he'd left by the cupboard and started for the door. There were others he wanted to bid farewell to before he went over the wall.

"Good luck, Mose."

Moses turned. James held out his hand. Moses shook it. And for a reason he could not explain, he took the red cloth with the *Légion d'honneur* medal inside from his pocket and placed it in the young Texian's hand.

"I can't take your medal," James said. "Wouldn't be right. You earned it."

There will be much blood here, mon ami, Moses thought. Beaucoup de sang. *More than you can imagine.*

"No," Moses said. "I believe you will earn it."

CHAPTER FIVE

Crossing the hard ground of the military plaza of San Antonio de Béxar, Colonel Juan Morales adjusted his white-plumed bicorn hat with his white-gloved hands and smoothed his unruly hair over the side of his head where his left ear used to be. He knew well there was a time when those scars would have been the result of what it meant to serve honorably in the Mexican army. Instead, they had become a constant reminder of his disillusionment with a man he'd admired and followed and trusted.

The military plaza, which was separated from the main plaza by the church, was nearly empty, except for a handful of sentries. The Mexican tri-color with its eagle in the center hung limply from the flagpole. Turning along Portrero Street toward the main plaza, he saw his good friend Colonel José Romero tying the reins of his horse to a post. Morales slowed his pace to wait for him. They had known each other since their cadet days in the Batallón de la Libertad and saw action hunting down Comanches in the northern provinces. Romero was stout, bull-necked, and walked with a swagger, while Morales was reed thin and stood a head taller.

"His Excellency awaits, no?" Romero said in his gravelly voice, brushing his white-gloved hands over the red bib of his blue uniform blouse to remove the dust from his ride into town.

"Did you see any movement at the Alamo on your patrol?" Morales asked.

Romero shook his head. "Strangely quiet. They usually shout their worst curses at us officers when they see us."

Morales chuckled. "These *americanos* are a bold lot, are they not?"

Romero grunted.

As they walked, Morales saw the other officers gathering. Like him and Romero, they were the field commanders who'd been summoned by His Excellency to his headquarters, the long adobe house on the north side of the main plaza. The family that lived there had "offered" it to His Excellency when he expressed his interest in it the day he led the first columns of his army into Béxar almost two weeks ago.

"I'll wager His Excellency has decided to wait for the twelve-pounders," Romero said. "They will be here tomorrow. Care to take me up on that bet?"

Romero enjoyed games of chance, but, whenever he became bored waiting, as he had for over a week now, he would bet on anything — the way the wind would blow, which haunch a horse would brush with its tail first, how many musket balls he could hold in his hand.

"I don't believe he will wait for the cannon," Morales said.

"*¿Por qué no?*"

"You've seen how irritable he's been the last few days."

"What are you saying?"

"I think things have changed."

Romero snapped his head at Morales. "*¿La mujer?*"

"Lower your voice," Morales said low. "Let us say the woman is more than a suspicion."

"Well, what have you heard?"

"He was bedding her two, three times a day."

"That was no secret. He bragged about it. *El hijo de puta.*"

"Yes, but now? *No más.*"

"How do you know this?"

"A friend of the woman who does his washing told me."

"And how do you know her?"

Morales shrugged. "She is a lonely woman while her husband is away."

"*Jesús Cristo,*" Romero said under his breath as they reached His Excellency's headquarters and followed their fellow officers inside.

La mujer was the name Morales and Romero used for His Excellency's new young "wife." The day Santa Anna rode into town at the head of the army, he'd seen her waving from the street as he passed. Morales and Romero had seen her, too. A beautiful girl of sixteen. His Excellency desired her "company," but the girl's *mamá* refused until a proper marriage could be arranged. It was anything but proper. All the officers knew it, just as they knew Santa Anna already had a wife and four children waiting for him at his home in Jalapa, as well as seven mistresses and a dozen illegitimate children from Mexico City to Matamoros. But that evening, Santa Anna had sent for the vestments of the church priest, Padre Linares. The next morning, he ordered a nervous junior officer to don the vestments and perform the "marriage." Deplorable as Morales found that, it wasn't the main reason he hated His Excellency.

Morales snapped to attention as did the other officers when His Excellency entered the large room, a goblet of wine in his hand. He had a wide forehead and combed the sides of his hair forward, like his idol, Napoleon Bonaparte. More silver filigree covered the high collar, shoulder epaulettes, cuffs, and front of His Excellency's dark-blue uniform coat than all the filigree on all of the uniforms of the other officers in the room.

"The time has come to chastise these *norteamericano* pirates and the Tejano traitors who side with them," His Excellency said brusquely as he sat in his ornate chair at the head of the long table. A fire burned in the fireplace nearby. He took a drink from his goblet.

Morales, standing at the opposite end of the table with Romero and the other officers, most of whom gathered around the sides of the table, relaxed his stance. The other officers, even Romero, Morales noticed, continued to stand stiffly in His Excellency's presence. That His Excellency did not offer wine to any of them was not a surprise.

"We await your orders, Excellency," Colonel Almonte, Santa Anna's coffee-eyed chief of staff, said. He sat at the table to Santa Anna's right.

As his fellow officers nodded, some more enthusiastically than the others, Morales raised his head and cocked it to his left side. It wasn't that he couldn't hear out of his left ear. His hearing was fine. But he knew it was advisable to at least appear to be in accord with His Excellency.

One officer, though, sat straight and still — the wiry-haired General Cós, Santa Anna's brother-in-law, sitting to his left.

"Let there be no mistake," His Excellency continued. "The lawless *norteamericanos* are not fit for the freedoms they have demanded, these same freedoms they take for granted in their precious *Estados Unidos.*" He shook his head. "I welcomed them as colonists. I gave them fertile lands. I allowed them every means to live in comfort. And how did they thank me? By taking up arms in a criminal attempt to dismember the republic."

Morales covered his mouth and coughed, a sour taste in his mouth.

Only a few months ago, he had been committed, a believer in His Excellency. He saw Santa Anna not only as a brilliant military commander, but also possessing a shrewd political sense and clever enough to know how to use both to his advantage. When Santa Anna declared himself absolute ruler of Mexico, Morales cheered, *"¡Viva Santa Anna!"* It was a great day! Morales believed Mexico needed a strong hand to run its affairs.

Most of the country had cheered His Excellency, as well. But not Tejas. And not the state of Zacatecas in central Mexico. Before dealing with the rebels in Tejas, His Excellency marched on the Zacatecas capital with his army. Morales was proud His Excellency had chosen him to lead three companies of *cazadores,* light infantry, of the San Luis Activo Battalion. "Zacatecas may hold its silver mines hostage, but it will not hold the supreme government of Mexico hostage," Santa Anna had told his commanders.

The day of the battle, Morales led the attack on the right flank of the four-thousand-strong militia formed on the plain outside the city. He broke the enemy line and their resolve with a wall of rifle fire and bayonet steel. But a blast of grapeshot from an enemy cannon caught him, taking off his left ear and leaving the left side of his face scarred and pitted. It was three days before he regained consciousness and heard that His Excellency had ordered his army to pillage the town. For two full days women were raped in the streets and random citizens executed. It would serve as a warning, His Excellency had said. Morales had vomited when he'd been told. Where was the honor? He had been a soldier, an officer in the Mexican army all his life. It was all he knew. Butchery was not the duty of an officer.

But the day might come to switch allegiances. There had been other presidents, other dictators. Santa Anna would falter. Revolts came. The people turned. Morales would bide his time. The army would always be needed. This was Mexico, after all.

Santa Anna glanced at his chief of staff. Colonel Almonte raised his white-gloved hand and motioned to Lieutenant Colonel de Labastida, who had been waiting against the far wall all this time. He wore silver spectacles and was Santa Anna's chief engineer. Stepping up to the table, he seemed nervous as he unrolled the parchment he held. Morales saw it was a map of the Alamo garrison with its odd L-shape. De Labastida's hand trembled as he placed several empty glasses he took from the nearby *tresoro* on the corners, in order to keep it flat. The dozen candles burning in the iron candelabra overhead cast a warm light over the table.

General Cós made no move to pull himself closer to the table, Morales noticed. But the same could not be said for some of the others, like balding Colonel Duque and General Ramirez y Sesma, who drew his finger across his thin lips as he leaned in to study the map.

"The attack will begin at four o'clock tomorrow morning," His Excellency began. "A bugle will sound. The four columns will advance simultaneously. That is imperative. Surprise is the key. The pirates will be asleep."

Morales saw His Excellency give a nod to de Labastida.

The Lieutenant Colonel unsheathed a pearl-handled dagger hanging from his side and pointed, as steadily as he could manage, to each place on the map, as His Excellency presented his plan of battle.

General Cós would attack from the northwest with three hundred-fifty regular *soldados* and *cazadores,* the light infantry. Colonel Duque would lead four hundred *soldados,* from the northeast. "Drive the pirates from the north wall," Santa Anna told them. Colonel Romero would strike from the east with four hundred-fifty men.

Only one obvious place left. Morales knew

where His Excellency would order him.

"Colonel Morales, the hero of Zacatecas . . ."

Morales wished he could wring the pox of His Excellency out of his uniform.

"You," Santa Anna continued, "will have the honor to attack from the south with three companies of *cazadores.*"

De Labastida drew his dagger from the main gate of the garrison across to the wooden palisade.

Mierda, Morales thought. Three light companies. That only amounted to about a hundred and twenty men.

"You will break the pirates at their weakest point," Morales heard Santa Anna say.

Give me three hundred-twenty men, and the "weakest point" could be overrun with ease, Morales thought disgustedly. Glancing at His Excellency, he saw the congratulatory look on his face and nodded his acceptance. It was the prudent thing to do.

"General Ramirez y Sesma," Santa Anna said, "you and your cavalry will see to it that none of the pirates escape from the garrison."

"Of course, Excellency," the general said.

"And," Santa Anna continued, raising his forefinger, "if any of our *soldados* should turn and run, you will see to making an example of them to the others. Do you understand?"

"*Completamente,* Excellency."

"Lastly, I will be watching from the north batteries. Five hundred *granaderos* will be held with me in reserve. Should any part of the attack falter, they will be sent in."

Morales resisted the temptation to remind His Excellency that on the first day of the siege, when Colonel Travis, the leader of the rebels inside the Alamo, answered an offer to surrender with the roar of a cannon, His Excellency proclaimed that he personally would lead the attack.

"Again, surprise will be paramount," His Excellency said. "You will see to it that the attack does not fail. I expect that every man will do his duty."

A moment passed. A cool breeze wafted in through the open windows that faced the courtyard on the backside of the house where a barren cypress tree stood. The candlelight overhead flickered.

Morales knew everything about this attack was a mistake. It was a mistake because it was unnecessary. That irritated him greatly. But His Excellency had made up his mind. To disagree at this point would only antagonize him. He heard Romero suck in a breath.

"Your Excellency," Romero said, "our twelve-pound cannons are expected tomorrow. With them we can punch holes in the north wall large enough for the army to march through."

"I will wait no more," Santa Anna said.

Morales caught Romero glance his way, a sheepish look on his face.

"Excellency," General Cós said, his tone careful, Morales thought, so as not to sound disagreeable. "Perhaps we should try one more time to offer terms of surrender. These men are not —"

"They are pirates," His Excellency said.

"Of course, Excellency," Cós said, "but I am thinking of the loss of our *soldados.*"

Sitting back in his chair and raising his chin, His Excellency considered Cós for a moment. "Tell me, General, do you remember what Napoleon said about a general's first duty?"

"No, Excellency."

"He said it is to maintain his honor and his glory. Compared to that, the cost in troops is unimportant." Santa Anna waved his hand dismissively. "A trifle."

"Forgive me, Excellency," Cós said, "but I believe the cost will be significant."

Santa Anna rose up from his chair.

"And which will cost me more, General,"

68

His Excellency asked evenly, looking down at Cós, "appearing weak to these pirates or showing them no quarter?"

Cós, who did not raise his eyes to His Excellency, nodded then asked, "Would Your Excellency reconsider the taking of prisoners?"

"No!" He slammed his fist on the table. "There will be no prisoners."

"But it would demonstrate to the people of Mexico your benevolence, your forgiveness."

The dark look that crossed His Excellency's face made Morales think Santa Anna might order the arrest of General Cós. But His Excellency cast his eye around the table at each officer and said, "There is no forgiveness without bloodshed."

His Excellency turned and strode out of the room.

Morales bolted out of that house. He didn't care that Colonel Almonte wanted to speak with the officers. All Almonte would do is tell them again what His Excellency had just told them, and that a written order would be delivered shortly to each commander. It would change nothing if Morales weren't there. Orders had been given. Morales wanted a drink. He also wanted to find Padre Linares, but he wanted the drink first. He was nearly halfway across the main plaza, headed for the cantina, when he realized Romero had caught up with him.

"That man is a fool," Morales said, barely keeping his anger in check.

Before Romero could respond, they heard the bugle call sounding retreat. Down the street next to the church leading to the military plaza, they could see the color guard slowly lowering the Mexican tri-color. Coming to attention, they raised their hands in salute. Respect for country had not waned. A couple of *soldados* hauling a donkey cart had halted near the corner and snapped to attention, as well.

"You know this attack is a mistake," Morales said, keeping his voice low.

"Of course," Romero said. "I said we should wait for the big cannons."

"It's more than that," Morales said. "For twelve days he batters the north wall when he could have easily blasted apart the timber palisade on the south. For over a week we've had almost three thousand men sitting and waiting."

Morales saw Romero nervously shift his head around to see if anyone was close by, listening.

"Assaulting the fort a week ago would

have been honorable," Morales continued. "Instead, we waste time and powder and opportunities. Now we'll waste good men, all because His Excellency allows the little *verga* between his legs to do his thinking for him."

"Keep your voice down," Romero whispered.

"I tell you, he will send *la mujer* away very soon. Her and her *mamá.*"

The bugle call ended and Morales and Romero lowered their salute. But there was a strange sound in the distance. Like two cats fighting. It was coming from the east.

They moved off the plaza, past Santa Anna's headquarters to an open area between several adobe houses. About three hundred yards beyond the river, they saw, in the lengthening light, two men on top of the Alamo west wall at the cannon emplacement. One played a fiddle, the other a colorful set of bagpipes. Others joined them on the wall. Some appeared to be dancing.

"Look, they're pulling down their flag," Romero said. "Maybe they've decided to surrender."

"I don't think so," Morales said as he watched the rebels raise a new flag atop the two-story adobe building, what he'd been told was an old convent. A breeze caught it.

This was a big flag, much larger than the others Morales had seen flying over the Alamo. On the blue field of this flag was what appeared to be a large single white star. "There's something else under the star, I think. Perhaps a word."

"You know their English better than me. Can you make out what it says?" Romero asked.

"Too far away," Morales said.

"Independencia."

Surprised by the voice behind him, Morales turned and saw Colonel Almonte, a spyglass raised to his eye. Standing next to him was His Excellency, his face hard as stone.

Morales hid his smile. The English word was almost identical to the same one in Spanish.

"Shall I order the 'Degüello' and our gunners to commence a bombardment, Excellency?" Almonte asked, lowering the spyglass.

Morales could see Santa Anna considering it.

"No," Santa Anna finally said. "My orders stand. But someone *will* bring me that flag." He turned sharply and headed back to his headquarters.

"I shall see to it personally, Excellency,"

Almonte said, following close behind.

"Those rebels are a bold lot, I'll give them that," Romero said.

"That is true, *mi amigo*," Morales said and smiled as he continued to watch the men on the Alamo wall. These *americanos* did not know the meaning of fear. They were doing what he would do if he were in their place.

CHAPTER SIX

"Kiss my ass, Santa Anna, you son of a whore!" James shouted from the eight-pound battery at the northwest corner. Damn, he felt almost giddy, what with Travis's flag and David Crockett and Johnnie McGregor playing "Yankee Doodle Dandy." A spirited little tune, that.

As far as James could tell, nearly everyone in the garrison appeared to be prancing lively or clapping along, dancing away all that weariness they'd been feeling, the tenseness from lack of sleep. He commenced a sprightly step of his own to taunt the Mexican soldiers. It worked, too. One made a hand gesture at him and hollered something in Spanish. James couldn't make out what he was saying but decided it was coarse and lewd. He opened his mouth wide and laughed.

"What are you laughing at?" his brother Edward asked, appearing next to him.

"A Mexican over there trying to rile me. I'm aggravating him by laughing at him."

"Travis's new flag is aggravating them Mexes plenty, I expect."

"Hell yes," James said. "You know where he got it?"

"Somebody said Lieutenant Zanco had something to do with it."

"Resourceful little cuss, isn't he?"

"All I know is that flag must be spoiling Santa Anna's plate of beans. Speaking of which, you ought to go down and have yourself something to eat. Only more corn stew, but Georgie's down there."

"You come, too," James said.

Edward shook his head and snorted. "My watch."

"I thought Wussler was supposed to be on sentry duty."

"He's in the hospital. Came down with the flux. Captain told me to take his place. Just my luck he saw me first."

Ever since they were boys, James knew well Edward's tendency to complain. He was about to point that out when he caught sight of a column of Mexican cavalry forming at the woods near the edge of town. They carried nine-foot wooden lances, the sharp steely points flashing in the long light of the setting sun.

"You see that?" he asked Edward.

" 'Course I do. The Mexes are deadly with those frog stickers."

Neither said a word for a moment.

"You know," Edward said, "I'd feel better if I saw Fannin and his men marching over Powder House Hill about now." He turned and looked out to the east, beyond the chapel, where Powder House Hill stood with only a scattering of Mexican soldiers in evidence. "A whole sight better."

We'd all like to see that, James thought, but he refused to allow melancholy to set in on him.

"Yankee Doodle Dandy" ended with a flourish, and Crockett and McGregor started another tune. It was one of James's favorites.

"Yes sir, 'Turkey in the Straw' sure beats the hell out of that damn 'Degüello,' wouldn't you say?" James said as he headed down the dirt ramp lined with timber posts.

He found Georgie having a plate of corn stew. Cleland Fleet, Hardin Bishop, Preacher Garnett, and a few other men from the north wall were spooning helpings into their mouths, too. They were sitting near the *acequia* ditch that ran the length of the compound, from under the north wall and out again under the south wall. It was

76

fed by the San Antonio River but was near dry, thanks to Santa Anna's engineers damming up the tributary. Fortunately, Travis had seen to having a well dug near where the west and south walls met, so the garrison had fresh water.

"James, how about some food?" Georgie asked. "Can't compliment the cook, but it'll keep your belly from feeling cheated."

Hardin took another spoonful and grimaced. "I'd swap this for a taste, a thimble full mind you, of old homemade corn liquor," he said in his squeaky voice. He was gangly, and his left eyelid drooped.

Georgie grinned at James. "Be nice about now, wouldn't it?"

"More than that," James said.

"Come on and eat," Georgie said.

"Maybe later," James said.

Truth was, he wasn't in the mood for more corn stew. At least that's what they called it, though it was more like corn mush. Some eighty bushels of corn had been stored in the granary rooms inside the long barracks on the east wall. No beans. No bread. Just corn. Corn mush was the only thing they'd eaten for over a week. Every meal.

They'd had less than a dozen head of cattle in the corral on the east side to begin with, each one of them scrawny at best. With about two hundred mouths to feed, that beef hadn't lasted long. And though the meat had been on the stringy side, James would've relished a bite or two about now.

"All I know is I'm glad it's our own music serenadin' us and not them Mexicans," Cleland said. "Oh, hell," he added, realizing he'd dribbled corn mush onto his dark full beard, and he wiped it off with his hand.

"Lord knows we've had little rest and little reason to be cheerful," Preacher said.

"Well, I like this song," Hardin said. He set aside his plate, dusted off his homemade trousers and started a high-stepping dance with his long legs. "C'mon, Preacher."

Preacher joined him, and they locked arms. Preacher was a big barrel of a man with a bulbous nose, and he wore bifocals. Considering his stockiness, James thought him surprisingly light on his feet. Hardin threw his floppy hat down and whooped loudly.

Watching the dancing and laughing reminded James of the night he and his brothers arrived in San Antonio. Nearly everyone inside these walls was celebrating George Washington's birthday over in the main plaza of town. Texians and Tejanos both. Went all night, that party. Lots of women to dance with. And the corn liquor flowed.

And the next morning, when Santa Anna rode in with his army, every volunteer came running, and a few stumbling, into the Alamo for cover. A handful of them managed to grab a jug or two along with their other possibles. Sadly, most of those jugs hadn't been full. But every one of them was empty by the third day of the siege. Some of the men grew downright tetchy about it, saying that with some eighty bushels of corn in the granary rooms on the east wall there was plenty available for making corn liquor. Travis ordered that the corn would only be used for cooking meals. There were those who disagreed, strongly, but Travis said food was the priority. Edward was bitterly disappointed. "Makes a man wonder if this here war is worth fighting," he'd grumbled. Others joined in that sentiment.

James hadn't heard men grousing and moaning that much since Edward blew up Pa's still.

James wasn't more than six years old when Pa came to the conclusion that Perry County, Tennessee, was too crowded and too civilized to his liking. Being cooped up in a trading post didn't suit him, either. He moved the family to Texas, where new prospects beckoned.

Pa settled the family at Round Point near Trinity Bay. He saw all that blue water and fell in love with it. With a dugout canoe he took up a new life as a trapper and hunter. "A man can prosper here if he's blessed with the proper wit and fortitude," he said. His pelts were always the finest, and he never gouged on the price. He was an honest man and well liked.

A few years passed. Money was coming in steady, and that was helping the whole family. Besides Pa and Ma and Edward, James, and Georgie, there was older sister, Cecilia, and, since coming to Texas, Ma had her younger brother, Robert, and little baby, Nancy.

However, there was one drawback about Mexican Texas in Pa's mind. While he happily agreed to become a Mexican citizen and abide by Mexican laws, he missed the taste of homemade corn liquor. While families were encouraged to make their own wine, Mexican law outlawed folks distilling liquor. But Pa decided not to let that stop him.

He had operated a still back in Perry County, selling his corn squeezings over the trading post counter by the glass and by the jug. While he'd had to leave the still behind with no room to pack it for the move to

Texas, he did make the acquaintance while trading around Trinity Bay of one of Jean Lafitte's buccaneers who continued to operate along the Texas coast. He ran goods, American and Mexican, legal and illegal. Pa managed to barter a good-sized copper pot from him. As a matter of fact, Cecilia, by then sixteen and the oldest of the six Taylor children, married that old buccaneer.

With the copper pot, as well as a coiled condenser he fashioned himself from other parts, Pa commenced distilling. Texians from Galveston to Nacogdoches called his corn liquor Round Point Bounce. It wasn't rotgut, but it wasn't sipping whiskey, either. However, one swig and a man would swear he was ten feet tall and could leather the tar out of anyone and anything. Most important, though, nobody ever went blind drinking Pa's corn liquor.

When Edward saw the contraption, he believed he'd found his calling and pestered Pa to let him help. Pa said he was too young, being only eleven, but promised when he turned twelve he'd show him how to work the thing.

When that day came, Edward was almost dizzy with excitement. He even bragged to James that he would be the best maker of corn liquor ever. James didn't care. Though only ten, he already had his mind set on other pursuits, like maybe the law. Not a damn shyster neither, but a real lawman.

Pa showed Edward the importance of keeping a proper fire under the still, a sharp eye out for leaks, and never letting the liquid spill over.

Edward did fine for the first couple of weeks. Then he forgot to take his afternoon meal with him one day, got hungry, and ran home the half mile to fetch it. But before heading off, he built the fire up high, not wanting to take the chance of it going out. On reaching home, he found the cloth sack of food he'd left on the table. Taking it in hand, he stepped out the cabin door to hurry back to the still and heard the explosion. Folks living miles away heard it, too.

The Mexican authorities over in the town of Anuhuac came to investigate. It was sheer luck none of them was familiar with stills. Pa did some fast talking, claiming he knew nothing about this contraption and saying somebody must be trying to get him into trouble. He didn't hear anymore from the authorities after that and decided his distilling days were done. Edward said he was real sorry, but later told James that distilling liquor was too much like work, hard work, and had concluded it wasn't for him anyway.

Sitting inside the Alamo this night, James was certain a little corn liquor would taste real fine right about now . . .

And suddenly the gloom crowded in on him. Maybe it was thinking about Pa that brought it on. But there it was. Everything he didn't want to think about. No corn liquor. When was Santa Anna going to attack? Where was Sam Houston and the army of Texas?

He pushed away the melancholy and told himself to think about what needed doing. Winning this battle. Freeing Texas. Finding Thomas Jefferson Chambers, the man who had killed his pa.

Ma, mercifully, had died from consumption back in April of '31. Mercifully, James thought, because she could not have taken Pa's murder three months later. Someone shot him in the back of the head. No one knew who had done it or why, but James was certain that scoundrel, Thomas Jefferson Chambers, had something to do with it.

James, who was going on seventeen then, had made it his business to find out everything he could about Chambers. First off, Chambers was a damn lawyer. He had come to Texas in the winter of '30. It was said he had left Alabama suddenly. The exact cir-

83

cumstances surrounding his hasty departure were unclear. Stories circulated of his attempts to bribe witnesses, including a county magistrate in a fraud case in which he represented the defendant, who happened to be his cousin. There was also the story of a brothel madam in Mobile who was convicted of keeping a riotous and disorderly establishment and ordered to post a five-hundred-dollar good behavior bond. She said she had the money at her establishment, but the judge refused to allow her to leave the courtroom before the fine was paid. Chambers, it was claimed, had been in the courtroom on another matter and offered to retrieve the sum for the madam. Knowing full well that Chambers was a frequent customer at her brothel, she accepted his chivalrous offer and told him she kept money behind a wall panel in her bedroom. Chambers promptly exited the court, took himself to her room, pried open the panel, and absconded with all her money, perhaps as much as six thousand dollars. It was said he crossed the state line minutes ahead of a posse and made a beeline for Mexican Texas.

Shortly after his arrival, he ingratiated himself to Jose Victor Padilla, the newly appointed land commissioner for eastern

Texas, who gave him the post of surveyor general. He walked around telling folks he deserved it on account of his "exceptional fitness, learning, and probity." James had never heard the word *probity* before and someone told him it meant honesty. If a man insisted on telling folks how honest he was, James figured he had to be lying.

Word had it that Chambers wanted land for himself and lots of it. To insure that happened, he bought off certain men by giving them jobs as deputy surveyors. One, Bartlett Sims, surveyed a tract of land stretching from the Trinity River to Double Bayou — six leagues of land in all that included Round Point. One of those leagues was the property that belonged to Pa. Sims told him there would be no problem. He would mark Pa's land and then settle it at the office of the land commissioner. First there was confusion over the measurements, something to do with Sims's surveying chains not being the proper length. That meant some claims overlapped, and others came up short. As far as James could tell, keeping folks confused and confounded was how Chambers operated.

New surveys were recorded, official documents put in order, and, suddenly, Thomas Jefferson Chambers held title to all six leagues. Six goddamn leagues! That was over twenty-four thousand acres!

Pa fought that greedy son-of-a-bitch in court beginning the following January, but it was clear the Mexican judge said whatever Chambers told him to say. "All parties are not present, so we have to adjourn until *mañana*" or "A document can't be located, so everybody come back *mañana.*" Hell, *mañana* didn't mean tomorrow in that court, it simply meant *not today.* They were hoping Pa would give up and go away, but he dug in like a Tennessee tick. Pa wasn't fancy-educated like Chambers, and he didn't have a high-sounding title like *jefé político,* but he knew when somebody was pissing in his boot and calling it rain.

And then, come late July, Pa was shot in the back of the head while tanning a hide. His blood and brains were splattered on that deerskin. James and Edward found him lying in the dirt, unconscious. They took him to Doc Labadie, where he held on for a day and a night before he died. Doc Labadie said he was in a comatose state. All James knew was that his Pa never came to or spoke another word.

Suddenly, all those court documents appeared along with every one of Chambers's witnesses. The Taylors didn't stand a chance in that Mexican courtroom. The proceedings took less than an hour. The judge made his ruling, and Chambers became the legal owner of Pa's land, and those other five leagues, too.

James and his brothers had no choice but to send Robert and little Nancy to live with their sister Cecilia down in Matamoros.

But James vowed to get their land back. Dragging Sims into an alley one night, he gave him several sharp raps about the head with the heavy butt of a flintlock pistol to aid him with his clerical recollections. Sims admitted Chambers's scheme to bribe Mexican judges and other officials so he could steal land. James went looking for Chambers, but the son-of-a-bitch had run off, a guilty man hiding like a scared dog. There was room to hide in Texas, that was certain, but James vowed to find him. And when he did, he would make him wish that Alabama posse had caught him and hanged him. That would have been a hell of a lot quicker and less painful than what James planned to do to him. Yes indeed . . .

James saw Georgie jump up and dance a little jig, motioning to him.

By damn this was a shivaree, a real celebration! James joined Georgie in a spritely gambol. He caught sight of Moses Rose passing by.

"What do you say now, Mose?" James asked.

"I think," Moses said slowly, "I heard there was a dance in Brussels the night before Waterloo."

CHAPTER SEVEN

Inside the cantina near the main plaza, Colonel Morales and Colonel Romero drained the last of the wine from their glasses.

"To long life," Morales said.

They sat near the open fireplace, as there was a chill in the air. The cantina was quiet and nearly empty except for Morales, Romero, and the old surly barkeep who'd been smart enough to keep his mouth shut about the lack of business. Since His Excellency's arrival, the citizens who had remained in town had tended to stay away from the plaza, except for Mass on Sunday morning. Also, Santa Anna had banned his *soldados* from the cantina during the siege. Whenever the pirates inside the Alamo looked out, he'd said, he wanted them to see the growing ranks of his army surrounding them. Santa Anna had placed no such restrictions on his officers, however.

Stepping outside, Morales looked up at the purpling twilight and listened a moment.

"Do you hear that?" he asked.

"I hear nothing," Romero said.

"The *americanos* have grown quiet."

As they prepared to mount their horses, Morales saw Padre Linares come out of a house across the way. Outside the door, two weeping women dressed in black bent down and kissed his hand as he departed, holding his Bible to his chest. Morales guessed someone in the house was dying and Linares had performed the sacrament of the Anointing of the Sick. It struck him that the padre probably didn't know it at this moment, but he would be very busy tomorrow, after this battle. Morales turned to Colonel Romero, who was already mounted, and said he wanted to speak with the padre.

"Of course. Good luck tomorrow, my friend," Romero said.

"And you," Morales said.

Romero rode out as Morales approached the black-robed padre and told him he needed a word. "I want you to hear my confession. I need to make it now, Padre. *Con su permiso.*"

Linares had a thick shock of graying hair that fell to one side, and dark, weary eyes

90

that suddenly turned flinty. He turned his head, looking toward his church.

"I want that . . . flag off of my church," Linares said in a low voice. *"Con su permiso, Coronel."*

Morales couldn't blame him. His Excellency's "no quarter" flag of death flying from the top of the church dome was like a slap across the padre's face. This was also the priest whose vestments had been demanded and used for Santa Anna's jest of a marriage ceremony. Another grotesque insult.

"As do I, Padre," Morales said. "But it is out of both of our hands."

After a moment, Linares gave him a sharp nod, and they walked wordlessly to the church. On entering, Morales saw the glow from the flames of two thick candles in silver candlesticks standing on the altar. Linares lit a smaller candle he kept on a table inside the main doors and led the way to the confessional box, where several racks of votive candles burned on either side of it.

Morales knelt on the cold stone floor inside the confessional box. He watched through the opening in the wooden partition as Linares set his candle on the end of the arm of his worn chair, took a purple stole from his pocket, and sat down. Holding the stole in his hands, he kissed the small, embroidered cross at the middle of it and then placed it around the nape of his neck. Linares sat back, tucked his thumb under his chin, and curled his fist against his mouth.

"Bless me, Padre, for I have sinned," Morales said as he made the sign of the cross. "It has been at least a year since my last confession. These are my sins. I have taken God's name in vain many times. I have sworn profane curses everyday. I have killed many men."

He heard Linares make a low sound.

Morales continued. "There have been at least twenty, perhaps forty women I have fornicated with."

"These women," Linares said, "were they —"

"*Prostitutas, sí.* Well, most of them. Some were . . . are married."

Linares let out a long sigh. "Go on, my son."

"I am not a handsome man, Padre, but I am a man."

Linares dropped his hand and cocked his head to look at Morales. "Everyone carries scars, my son. Some on the soul, some on the body. But God knows we are all sinners. We have our weaknesses." He sat back in

92

his chair. "Do you have more to confess?"

"There are other sins I have committed, Padre, but I can't remember them now."

"These men you killed, was that in battle or — ?"

"It was in battle. I was performing my duty. If I did not kill them, they would have killed me."

"That is understandable in the eyes of God. As for your other sins, you must be truly sorry, and you must try not to commit them again, if you truly seek forgiveness. Will you do that?"

I'm a soldier, not a saint, Morales thought. "I want absolution, Padre," he said. "Time grows short. I do not want sins on my soul when I stand before God."

"*Entiendo.* But if you are not sorry for your sins, if you will not try to avoid temptation, I cannot give you absolution."

"As you say, we are all sinners."

"But we must also be humble and ask God for His help if we wish to attain our reward in heaven. Now, tell me truthfully, are you sorry for your sins?"

"If I am not killed in battle, I will fornicate with women again. I will take God's name in vain again. I will commit more sins. That is the truth, Padre. And if I say here in this place at this moment that I am sorry for my sins, I will be sinning by telling a lie."

Linares leaned forward, and Morales met his eyes. The priest wore a peculiar look on his face, as though no one had ever spoken to him this way before. Perhaps no one had. But Morales didn't care. He would not speak a lie, in church, to a priest. And if this padre refused to grant him absolution, he would leave and ask God to have mercy on him if he fell in battle. Then he heard Linares grunt.

"God hates a coward," the priest said. "And He loves a sinner. I can give you absolution. But it will be God's decision if He wishes to grant you pardon."

Morales nodded.

"For your penance say twenty Our Fathers and twenty Hail Mary's," Linares said. "And pray for God's mercy."

Morales bowed his head and asked God for His pardon while Linares whispered a prayer in Latin. Then Linares blessed him with the sign of the cross while saying, "*Ego te absolvo a peccatis tuis in nomine Patris, et Filii, et Spiritus Sancti.* Amen."

"*Gracias,* Padre. And may I ask for a small favor?"

"If I can."

"Say a prayer for us this night."

"So, it finally comes," he said. "I suspected

as much when you demanded I hear your confession. *Sí.* I will offer a prayer. For your *soldados* and those poor wretches inside the fort."

CHAPTER EIGHT

With Angelina secure in a cloth sling she had tied over her shoulder, Susannah sat in an anteroom near the main doors of the church. The small room used to be where the priest would baptize children. That's what Ana Esparza had told her, anyway. But now it and the anteroom across from it was where all the ammunition and gunpowder was stored.

Reaching into a long wooden box, Susannah scooped out another handful of paper cartridges and placed them into a bucket. She'd lost count as to how many buckets she had filled in the last hour. All that mattered to her had been to keep busy. She had seen the men breaking open the boxes and filling the buckets with cartridges and realized there were other more important things they could be doing. Finding Major Robert Evans, the tall Irishman with curly, black hair whom Travis had put in charge of all the guns and cannons and powder, she had insisted he allow her to assist with this job. "You're a willful woman, Mrs. Dickinson," he had said with a smile. She liked Evans, even though she saw a glint of the devil in his eye.

A fellow from Kentucky came by and lifted the bucket by its rope handle. "You've been a big help, ma'am."

Angelina started crying and fussing. Susannah knew it was past her feeding time. She told Major Evans she needed to see to her daughter.

Nearing her sacristy room, she heard voices coming from inside and on entering was surprised and pleased to see her husband sitting at the table where a candle burned, laughing and eating a bowl of corn mush along with Lieutenant Bonham and two other gunners, a ruddy-faced man named Shied, and Rutherford, whose hair had thinned considerably. So often Almeron and his gunners ate at their post. When she asked where the other men were, Almeron said three were on work details, and that Ana Esparza had brought her husband and the other three gunners their meals while they remained at the guns on the top of the ramp.

Scooping a little corn mush from Almeron's bowl into another bowl, Susannah sat down on the edge of the bed and tried to feed Angelina. At the same time, she listened to Bonham finish his story about a court case he handled back in South Carolina.

"I'd only been a lawyer for a few months when Mrs. Crawford comes to retain my services," he said. "She was the owner of Crawford's Ice House, inherited from her departed husband, and was being sued by one Woodrow Fulkes. He claimed that she had not sold him ten full pounds of ice, for when he got it home and weighed the block, it was only eight and one-quarter pounds." Bonham set his empty bowl aside.

"We convened in Judge Gillum's court-room. When Mr. Fulkes took the stand, I questioned him and was able to elicit certain facts. That he lived some three miles away from Mrs. Crawford's establishment, that he carried the block of ice in an uncovered cart, and that he made his purchase at midday, in the month of August, when the heat of summer is particularly vicious."

Almeron shook his head, and Shied and Rutherford chuckled.

"Blockheaded fool," Rutherford said.

"Precisely," Bonham said, jabbing the air with his finger. "And it was at that moment that Mr. Fulkes's attorney, a loutish man, made a callous remark about Mrs. Crawford, one I will not repeat for it was most ungentlemanly." He nodded courteously at Susannah. "I immediately demanded he retract his uncalled for statement and apologize to Mrs. Crawford. When he refused I was left no alternative but to rap him soundly with my cane."

"You struck him?" Susannah said.

"Above his left ear. He then apologized. However, Judge Gillum called me a disreputable scoundrel for disrupting his court proceedings. I advised him to watch his tongue. He sentenced me to ninety days in jail. Contempt of court."

"Oh, no," Susannah said.

Bonham waved away her concern. "Not only did the ladies of the community take pity on my situation, daily bringing me the finest meals and engaging in witty conversation to help me pass the time, but on my release I returned to Judge Gillum's court and won the case."

Susannah and the men laughed. It was wonderful, if only for a moment.

A bearded fellow stuck his head through the doorway.

"Officers' call, Captain Dickinson. Lieutenant."

"Thank you," Almeron said and wiped his mouth.

The bearded man turned and left.

"Another officers' call? You haven't even had time to finish your supper," Susannah said to Almeron, annoyed that Travis had to summon all the officers again to his quarters. They'd had an officer's call not even two hours ago.

"I should think I'll be back very shortly," Almeron said as he took another spoonful of corn mush, rose from the small table, and reached for his hat. He leaned down, kissed her and Angelina, and left their sacristy room followed by the others, who thanked her for her hospitality.

Susannah picked up Almeron's wooden bowl. He had eaten only about half of his meal. Susannah took a spoonful for herself but found she had little appetite. It wasn't the corn mush, though she had had her fill of it days ago. And although Almeron had eased her fears about their reasons for coming to Texas, there was still the attack she knew — they all knew — was to come.

Holding Angelina, Susannah scraped a little mush onto the end of her spoon and raised it to her daughter's mouth. Angelina jerked her head away and Susannah trailed her mouth with the spoon.

"One more bite, darling," she said, but Angelina would have none of it, twisting her head to the other side.

"Maybe that's enough, then," Susannah said. She laid her baby on the bed and brushed her hair with her fingers. Then Susannah turned and looked up through the roofless chapel at the darkness above. The first stars would show shortly.

Wanting to stretch her legs, she stepped out into the nave. A few torches mounted on the walls burned brightly. No candles burned in the old monk's quarters where Ana Esparza's family stayed.

Susannah decided she might see if they were out in front of the chapel and was nearly to the main doors when Gregorio Esparza came out of the anteroom. On his shoulder he carried a hammered tin cylinder.

"Con su permiso, señora," he said, as always.

"Of course," she replied, stepping aside to allow him to pass.

"A little gift to return to His Excellency's *soldados.*" He grinned and patted the tin as he started up the wooden ramp to the gun emplacements at the top. "They left this one and others behind when we drove them out of Béxar," he said. "I will be happy to give it back to them."

She knew from Almeron the tin Esparza carried was canister shot, dozens of lead balls packed into the cylinder. When it was fired, he said, it was like a big blast from a shotgun. The Mexicans had left plenty of canister shot inside the Alamo after Almeron and a couple hundred other Texians had run them out of San Antonio after the battle for the town back in December.

Those Mexican soldiers also left scores of rifles and muskets, pistols, all the cannons, including the big eighteen-pounder, and over a hundred kegs of gunpowder, he said, "Enough to hold this place for six months or until Sam Houston marches in with his army, whichever comes first."

A clanging sound coming from the other side of the ramp drew her attention, along with, "Oh hell! This is the most contrary damn horseshoe."

Making her way around to see what the commotion was, she saw Anthony Wolf's two tow-headed youngsters, Nathan and Aleck, come hurrying through the main doors. Nathan carried a coffee pot that was missing its lid, and Aleck had a wooden bucket in his hands. They headed straight toward the commotion.

Susannah followed and saw their father

and Private Tylee, both of her husband's battery. They sat on the flagstone floor beneath one of the torches on the wall. Anthony Wolf had a hatchet he was using to chop apart some old horseshoes. Tylee, a cigar stub clenched between his teeth, was prying the rusty hinges off a broken door. The boys set down their containers.

"We didn't find much, but we brought you everything we could, Pa," Nathan said.

"Here's a piece of chain," Aleck said, taking it out of his bucket and holding it up like a prize fish. "Found it under a busted chair."

"That's real fine, boys," Wolf said as he picked up a piece of kindling, held it to the torch, then used the lit kindling to light his clay pipe. "I doubt there's a chunk of loose iron left to be found in this old fort. And believe me, every Mexican out there that gets a belly full of this will know what hurting means. Did you have some supper?"

They both nodded.

"Good. Sit and rest a bit," Wolf said, and the tired boys plopped down against the ramp wall facing their father and Tylee.

For over a week, Susannah had seen the gunners in the fort gathering every nail, chain link, twisted hasp, and any other rusty piece of scrap they could find. When she'd asked Almeron about it, he said they would fill canvas bags with the stuff and use it along with the canister shot. He called it *langrage* and said it was better than cannonballs for playing hell with Santa Anna's Mexicans.

Wolf and Tylee did not see her as they dropped the pieces into a big wooden barrel set between them.

"As I was saying," Tylee said, "all I know is I want this thing settled. Then I'll only have to worry about rattlesnakes and centipedes."

Wolf stopped his chopping with the hatchet and stared at him. "What?"

"I don't dare slip into a pair of boots or pull on my pants without shaking them out first, and vigorously," Tylee said.

"Hellfire," Wolf said, yanking his pipe from his mouth, "that's about all Texas has, all manner of things that'll stick you or sting you."

"Nothing like them where I come from in New York, I can tell you. And if ol' Santy Anny attacks tomorrow, it'll prove certain he and his men are a godless bunch."

"And why's that?"

"Tomorrow's Sunday, the Lord's day, a day to rest," Tylee said, pausing to rub his lazy eye.

"Now you did plenty of work last Sunday," Wolf said, putting his pipe back in his mouth. "I seen you hauling dirt and sweating right along with me and a whole pack of others." He twisted a chunk of horseshoe loose and dropped it in the barrel. It made a sharp sound when it landed.

"But that's so I can show the Lord I ain't no wastrel. Besides," Tylee said, tugging hard on the hinge, "that work was necessary."

"It's still working on Sunday."

"Yeah, but it ain't like I got a choice in the matter. Come out of there, you miserable damn thing," Tylee said as he pulled the stubborn hinge loose. "Like I said, that work was necessary. That makes the difference. Santy Anny don't have to come tomorrow, not if he's a God-fearing man." He tossed away his chewed cigar stub.

"You know, time comes, I hope I don't end up behind you at the gates of heaven."

"What do you mean?"

"On account of you'll be arguing with God forever, and I hate to think about what I'll be saying if I have to wait. Probably end up in hell for it. And it'll be your fault."

Though she disapproved of cursing, Susannah covered her mouth with her hand so they wouldn't hear her laugh and went back to her room. Once inside, she held Angelina and laughed again. Laughing was wonderful indeed.

Sitting at the table, she busied herself threading a needle. The men would surely be coming by soon to see about their clothes and such. She'd already scrubbed a number of shirts, sewn up a hole in her husband's coat, and patched the pocket on Tylee's vest. Pulling the candle closer to see better, she began sewing a button that had come loose on David Crockett's shirt.

CHAPTER NINE

Moses ran his finger underneath both sides of his long moustache and then knocked on the door of Jim Bowie's quarters. Holding the barrel of his rifle, he rested the butt on the ground and waited. Nearby campfires made his tall shadow shimmer across the door. And, glancing up, he noticed for the first time the cross cut into the stones over the doorway of the small house.

The door opened, and he saw Juana Alsbury looking up at him. Her dark hair was pulled back away from her frowning face.

"What do you want?" She sounded agitated.

"I would like to see the *Colonel*," he said. "I am leaving and wish to say good-bye."

"He is not well. I will tell him your message. Now go away." She started to shut the door on him.

"Please" he said, placing his hand against the door. *"Seulement un instant."*

"*¿Que?*"

"*Pardonnez-moi.* I ask to see him only for a moment."

Annoyed, Juana told him to go, but Moses heard a voice inside and saw a small hand reach out and touch Juana's arm. In the campfire light Moses saw the hand belonged to Gertrudis, Juana's younger sister. She held a sleeping baby in her arms. Moses knew it was Juana's child, a boy. She had married H. A. Alsbury only last January, and the child was from a previous marriage. That husband died. An accident, he'd heard. But Moses figured Juana had to be very worried, as her new husband had been dispatched by Travis the first day of the siege to find Houston, and he had not returned or sent any word. Every soul in the fort knew Juana's father was what Moses called back in France the *grand homme,* but here in Texas he was the *jefe político* of San Antonio de Béxar and a friend of Santa Anna's. And she was having to help care for her sick brother-in-law, Jim Bowie. Moses could not blame her for being irritable.

Gertrudis whispered something to her sister. It was in Spanish, but Moses didn't hear it. He understood Spanish and could speak it fairly well, especially the swear words. Juana spoke English and Spanish, but her sister knew only Spanish.

Juana opened the door, averting her face from him. Probably out of embarrassment, he guessed. He stepped inside the two-room place and removed his floppy hat but held onto his rifle.

Gertrudis, her black hair hanging soft around her shoulders, indicated the other room, where a fire burned in the fireplace. Stepping through the archway to the room, Moses saw Bowie lying in his bed. The same blanket from earlier in the day still covered him. His big knife lay on top of a wooden table by the bed. Moses had never seen such a blade until coming to Texas. Candles flickered in holders in the wall placed on either side of his bed. A gilt-edged crucifix hung on the wall above it.

Moses noticed Gertrudis and Juana busy themselves at the far end of the main room with the baby. He was grateful, as it would give him a little privacy. Bowie's room felt close and stank of sweat. And something else. Moses had smelled it before, years ago, in the awfulness that was Moscow. It was the smell of diseased men, dying men, haunted men.

He went to Bowie's side. In the candle-light, the big man was a shade of himself.

His shirt was damp and stuck to his arms and chest. His face and neck were beaded in sweat, his cheeks drawn, eyes sunken and closed. Moses believed he might be asleep and thought to leave, but the colonel's grey eyes opened; it was a moment before he recognized Moses.

"Well, my friend," Bowie said, raising his arm. There was a wheeze in his voice.

Moses shook his hand. Bowie's grip was fair and his hand moist with sweat.

"I have come to say *adieu, Colonel.*"

"Thank you for that, Moses. Been an honor to know you."

"The honor is mine."

"Help me sit up, will you?"

Moses took his arm as Bowie pushed himself up with some effort to set his back against the wall.

"Better," Bowie said. He reached clumsily for the empty glass on the wooden stool next to his bed. "A drink, Juana, *por favor.*"

Moses heard Juana step softly across the floor. She held a bottle wrapped in a cloth in her hand. From the way she tilted the bottle and poured, he could tell it was close to empty.

"Have a drink," Bowie said.

"*Merci,* no."

Bowie drank down the amber liquid in his

glass, closed his eyes, and rested his head back against the wall. "Can I ask you something, Mose?"

"Of course."

"You have any regrets?"

He recalled the face of his friend who had died in battle . . . the bitter retreat from Moscow . . . the tragedy of the emperor. "A few," he said.

"There's one I got been gnawing at me." Bowie raised his glass to his mouth and realized it was empty. "Another drink, *por favor.*"

As Juana arrived and poured, Bowie said, "Wish I could've settled all this business with Santa Anna myself. You know how? A duel. Him and me. His choice. Pistols, swords. Knives."

He reached over, fumbling a bit as he took his big knife from the table. Holding that wide blade before his face, Bowie said, "Winner takes Texas." He closed his eyes, his arm dropped, the knife falling onto his lap. "Would've been a fight to see."

Not since the retreat from Moscow had Moses seen a man so ill and so broken. The end was coming soon for Bowie, if not in battle, then in his bed. Moses could not blame him for wanting to die like a soldier, standing on his own two feet.

Bowie opened his eyes and raised them to look at Moses. "Did you know he had me arrested once?"

Moses shook his head and listened.

"Claimed I had too much land. Threw me in some godforsaken jail in . . . hell, can't recall now. Can still smell the stink. But I got out. Slick as you please. Walked away when they weren't watching." He chuckled weakly. "Calls himself the Napoleon of the West. Popinjay, more like it. You knew Napoleon, the real one, didn't you?"

"*Oui, mon Colonel.* The emperor would not waste his spittle on this *imposteur.*"

Bowie chuckled again, but it turned into a harsh, rasping cough.

Moses glanced over at the women. Juana started toward them, but Bowie waved her away. His coughing stopped, and he leaned back against the wall as he tried to catch his breath.

Moses was about to take his leave when Bowie brought the glass to his lips and emptied the liquid into his mouth.

"I drink too much," Bowie said. "Makes me ornery. Expect I'll need that orneriness come tomorrow. My wife used to tell me I was so" — he tried to take a full breath — "so cussed ornery I had to live in Texas. No" — he coughed weakly — "no other place was fit for me. You know, I always thought my orneriness was a gift from a . . . a lifetime of sorrows." His glass slipped from his fingers.

Moses saw a profound sadness pass across his face.

"I'd rather die fighting out there . . . on the walls than sweating . . . in . . ." Bowie's eyes fluttered; his voice dropped to a raspy whisper. "Just me and Santa Anna. Winner takes . . . hell of a day, on that sandbar. Hell of a . . ."

Moses leaned over and gently kissed Bowie on the forehead. He could still hear him mumbling as he thanked the women and said good-bye.

Chapter Ten

Standing at the twin battery earthworks near the Alameda, the cottonwood-lined road that angled southeast toward Gonzales, Morales, his three company commanders — Captains Reyes, Escobar, and Victoria — and Colonel Miñón scanned the south wall of the Alamo. It stood about two hundred yards away. The Mexican gun crews on the twin battery had left to have supper, making it a quiet spot for the officers to confer.

"Study it well, *señores*," Morales said, rubbing his white-gloved hands together against the cold air. The gloves helped some. Reyes, Escobar, Victoria, and Miñón also wore white gloves. All of Santa Anna's officers were required to wear them. Even in battle.

A full moon was rising, casting a bright, but cold light. Campfires inside the Alamo on the other side of the wooden palisade added an orange glow to the chapel façade.

The palisade stood dark and ominous in front of that flickering firelight. While he could not see them, the burned-out remains of a handful of *jacales* sat in a rough line about halfway between the Mexican lines and the palisade. Used by the local villagers for storage, those *jacales* were nothing more than mud-plastered hovels with grass and stick roofs. But *soldados* had used them as cover in the early skirmishes with the rebels. And then the rebels had snuck out and burned them down. They were but patches of scorched earth now, but still to be avoided in his plan. And the abatis, that barrier of felled trees spread out in front of the wooden wall, took on an eerie cast in the moonlight. Like claws. *Garras del diablo.* Avoiding it was important, as well.

Morales picked up movement at the big cannon, the eighteen-pounder, at the southwest corner. A new sentry coming on duty. Less than ten yards to the east from that corner of the wall stood an abandoned old stone house. Its thatched roof lay partially collapsed.

Inside the lunette of earthworks and sandbags jutting out from the main gate like a spearhead, a small campfire burned. The rebels had placed two cannons, eight-pounders, there. One faced south to cover the flat, wide, open ground — the Plaza de Valero it was called — that stretched from the south wall out to the Mexican lines about two hundred yards away. The other cannon concerned Morales more.

"When the bugle sounds at four o'clock tomorrow morning, we will attack the south palisade," Morales said. "It is His Excellency's belief that all the rebels will be asleep and caught by surprise. I will lead the attack. In reserve here will be *Coronel* Miñón ready to take command should I become unable to continue."

Miñón graciously nodded at Morales.

"It will be a coordinated attack concentrating on the north, east, and south walls," Morales said, noticing Reyes's frown. "Something, *Capitán?*"

"They may be asleep, sir," the flinty-eyed Reyes said, "but unless our men start right away, we'll be fortunate if any of them are even halfway through that abatis. Finding a way through those damn dead trees can make plenty of noise and take much time. And in this moonlight we will make easy targets."

"Excellent points, *Capitán,*" Morales said. "First, if you will look over toward the east, you'll see clouds gathering. With luck, they will give us plenty of darkness. But whether

116

the clouds come or not, I have decided to have thirty skirmishers take up position close to the palisade prior to the attack."

Morales noticed Reyes and Escobar, whose light complexion betrayed his Spanish roots, exchange surprised looks. Heavy-jowled Captain Victoria, holding a tin cup in his hand, calmly took a sip of his coffee.

"They will move under cover of darkness as quietly as possible around the edges of the abatis to the palisade, being careful to avoid the *jacales*. Breaking a piece of burned wood underfoot, we might as well tie a cowbell around each man's neck," Morales continued. "Reports say the rebels have dug a ditch in front of the palisade. Perhaps three or four feet deep. I am awaiting word on ladders. If we do not have them, the men will have to climb the palisade wall. Whether we have ladders or not, when the bugle sounds, our advance skirmishers will storm the wall through the embrasure the rebels have cut for the cannon at the center of the wall. That surprise assault should give us time for the main force to quickly advance, making our way around both sides of the felled trees in a pincer movement, storm the palisade, and enter the garrison." He intended to bring as many of his men through this battle as he could.

"A bold and clever plan, *Coronel,*" Victoria said after a moment. "If I may?"

"Digame," Morales said.

"The east-facing cannon inside the lunette at the main gate can flank our attack. Perhaps send a detachment of men to take the lunette, and, on doing so, they might even be able to open the gate. With two cannons there, the rebels will have gunpowder for them. There should be enough to blow the gate open."

As much as Morales dreaded the idea of making a run past that east-facing cannon, a cannon the rebels will have no doubt loaded with damned grapeshot, he knew he was already taking a chance with his plan. "The palisade is the weak spot," he said. "Committing a fifth of our men to a surprise assault on it is already a risk. Committing another fifth at least to assaulting the lunette, essentially splitting the command, might well prove to be too much of a gamble. Especially as we have no way of knowing how many rebels defend the lunette."

"If we had more men . . ." Victoria offered.

"His Excellency has given us our orders,"

Morales said.

Victoria grunted quietly.

"Coronel," Reyes said, "by concentrating our attack on the palisade, what of rebel gun fire from the south wall? The rebels will come to the aid of their comrades."

"Surprise will be our advantage. You will choose the ten best sharpshooters from each of your companies. They will act as the advance skirmishers and must keep the rebels in the lunette and on the south wall pinned down while we make our assault. We must take the Alamo by storm. The more quickly we accomplish this, the better. As you all know, His Excellency will tolerate no retreat."

"Of course," Victoria said flatly.

Escobar spoke up. "It is said that Crockett is on the palisade wall."

"I have heard that," Morales said.

"In the skirmish we had a few days ago," Escobar continued, "one of my sergeants reported seeing a rebel attired in what he said was a strange fur hat and buckskins firing from the palisade the whole time. This man stood there with his long rifle, firing and reloading. The sergeant said he and his men fired at him. Not only was he never struck, the man didn't even appear concerned. And he almost never missed what he aimed at."

"If that is the case," Morales said, "and he takes aim at any of us, we shall have no more worries to concern us."

The officers laughed.

"Now, whether that man was Crockett or not, he is one man," Morales said, "and he and his fellow rebels cannot stop the sixty-one-caliber lead ball of the British Baker rifles our *cazadores* carry." All of them at some time had witnessed the terrible damage the Baker rifle could inflict. That ball could make a fist-sized hole in a man or take off an arm. "But make no mistake, once we're over that wall, the bayonet and the sword will decide this battle."

Victoria tilted his head back and drained his coffee cup.

"About the skirmishers, sir," Escobar said. "Would there be any objection to asking for volunteers?"

"No, but they must be reliable men, men who will not panic. *Capitán* Reyes?"

"Yes, sir."

"You shall lead the advance skirmishers."

"It will be my honor, *Coronel.*"

Morales detected no reservation in Reyes's expression.

"And one more thing, *Capitán,*" Morales said. "There is the matter of the forward sentry at the south wall." They were all aware that every night a rebel sentry was posted in a small trench behind a dirt embankment set about fifty yards outside each of the four walls of the Alamo. "It would not do to have the rebels alerted before the attack begins."

"I will see to it."

The sound of someone approaching drew their attention.

"Con su permiso, Coronel," a young messenger said and reached into the satchel he carried slung over his shoulder. Pulling out a parchment scroll tied with a thin red ribbon, he handed it to Morales. "From His Excellency."

The messenger turned and left.

Morales invited the officers back to his command tent across the way. In the lantern light he read His Excellency's orders to all commanders. Morales told them His Excellency stated that each man would be issued two packages of cartridges and two flints.

Indeed, Morales thought, *the bayonet* will *most certainly decide this battle.*

His Excellency had also ordered that each man wear proper brogans, that chin straps be tight. *He treats us as if we are children,* Morales thought with disgust.

"The order also states," Morales said,

" 'The men will wear neither overcoats nor blankets nor anything that may impede the rapidity of their motion.' "

"If tonight is like last night, it will be a cold one," Reyes said, shaking his head.

"We will have only two scaling ladders," Morales said, knowing six would be better.

"Are we issued any axes or crowbars?" Miñón asked. "The rebels have covered windows and doorways in the outer walls with brick. Breaking through them would give us an advantage."

"Eso es cierto," Morales said. "But unfortunately, it would appear only General Cós's column is designated to carry them. Well then, are there any other questions?"

"What are the instructions about prisoners?" Victoria asked.

"No prisoners will be taken," Morales said, rolling up the parchment. "His Excellency was very emphatic about it."

"But if they wish to surrender?"

"His Excellency said he expects every man to do his duty."

After the officers left, Morales stepped outside into the moonlight. It was quiet along the Alameda. He liked it here; he liked the big cottonwood trees. Many of them still held their leaves, sustained by the stream flowing nearby.

To the southeast near a sharp bend in the river, cooking fires burned in La Villita, a scattering of old mud huts that had been an Indian village long ago. Some of the men slept inside those huts, the ones who did not mind the smell, anyway. Dead animal carcasses and God knew what else had been cleared out of them when the army arrived. Reyes, Escobar, and Victoria would assemble their companies at La Villita in preparation for the attack.

Morales knew the rebels in the Alamo would all be dead by sunrise. They were outnumbered. They would be shown no mercy. But he also knew they would fight to the death. Were they all as stubborn and dedicated as Travis? They must be. But Morales would do all he could to bring as many of his own men through this battle as possible. His three captains were good men, good officers. As far as he knew, they were dedicated and loyal to Santa Anna. It may have been out of fear or perhaps zealousness. Morales knew well that His Excellency could promote both in his subordinates. But whether Reyes, Escobar, and Victoria felt as he did about Santa Anna was unimportant at this moment. The upcoming battle was what mattered, and Morales felt confident each of his officers would indeed do his duty. His Excellency had committed himself to making an example of these rebels. And Morales was obliged to carry out his orders. But he would do it his own way.

A light breeze came up, rustling the leaves. He heard the gentle murmur of the stream. For a moment, they offered a temporary tonic to the coming battle.

Chapter Eleven

"Brace is nearly in there, boys," Captain Jameson grunted.

James, his brothers Georgie and Edward, and Cleland Fleet and barrel chested Preacher Garnett strained against the heavy timber post, its base scraping along the ground while Captain Jameson and Hardin Bishop were above on ladders, working it into place with mallets and sweat.

"A little bit more now," Jameson said.

"Get in there, dern it," Georgie puffed.

"Quit lollygagging, Cleland," Edward said.

"You quit," Cleland said, his voice straining. "I'm doing your work and mine."

James heard the beams of the roof moan as he put his shoulder hard into the timber and shoved. They were inside a small house some of the officers bedded down in. It was on the west wall next to the northwest corner gun battery. Three of the roof beams had split badly, and a fourth was in danger of breaking apart. It wouldn't do to have the roof collapse under the feet of the men posted there, Travis had said. The sound of the mallets pounding increased and suddenly stopped.

"That got it?" James called out.

"It'll hold," Captain Jameson hollered, and he and Hardin Bishop climbed down. Jameson inspected the work while James and Georgie and the others stood back, tired, sore, and sweating. Preacher pulled out a cloth to clean his bifocals while Cleland bent over, his hands on his knees.

"By God," he said, panting hard, "when I pulled up stakes from Louisiana to seek a new establishment for myself, I felt a great desire to render service to the freedom of this new country. But this soldierin' business has been damn hard work."

"That should do fine," Captain Jameson said. "Good work. Back to your posts now."

As they picked up their rifles and headed for the door, Hardin said, "Tell me something, Cleland, what was it you said you was figuring to do here in Texas?"

Cleland straightened up. "Maybe become a judge. Hearing cases."

"You never mentioned you knew anything about law," Preacher said, putting his bifocals back on.

"Well, I, I don't exactly but —"

Edward cut him off. "And I don't recall hearing you speaking no Spanish, neither. Lot of folks here don't speak English, you know."

"But when Texas is ours, everybody'll be speaking English," Cleland said.

"Well, they won't be learning it overnight."

"I picked up some Spanish," Cleland said, a touch of indignation in his voice. "Don't you concern yourself about that."

"All right then 'Judge' Fleet," Edward said, "tell me something in Spanish."

James knew Edward was throwing down a challenge. He also knew his brother had learned damn little Spanish in all the years they'd lived here. Except for some cuss words.

Cleland narrowed his eyes at Edward and said, *"Al diablo contigo,"* and walked out.

"Did he just tell me to go to hell?" Edward asked no one in particular.

Preacher said, "I believe he did."

"Doesn't sound like any proper courtroom talk to me." Edward laughed as he went out the door.

James remained behind. There was a bricked-up window in the west-facing wall. Picking up a mallet, he gave those adobe bricks a couple of hard whacks. They held solid, and that was a good thing. Travis had ordered all the openings along the outside of the walls sealed up that first day inside the Alamo. He said every one of them was like an invitation to Santa Anna to come in. Houses and kitchens and storerooms and such, all built side by side, made up the better part of the walls of the Alamo. Almost every wall had doorways and windows that required sealing. Even the chapel had a couple of small windows high up on the side of it, and they were bricked and mortared shut.

That first day, James and Edward and a few others had been assigned to seal every opening in the west wall. James counted fourteen windows and two doorways. But then Travis ordered that one wide window, part of the ruins of a roofless, crumbling adobe hut, would stand open, and a cannon was wheeled to it to help defend the wall.

The house Travis had taken for his headquarters, situated about the middle of the west wall, had a doorway that needed bricking up. A heavy wooden bar that slid into a couple of brackets on either side was all it had to keep it secure. In case of an Indian attack, that was fine, but an eight- or ten-pound Mexican cannon ball was another matter. James and the rest had gathered adobe bricks and stones from the ruins of other buildings inside the garrison to shore it up, along with all the other openings. It took them better than a full day to complete, but, once dried, those gaps in the west wall were good and solid.

But what they could not attend to were the thatched roofs on three of the buildings along the west wall. One was a long building with a pitched thatch roof that sat to the right side of Travis's headquarters. The remains of three curved archways stood in front of it. Some of the men used the rooms inside as a barracks. To the left of Travis's quarters was an open section of wall, another flat-roofed house, and then a wooden platform atop a built-up mound of rubble. A ten-pounder cannon sat on that platform. One of those fellows from New Orleans commanded the gun. He was on the puny side and had bad teeth. On the other side of that battery was a small hut with a flat thatched roof. Next to it was what had been a kitchen. And beside it was a storehouse with a pitched straw roof. If the Mexicans climbed up on any one of those three roofs, they'd have little trouble chopping a hole through that straw and dropping down inside. Or setting them on fire. Maybe that New Orleans fellow and his men could stop them. Well, James didn't want to think about any of that now. Besides, they'd been lucky so far.

"Thank you, kindly!" a voice called out as James climbed back up on the wall to his post. The voice belonged to Captain Albert Martin, the commander of the northwest corner battery. He was one of the officers who used the house they were just working in as sleeping quarters. He walked with a limp. James had been told that during the fight for San Antonio, Captain Martin had managed to cut his foot with an axe. It had slipped while he'd been chopping down a door. He was now coming up the ramp, followed by some of his gun crew. They carried cylinders of canister shot and canvas bags of grapeshot. One held a small keg of gunpowder on his shoulder.

Captain Martin and his men looked bone tired, same as James and the rest of them. As good as it had been to dance and cut loose only an hour ago with the raising of Travis's independence flag, combined with so many near-sleepless nights for the last two weeks, the toll was showing.

Mexican curses drew James's attention to Sergeant Abamillo, who, with his Tejanos, was posted next to Captain Jameson's triple battery at the center of the north wall. Abamillo directed his Tejanos and other men as they lashed more ropes around the upright timbers in place outside the wall there.

James and Edward and Preacher and the others sat and began cleaning and checking their guns. They had their rifles and muskets and shotguns stacked. This section of the north wall was their post, along with Abamillo and his Tejanos. It went from Captain Martin's cannon emplacement to Captain Jameson's battery. There were no structures there, no houses or storerooms, only the ruins of them. James and the others had spent many days and nights with shovels and ropes and timbers packing dirt against the inside of that section of wall. They built it up and held it in place with timber braces inside and outside on account of the wall being in such a poor and weakened condition, according to Captain Jameson. Edward complained they must have piled half the dirt in Texas against it. There was walking space near the top but less than a foot of wall exposed to allow them any cover. Captain Jameson had said they needed to pile the dirt high.

"There must be eight, ten times as many camp fires out there as when this ruckus started," Hardin Bishop said, indicating the Mexican lines. "Good thing they left us all their extra muskets."

"These cheap Mex muskets ain't no Brown Bess when it comes to long range accuracy," Cleland said as he checked the flint of his own Brown Bess musket, "but they'll put a nasty hole in you up close."

"Being on the receiving end of one of these won't leave you in a good humor neither," Hardin said, patting the barrels of his shotgun.

Considering the whole damn Mexican army had surrounded them, James was glad to have been given three of those muskets his first day in the Alamo. Georgie, too. Edward was issued two muskets and a rifle. That rifle was an India Pattern carbine, Major Evans had said. Evans told them the Mexicans had purchased the carbines from the British along with these old muskets and other rifles. These extra weapons, the muskets mostly, were the ones the Mexican army had left behind when they surrendered after the fight for San Antonio. Travis and Bowie had ordered that every man be issued these firearms. The Mexicans had also left paper cartridges. Thousands of them. But they would only use them with the Mexican muskets.

"We can't be certain they use the same amount of powder for their musket that you use for your rifle," Travis had told the men. "Could be the difference between a misfire or your rifle blowing up in your face."

There were bayonets, too, but not so many. The Taylor boys each got one. So had Preacher Garnett. And they were glad to have them. That seventeen-inch lethal blade slid onto the end of the barrel and played hell with reloading. But tonight James couldn't help thinking those bayonets would come in handy, as there would be little time to reload anyway if the Mexicans got over the wall.

"Something strange here," James heard his little brother whisper to him.

"What is it?" James asked.

"I got an extra rifle. When we went down to help Captain Jameson, I only had four. Now I got five."

James glanced at his own pile and saw he had one more rifle than he did before. Then it struck him. "Moses. He must've left us his other rifles."

"I got one, too," Preacher said.

"Hell," Edward griped. "Didn't leave me one. Old bastard."

"You know," Cleland said, "you are the most complainingest cuss I have ever known."

"Who the hell you think you are?" Edward

said, cocking his head to one side.

James chuckled. "He's telling you the plain truth, Edward."

With a disagreeable expression on his face, Edward grunted and pulled a blanket up around his shoulders.

The white moon had half disappeared underneath the clouds moving in, but, looking out over the edge of the north wall, James could make out the gentle waters where the San Antonio River made a bend toward the fort. The large pecan tree at the northwest corner just beyond the wall was harder to see. To the east stood the walled corral, a few horses remaining inside, and the gun emplacement there. He wondered if Santa Anna would attack everywhere at once or try diversions. Captain Martin had said as much earlier to his gun crew. Whatever Santa Anna did, James was as ready as he would ever be. One thing he wished, though, was that the Alamo had been built as a proper fort with parapets and bulwarks for cover up on top of these walls. In that skirmish the other day, he'd crouched down low and fired at those Mexican soldiers and picked off a few before they retreated. Peering over the edge of the wall now at the wooden braces and uprights they'd constructed to try to hold this old wall in place, it was mighty clear he and the rest of boys would have to stand up and lean over to take aim on anybody within ten feet of the wall.

Georgie tapped James's knee and pointed down into the courtyard. James caught sight of Travis coming their way, his Negro, Joe, trailing behind him. Travis strode up the ramp to Captain Jameson's center battery. His sword hung at his side, and Joe carried Travis's shotgun.

Travis looked out into the darkness. Of course, the Mexicans were still there, but James wondered what Travis was pondering. Maybe he saw something else, something James couldn't see.

Suddenly, Travis turned and called out, saying he needed a rider.

"I'll do it!"

James spun around to look at Edward, who had spoken. "What the hell?" James said. "Since when are you any good on a horse?"

"Just you watch me," Edward said, throwing off his blanket.

"What's he doing?" Georgie asked.

James shook his head. But before Edward could make it down from the wall, Travis chose a spry little fellow, not more than fifteen, James thought, named Allen, whose post was on the other side of Jameson's battery.

Edward grumbled an oath.

"I'm sending out one more messenger," Travis said. "If you have a letter, give it to him. Mr. Allen leaves in five minutes."

Neither James nor his brothers had sent word to their older sister Cecilia down in Matamoros since the Christmas before last. He recalled there was some paper in the corner room where he and his brothers and old Moses slept. Telling Edward and Georgie to think quick if they had anything they wanted to say to Cecelia, he ran down to the room, found a piece of paper, and came back to jot down his words.

Hardin, who didn't know how to write, asked Preacher to write his letter for him to his former neighbor. James couldn't help overhearing.

Hardin said, "Let me think now . . . put this down. 'About three months ago I stole a shotgun from your house and some clothes. A big coat and jeans and some socks. The shotgun was near new. I needed them as I was on my way to Texas. Please know I am heartily ashamed of my action. It was always my intention to send you the money for them once I made my fortune here, but that fortune may be delayed, or none at all, as things are looking grim. I hope you accept my apology for the theft. Signed, Hardin Bishop.' "

James noticed Cleland checking one of his rifles.

"You ain't writing a letter?" James asked.

"Got no one to send it to," Cleland said without looking his way.

James wrote quickly.

Dear Sister, This must be short as a rider waits. We may not see you again. We are surrounded and a fight is coming but we are ready. If we defeat this Santa Anna, the country will be ours. Should we fail, do not be sad for us. Pa always told us to live free and bend your knee to no man. No shame in that. I am watching the moonrise tonight. I take solace in knowing you may be watching it as well. My only regret is that if I or Georgie or Edward should not survive this battle, TJ Chambers will not be made to pay for what he did to Pa. He is a guilty man. I know this to be true though I cannot prove it. He should die a horrible death. Tell little Robert and Nancy to be good.

James looked over at his brothers. "Anything you want to say?"

Edward shook his head. Georgie asked him to tell them he loved them. Georgie looked distressed.

"You all right?" James asked.

Georgie nodded. "It's nothing. Just miss them is all."

James finished, then folded the letter and addressed it.

Allen was adjusting the bridle on his little mare as James rushed up and pushed the letter into his hand. A couple of other men quickly followed, and Allen stuffed all the letters into a satchel.

Travis appeared and told Allen, "Find Fannin. Tell him his countrymen need him, now." Travis ordered the main gate opened.

James watched as Allen rode out and the gate was quickly closed and barred. James noticed most of the men — in the courtyard, up on the walls — were also watching.

Returning to his post on the north wall, all James could think about was that there had been no rifle shots, no shouting from the Mexican lines when Allen rode out. Maybe he would make it to Fannin. Maybe Fannin was already close by. Maybe there was still hope.

As he sat down and picked up a rifle, James noticed Preacher, his Bible open in his hands, staring at it, a deep frown on his face.

"What's troubling you, Preacher?" James asked.

Preacher sighed. "I've read this passage from the Book of Psalms eight times, but all I can think about is I wished I'd written a letter to my wife before that rider went out."

CHAPTER TWELVE

Her shawl draped around her shoulders, Susannah walked to the cooking fire in front of the chapel. She held a blackened coffee pot in her hand, planning to boil the water inside to make tea. Tilting her head, she watched as the moon disappeared behind the clouds. Just for a few moments, that big, round, white full moon had reminded her of the china plates she had prized so, the ones all the way from Philadelphia, the ones now certainly lost. She pushed the bittersweet memory away. Angelina and Almeron were all she wanted to occupy her thoughts at the moment.

She greeted Ana Esparza with a nod of her head.

Ana and her children sat near the fire. It took the chill out of the air. Her boys, Enrique, Manuel, and Francisco, stared into the flames. Little Maria rested her head against her mother's shoulder, her eyes closed.

Susannah bent down and placed the pot on the edge of the glowing red embers. A black kettle simmered over the fire. Corn mush still bubbled inside the kettle.

Enrique moved to his mother's ear and whispered something. She nodded, and the three brothers leapt up and ran to the chapel.

"They say they are still hungry," Ana said to Susannah.

"Still some here. I think everyone's had their fill by now anyway," Susannah replied.

"Did you see?" Ana asked. "Travis sent out another rider."

"No," Susannah said surprised. "When?"

"Not long." Ana shrugged, pulling her *rebozo* closer. "Maybe twenty minutes ago."

Susannah said nothing. Travis had sent out so many riders. Some had come back. Some had not.

"I'm making some tea," she said to Ana. "Can I bring you a cup?"

Ana shook her head and quickly wiped away a tear.

"Ana, what's wrong?" Susannah asked.

This woman who seemed to always show such determination, a will of iron, turned away, embarrassed maybe to show her tears.

"It is certain," Ana finally said. "My husband's *hermano,* his brother. He is out there. One of the *soldados.*" She drew her lips tight. "I will not speak his name out loud."

Enrique and his brothers came hurrying back, bowls in hand. Their grins disappeared upon seeing their mother upset.

"*¿Mamá?*" Enrique asked.

Ana shook her head and spoke to them in Spanish.

Susannah guessed she was telling them everything was fine and they needed to eat. It's what she would have said. But then Ana faltered stepping toward the kettle, and Susannah told her she would take care of it. As she scooped a ladle of corn mush into each of their out-stretched bowls, they thanked her and sat down to eat. Enrique took a spoonful but didn't bring it to his mouth. Susannah could tell he and his brothers were worried about their mother.

Susannah moved next to Ana and asked how she knew it was her husband's brother.

"During the music playing," Ana said. "Gregorio was on top of the chapel, and he saw a *soldado* shouting at him, calling his name. The *soldado* took off his tall hat. Gregorio says it is him."

"But how can he be so sure?"

142

"His *hermano* called him by the name they used as children."

"Oh. I am so sorry."

Ana blew out a disapproving breath. "Don't be. That *hermano* is a . . . oh, how do you say? An idiot."

Susannah listened as Ana explained that the last time her husband and his brother saw each other was very bad. "The brother, he called Santa Anna the hope of Mexico. Gregorio told him he is a fool to believe that. It was terrible. The things they said, accusing each other of being traitors. They have not spoken since. A long time."

"Is he worried he might face his brother?"

"He doesn't say." Forcing a smile, she glanced up at Susannah. "It is sad and good together. *¿Sí?* On the one hand, a lost brother is found. On the other, he should have stayed lost."

Susannah heard the water boiling in the pot and said she would bring Ana a cup of hot tea. It was all she could think of to do.

"No," Ana said, "we will be fine." She put her arm around her daughter and hugged her close.

Gathering the folds of her dress in her hand, Susannah reached down and took hold of the coffee pot handle. Straightening up, she saw Travis approaching. Joe was not following behind him.

Travis said, "Forgive me, Mrs. Dickinson. May I have a word? In private, please?"

He seemed earnest in his request, she thought. But even when he was trying to be civil, he still sounded like he was giving orders.

Susannah glanced at Ana and saw that she had silently gathered up her children, and they were halfway to the chapel.

"Can I make you a cup of tea?" she asked Travis as she started for the chapel. She was only being polite and hoped he would say no.

"Thank you, yes," he said, following her.

Inside Susannah's sacristy room, Angelina lay asleep on the bed. Travis sat stiffly at the table. Susannah set down a dented tin cup in front of him and one for herself.

"I'm sorry I don't have proper teacups," she said as she poured the dark steaming tea, filling his cup.

"Many thanks," he said. "This will be fine." He took a sip and seemed to relish it. "Tea helps me, clears my head."

She was pleased that he appreciated the trouble she'd gone to for him. She poured a cup for herself and sat down on the edge of the bed. These were more words than he'd spoken to her since coming into the Alamo.

What did he want?

He kept his hands around the cup as though he were warming them. Then Susannah watched, puzzled, as he pulled his ring from the ring finger of his right hand. It was a beautiful ring of hammered gold with a black, polished stone, like a cat's eye. She couldn't remember seeing him wear it before. He set it on the table, reached into his jacket pocket, and pulled out a piece of straw-colored twine.

He did not meet her eyes as he ran the twine through the ring. "Your daughter is very precious," he said. "She may well be the future of Texas. It would be my honor to give her my ring, with your permission, of course."

"Colonel, we . . . we can't accept this," Susannah said, flustered.

"I am not the most . . . respectable man, Mrs. Dickinson, but I would . . . I need her to have it. This ring is the only thing I have of real value anymore. I would prefer to know that she has it, not some Mexican trollop who'd trade it for a drink."

At that moment, Susannah saw it, the plea in his eyes. Helplessness mixed with hopefulness.

"All right then," she said before even realizing the words had come out of her mouth.

He rose, came around to the bed and knelt on one knee. He leaned over to Angelina and gently looped the twine around her neck and tied it securely. Then he stood, appeared as though he were about to say something, and abruptly turned and left the room. No word of thanks. Not so much as a smile. Just up and walked out. But Susannah did not see it as his being rude or arrogant, those traits that were so easily second nature to him in her mind. And she did not attribute his gruff action to the burdens of command on this of all nights. No, she believed with absolute certainty she had witnessed the closest she, perhaps anyone, might be allowed to get to William Barrett Travis. She felt sorry for him, something she would have never believed possible before this.

"My Lord," she whispered as she brought her hand up to her neck and clutched her brooch.

CHAPTER THIRTEEN

"¡Oye! ¡Francés!"

Moses cast a look in the direction of the voice as he walked down the stone steps from the hospital roof. He knew Spanish fairly well. Someone was calling out for the "Frenchman."

Planting his feet on the compound ground, Moses saw Sergeant Juan Abamillo coming toward him. The big man had a hard face. He wore a serape, floppy hat, and old leather sandals. He and Moses had shot at Mexican skirmishers together from the north wall and shared water while on sentry duty. Yet Abamillo hardly talked much to him.

Moses also recognized the Comanche war hawk club Abamillo carried in his belt. A barbaric looking thing. So was Abamillo, if the stories Moses had heard were true. Where that savagery came from was the subject of rumor. However, one story was known. A few years ago, Abamillo had gone hunting along the Medina River some twenty-five miles northwest of town. A Comanche war party attacked him. Two days later, Abamillo, with three arrows in him, was found alive. He said he had crawled through the night. In his hand was the war hawk club, covered in dried blood. All he would say about the attack was that they had killed his horse, and he had left the bodies of the Comanches as a warning to the tribe. On hearing that story, Moses had almost pitied the poor Mexican *bâtards* outside the walls, the ones who would face Abamillo.

"Have you chosen your way out?" Abamillo asked.

Moses shook his head. Holding his long rifle in the crook of his arm, he adjusted the blanket roll he had tied and strung over his shoulder. "I believe this darkness is the only thing in my favor."

Abamillo grunted. "Where will you go?"

"East. As far from Santa Anna and here as is possible," Moses said. He told Abamillo that going over the corral wall looked promising, but a couple of large ponds had formed on the east side in the last few days when the *acequia* there overflowed. "I will only attract attention slogging through that mud."

Abamillo nodded.

"Finding a good place to cross the river would be the best," Moses said. "There's a spot near the north wall I've seen that does not appear too wide, I think. *Très possible.*"

"There is maybe a better place," Abamillo said.

"Dîtes-moi," Moses said. "I'm listening."

Abamillo told him to make his way along the south wall, pick up the *acequia* bed on the other side of the abandoned stone house at the southwest corner and follow it to the river. "It is a good place to cross. The water, it is only this high." He tapped a spot below his chest. "Trees are thicker on the other side of the river." He shrugged. "Then a short walk to town."

"How do you know about the water there?"

"Béxar is my home."

"I did not know."

"You can see my house from the west wall."

"Is your family there?"

Abamillo shook his head. "When we heard Santa Anna was coming, I sent my wife and three sons to stay with her father. His *rancho* is north, on the river."

"They're safe, then." Weeks ago Moses had seen many families fleeing San Antonio at word of Santa Anna's approach.

"*Sí, gracias a Dios.* But my house, a Mexican officer lives in it now. I have seen him there," Abamillo said bitterly. "My poor wife, she will return and scrub the walls, but they will not be clean enough. *El hedor,* the stench, it will still be there." He shook his head. "But that is not your concern."

Taking a bundle from under his serape, Abamillo held it out to Moses. "You must look like you belong here."

Opening the bundle, Moses stared at the scruffy pair of moccasins and straw hat that were wrapped up in a brown serape with white markings.

"I don't —"

"Bide your time, *Francés.* Do not be in a hurry. The *soldados* will not care about an old man. Especially one *sin importancia.*"

"Not important?"

"Put on the clothes."

"Whose clothes are these?"

"*Mi amigo,* Benito Cruz. He does not need them anymore."

Moses remembered seeing Cruz shot in the belly during the last attack on the north wall. Doctor Pollard said he might live. Apparently he had, but only for a few days.

"I'm sorry," Moses said. "About your friend."

"He is dead. Nothing more to say. He was a big man. Like you."

Moses had no qualms about wearing a dead man's clothes. He had pulled the heavy coat from the back of a dead French grenadier outside Moscow. And during that bitter retreat from Russia, he stabbed a fellow soldier in a fight over a pair of boots he'd taken off the feet of a frozen comrade. Moses didn't want to die then, either.

Setting his long rifle against the wall, Moses pulled the serape over his head.

"Leave your rifle," Abamillo said.

"But —"

Abamillo cut him off again. "If the *soldados* stop you, they will take it away. If you fight them, they will shoot you, or take you prisoner and execute you later."

Moses grudgingly handed Abamillo his long rifle.

"The powder horn and balls," Abamillo said. "They will take them, as well."

Moses untied the leather pouch from his belt and took off the powder horn that hung from the piece of twine. He wasn't about to mention the hunting knife he was carrying in a sheath behind his back. Holding the moccasins out to Abamillo he said, "I don't need these moccasins. I'm keeping my boots."

Abamillo shook his head. "Boots are prized by *soldados*."

Mumbling an oath in French, Moses steadied himself against the wall and pulled off his boots.

"They will let me keep my spoon and bowl, won't they? And my blanket?"

"Perhaps. Perhaps not."

"Maudits bâtards," Moses said.

"En español."

"Malditos bastardos."

"Your Spanish is good. You curse like one of us," Abamillo said. "And your skin, it is dark enough."

With the moccasins on his feet, Moses said, "Why do you help me? We have barely spoken before this."

"Let us say I am feeling generous. The first time in a long time. And cut off your mustache. It is too much." He indicated the long ends of Moses's moustache.

"No. *Absolument,"* Moses said. "Grenadiers in the *Grande Armée* can never do such a thing. Those were the orders of the emperor."

Abamillo walked past him. "Then keep your head down, and pray the *soldados* do not stop you."

CHAPTER FOURTEEN

"Thank you, ma'am," David Crockett said to Susannah in her sacristy room as she handed him his clean white shirt. "Looks about as new as the day I bought it."

"Oh, you're just being kind," she said. For one thing, she'd had no white thread to sew the button on his shirt and had to use blue instead, which she'd pulled from the hem of the cuff of her sleeve.

"No, I mean it. I'd been serving in Congress, and, what with all the backstabbing going on there, inside of a few months the shirt I had was so full of holes it wasn't near presentable. When the folks in my district saw fit to vote me out of that body — a happy day in my life by the way — I purchased this one, and it's done right well by me ever since."

She laughed. "I'm glad to hear it."

"Yes, ma'am. And, seeing that I expect to be killed tomorrow, I wanted to have on clean clothes for when they bury me. Seems the decent thing to do."

Susannah was startled. "Mr. Crockett, you're . . . I hope you're joking. Aren't you?"

He paused a moment and chuckled. "Tell you the truth, Mrs. Dickinson, I'm not rightly sure anymore myself."

She didn't know what to say.

"I did want you to know it has been a real comfort seeing you and your baby everyday. It's meant a great deal to me, and my men. Because" — he hesitated and glanced down at his feet and rubbed his thumb under his nose — "it reminds me of back home. My wife and children. Well, I wanted you to know that." He smiled at her and left the room, picking up his long rifle that he'd left at the doorway.

Susannah had seen that smile of his every day since coming into the Alamo. There was something always reassuring about it, even now, in spite of his strange comment. Crockett was known for his dry wit, Almeron had told her. She decided that's what it was. She also decided it was better to think of it that way.

CHAPTER FIFTEEN

James sat near the torch that burned by the cannon on the northwest corner. He put a sharper edge on his tomahawk and tried to think of anything except the Mexican army waiting outside the walls. Edward was cleaning a musket. Preacher, Cleland, and Hardin were busying themselves as well. One of the cannon crewmen stood guard on the corner, while his fellow gunners had propped themselves against the wheels, hats pulled low, trying to catch up on sleep. Everybody was being real quiet, and it was starting to bother James. It was like every pass he made sharpening his blade was running right along his nerves. He was glad when Georgie came running up the earthwork.

"I just saw old Moses," Georgie said.

"What the hell, is he leaving or not?" Edward asked.

"He's going, all right," Georgie said as he sat down next to James and pulled the bayonet off the barrel of his Mexican musket. "Looked like he was heading for the palisade, I think. Almost didn't recognize him."

"Why's that?" James asked.

"He was wearing a Mexican poncho and a straw hat."

Edward grunted.

"And he shaved off his moustache, too."

"Now that is something," Preacher said. "He say why he did that?"

"I didn't think to ask, I was so surprised," Georgie said. "But I did shake his hand and wish him luck. Told him we appreciated him leaving us his rifles, too."

Edward mumbled something.

"Moses wasn't carrying his rifle, come to think of it," Georgie said.

"Old fool bastard," Edward sniffed.

"Could be he's doing the smart thing all 'round, you know, looking like a Mexican and all," Cleland said.

"Maybe so," James said. "But if they were to catch him out there toting a gun they'd likely shoot him."

"That's right," Georgie said. "He can always get another gun. He'll have plenty of opportunity."

There was an awkward silence. James paused, still sharpening his tomahawk. Cleland stopped wiping down his long rifle. Holding his hooked needle, Hardin was sewing a piece of cowhide on the bottom of one of his moccasins. It had a hole the size of his thumb.

"Sorry," Georgie mumbled as he took out his whetstone and began putting a sharper edge on his bayonet.

James leaned over to him and said low, "Don't worry about it."

A few moments passed as the screech of blades being sharpened and the distinctive clicks of gun hammers being cocked and checked mixed with the soft crackle of the torches.

James noticed Georgie fanning his thumb over his bayonet blade.

"You not getting an edge on it?" he asked his little brother.

"I don't know," Georgie said without looking up.

"You don't know?"

"No, I mean I never used one of these before."

Preacher said, "You make sure it's on that rifle tight, you point it at the Mexican, and stick him in the belly."

"Good and hard," Hardin said, yanking the needle through the moccasin.

"First time I used one was in that fight in

San Antonio," Preacher said. "My flintlock misfired, and this Mexican came at me. Made a lunge and sliced my hand with his bayonet." He turned his hand and displayed the long white scar below his knuckles. "I tossed away my gun and snatched a musket from a dead Mexican and turned it on him. We did a lot of hollering and jabbing at each other, until I stuck him."

"That is right," Hardin said. "We went house by house, driving those bastards out into the street."

"The Lord will smite the wicked," Preacher said.

Georgie leaned forward. "But —"

"Believe me, you'll know what to do," Preacher said.

"That blade's better than a foot long," Hardin said. "You stick that in him, he'll know he's been stuck." He tied off the heavy thread he was using and slipped his moccasin back on his foot. "Much better," he said, admiring his handiwork.

James could see the concern on his brother's face. "If you're worried about it, leave the bayonet off, take a firm hold to the barrel, swing it like a club, and you cut a path through them Mexicans all the way to Santa Anna himself. Then you hit him so hard with it you send him rolling all the way back across the Rio Bravo."

While the others laughed, Georgie gave him a lopsided grin.

"I like that," Edward said. "Like to get a bead on that son of a bitch myself."

"What time do you have, Georgie?" James asked, looking out into the compound.

Georgie pulled out his silver pocket watch. "About half past nine."

"Travis is making his third round tonight," James said, seeing Travis and Major Evans below him as they headed up the earthen ramp to Captain Martin's battery.

James liked Evans because he called almost everybody "lad." Travis and Evans were asking Martin about something to do with the grapeshot. At least that's all James heard. Satisfied, Travis and Evans went down the ramp and over to Captain Jameson's battery. Probably with the same questions.

A fellow missing his front teeth and wearing a grey hat scurried up the earthwork toward James and the others. He was carrying a couple of buckets in his hands. His name was Pettis.

"Got cartridges and balls here, if'n you need more," he said, setting the buckets down. James gladly helped himself to both.

"I'll take some," Georgie said and squatted down by the buckets.

"Help yourselves there." Pettis stole a glance over toward the center battery, where Travis and Evans stood. "Sure wish Colonel Bowie was still in command," Pettis said, his voice low.

James shot him a look. "What are you saying?"

"I come in with Bowie," Pettis said, "and there ain't a better born leader here. Well, him and Crockett, I guess. But you take Bowie — tough as hickory bark, he is. Killed that feller in that sandbar scrape. You know about that?"

James nodded. "Some."

"Bowie stuck that feller with that big knife of his after he'd been stabbed and shot twice," Pettis said as Edward and the others came over to collect more cartridges and balls. "All I knowed Travis to do was to set fire to prairie grass, and for what? Burn up forage to slow down this Mexican army? That kinda failed, you ask me."

"Well, we're still here, too," James said.

Preacher said, "Travis has done pretty well so far."

"Maybe so," Pettis said, "but I hear the man's a scoundrel. Left his wife and family and lies with whores. But he's paying for it now, pissing pins and needles."

"What are you talking about?" James asked.

"The clap."

"What's that?" Georgie asked.

"Guess you ain't been around much," Pettis said. "He gets a powerful burning in his prod when he pisses. Hurts like sin, or so I'm told."

"If you don't like how Travis has handled things, why didn't you leave with old Moses?" James asked.

Pettis snorted. "On account of I ain't never run from a fight in my life. And I ain't starting by turning tail in front of a bunch of damn Mex. Hell, I'd just as soon spit in their eye as look at them. One Texian's worth ten of them. You best remember that." He said that last looking square at James.

"Maybe you best move on, mister," James said, an edge in his voice.

Pettis picked up his buckets. As he headed down the embankment, he mumbled that a man's character is all he's got in this world.

"Stupid bastard," Edward grumbled. "Telling us what we ought to remember."

"Sounded to me like he's just angry about Bowie," Cleland said.

"Might be," James said, but he was thinking about the look he saw on the man's face.

Somehow it appeared to him that man was more scared than angry.

Preacher stood, rifle in hand, adjusted his bifocals, and said he wanted to stretch his legs. Hardin said he'd join him.

As they left, James glanced up and noticed Cleland was talking to one of the gunners at the center battery. Georgie added the lead balls to his shot pouch, and Edward sat back and closed his eyes. James fanned his thumb over the new edge he'd put on his tomahawk and decided it would do fine. As he slipped it back into his belt, Georgie said, "I was thinking, James, about something you said a while back."

"What did I say?"

"Well, about becoming a Texas Ranger when this Santa Anna business is settled."

"I did say that."

"But you meant it, didn't you?"

" 'Course I did," James said.

"I'm glad to hear it, because I wanted to say I'd like to join up with you, if you wouldn't mind."

"Sure, Georgie. That sounds like a good idea."

James figured Georgie was looking for something promising to hang on to about now. Couldn't blame him for that. James figured a lot of the men were likely doing that very same thing. Thinking about the good things in their lives . . . things they've got, things they want . . . things that mean something . . . important things.

"You talk to Gertrudis?" James asked his little brother.

"Oh . . . ah, no. There's been so much to do."

"You ought to, you know."

Georgie shrugged. "I'd like to. But that sister of hers keeps a pretty keen eye on her."

"Well," Edward joined in. "I seem to recall you and Miss Amanda Dorsett making eyes at each other."

Georgie bristled. "And that didn't exactly work out, if you remember."

That was true enough, James thought.

Amanda Dorsett was the daughter of Captain Theodore Dorsett and his wife, Mary. They had a farm situated along the Trinity River near the town of Anahuac on the north side of Trinity Bay. Captain Dorsett was a Texas Ranger, one of a dozen or so men Stephen Austin had asked to help protect all those hundreds of families that had come to Texas to start new lives. Pa knew Dorsett because he'd done business with him over the years, selling him pelts and such, and also because Pa had helped Dorsett with his Ranger duties by acting as a scout, since Pa knew much of the land in these parts.

Following Pa's murder and the family being forced to split up after losing their home to that Thomas Jefferson Chambers bastard, James and his brothers decided they would stick together. Soon, hunting and trading pelts became wearisome to the brothers. In another effort to make money, they took various jobs in taverns, stables, and stores, but none lasted.

A couple of years passed, and Captain Dorsett offered the brothers work on his farm. That included bed and board. The boys readily accepted.

Captain Dorsett's business was raising and selling cotton, and he'd profited well by it. James and his brothers quickly discovered it was hard, backbreaking work, especially Edward, who complained bitterly, but only to his brothers.

And then Edward came up with a plan. It was illegal as hell in Mexico, but Captain Dorsett believed that strong dissatisfaction with new laws passed by the Mexican government — like the excessively high tariffs on goods imported from the United States — meant changes were coming for Texas, possibly even independence. And if that was to be the case, then Edward's plan to smuggle in two hundred barrels of bourbon whiskey sounded like a damn fine idea, particularly since Edward offered to cut Captain Dorsett in for a share of the profits. Captain Dorsett also longed for "a nip or two of fine ol' bourbon," being that he hailed from Georgia. He loaned Edward the money.

Edward had hoped to have his brother-in-law smuggle the stuff in, but the old bastard had "retired" from buccaneering and moved to Matamoros, thanks to his wife, who opened a dress shop there. That left Edward to make his own inquiries. He contacted Buchanan & Tetlow in New Orleans to act as the shipping agent and sent them the money to cover the cost of the bourbon and delivery. The proprietors were very sympathetic to the Texas cause and saw to it that the barrels were fitted with false tops, placing bibles in some, sugar in others. They had the barrels loaded onto the *Rachel Louise,* a privateer. That pleased Edward, because the skipper of the *Rachel Louise* came highly recommended, as he'd been running contraband goods into Mexico for some time. He provided counterfeit Mexican bills of lading printed for bibles and sugar coming from Veracruz and marked the barrels accordingly.

Unfortunately, Mexican authorities had caught on to the skipper's schemes, and the Mexican ship *Bravo* intercepted the *Rachel Louise* as it entered Galveston Bay. The skipper was imprisoned and the *Rachel Louise* impounded, its confiscated cargo becoming the property of the Mexican government. To make matters worse, Buchanan & Tetlow had made no provision for insurance since Edward had not specified a request for insurance. James and Georgie offered to help pay off Edward's debt to Captain Dorsett. It would keep all three brothers on the Dorsett farm for the next few years.

And then Amanda Dorsett came home. She had been away at a fancy school in South Carolina. It was the same school Mrs. Dorsett had attended. Amanda's hair was a mass of golden curls and her eyes big and blue. Georgie was smitten. And, after a short time, so was Amanda. But before Georgie would make any offer of marriage, he insisted he and his brothers be free of their debt. Amanda said she would wait.

A week later, this ruckus started up with Santa Anna.

James and his brothers announced that they had to fight and needed to join up with the army Sam Houston was raising.

Mrs. Dorsett and Amanda burst into joyful tears at the news. Captain Dorsett was proud of them, so proud, he forgave the balance of their debt. "If I was a younger man, I'd be joining you boys," he told them. "Give that Santa Anna a lick for us. Thinks he can run roughshod over us however he pleases. Not by a jugful!"

James and Georgie were astonished when Captain Dorsett presented each of them with a new long rifle, shot pouch, and powder horn. Edward already had Pa's rifle. He had considered selling it for gambling money after their pa's funeral, but James had talked him out of it. First, because it was Pa's, and he called it "My Lizzie" after Ma. Pa had even gone to the trouble to carve "My Lizzie" into the stock of the rifle, and quite handsomely at that. And, second, James told Edward if he sold Pa's rifle, he would buy it back and shoot Edward himself.

Mrs. Dorsett took Georgie aside and gave him a silver pocket watch. She said it had belonged to her father. She also gave him a new pair of buckskin breeches, saying it wasn't proper he should go off to fight looking like he had already been in one. Picking cotton was long, hard, sweaty work.

And sometime during that last night

before leaving the farm, Georgie and Amanda had some kind of mishap. When James asked him about it, Georgie refused to say. As the captain had no horses to spare, James and brothers had to walk. For the first three days, Georgie didn't say much of anything, keeping his own counsel, blue as it was.

On the fourth day, while they were crossing a streambed, Georgie finally told him and Edward what had happened. Amanda tried to convince him to stay behind at the farm, as she did not want him to go. She said that since her father had forgiven the debt, Georgie could marry her. Georgie said he told her it was his duty to fight, and she told him his duty was to her. James asked him if he and Amanda had engaged in relations, and Georgie swore they had not. James believed him. Edward, however, grunted and walked on ahead. James heard him mumbling about how he wished he had a horse. Or a mule.

When James asked Georgie if he thought there was any hope with Amanda, Georgie surprised him by saying, "If she was going to act that way, trying to make me shirk my responsibilities, she's not the girl I thought she was, and she can find herself some fancy fellow."

Glancing at Georgie now, sitting next to him on this wall, James realized that, after walking nearly two hundred miles to the Alamo and then working day and night shoring up the north wall, Georgie's new buckskin breeches had long lost their yellow newness, having become grease-coated shiny and sweat-stained hard.

"And I also recall that cousin of the Dorsetts took quite an interest in you, James," Edward said. "A fine looking woman."

"That she was," James said.

Charlotte Booth, a cousin of the Dorsetts who was visiting from South Carolina, had the blackest hair and the whitest skin and the greenest eyes he'd ever seen. She had the look of a wildcat in those eyes. Especially when she pressed herself against him. Oh, she and James did have a time. Captain Dorsett nearly caught them once up in the hayloft. They were peeled pink naked, and Charlotte commenced giggling. James clapped his hand over her mouth, and she bit him. Not so that she drew blood, but hard enough that it made him almost cry out. He looked at his hand now and thought he could still see the mark she'd left on the fleshy side of it. When he and his brothers said they were going to fight Santa Anna,

Charlotte told him she'd wait for him. He had sent her a letter with one of the first riders Travis dispatched from the Alamo. He wrote that he believed this business would be over in a few weeks, and that he'd be coming back to the Dorsett farm and had something important he wanted to ask her.

Glancing out across the darkness at the campfires scattered throughout the Mexican lines, James pushed away the thought that he would not have the chance to ask her his question. Now she was two hundred miles away. Or maybe Captain Dorsett had sent her back to South Carolina. James thought of the many times he could swear he caught the scent of her hair in a passing breeze and wished he could see her one more time. Damn, he missed her.

"Look there," he heard Georgie say.

James followed his gaze and saw Gertrudis and her sister walking across the compound. Juana held her baby, and Gertrudis clasped a cloth bundle in her arms. A couple of Bowie's men followed, one on each end of a large wooden trunk they carried between them. James and Georgie watched as they entered the flat-roofed adobe house where they had earlier braced the roof. It butted up against the gun emplacement at the corner.

"I thought they were looking after Colonel Bowie," Edward said

"Something's changed, I reckon," Georgie said.

"You should go talk to her, find out," James said. "Offer to help."

Georgie grinned. "Maybe I will."

James saw the disgusted look on Edward's face as he watched Georgie jump down from the earthworks and head for the house.

"Something bothering you, Edward?" James asked.

"Just don't know what he sees in that Mex girl, is all."

"What does that matter now?"

"I ain't partial to Mexes. You know that."

"You've mentioned it." James sighed.

Edward snorted. "Well, you tell me how the hell you can trust somebody who stinks like a mule, got skin the color of dried tobacco, and, when you look them in the eye, you can't tell what they're thinking. Can't trust somebody you can't tell what they're thinking, simple as that."

"Just let it be."

"And where did this ranger idea of yours come from?"

James gave him an exasperated look.

"Maybe because Captain Dorsett is one and . . . and maybe I like the idea of riding around this country, not being tied down." He shook his head ruefully. "No more farming for me. That was more work than I cared to do."

Edward chuckled. "I did like Dorsett's place."

"Hold on. All that complaining you did, and you want a farm?"

"You bet. Just like Dorsett's, only bigger."

"What's got into you?"

"Oh, big plans," Edward said. "I figured to grow cotton, but I wasn't planning to be the one to pick it. No more welts and cuts on my hands, fingers bleeding, knees raw to the bone, back bent over all day lugging those heavy sacks. No, I'd buy some niggers. Have them do it. That's why I was willing to fight, on account of Santa Anna outlawing having slaves." Edward set his rifle aside. "I was thinking I'd ask you and Georgie to come in with me."

"Me and Georgie?" James said, surprised.

"Austin promised every man who fights six hundred and forty acres of land. I figured the three of us could throw in together. We'd have a good spread."

"Out of curiosity, where is all this land you figured on having?"

"You recall that stretch of ground we came through along that creek, the one about midway between here and Gonzales?"

"We crossed a lot of creeks getting here."

"The one I said that if Pa had seen it, he'd of packed us up and moved us? I could see acres and acres of cotton growing all along there."

James did remember. It was a pretty spot, with canebrakes and green trees taller than what they had left back in Tennessee. A man was nothing without land, Pa used to say. You were somebody when you owned land.

"We'd've made a lot of money. Makes no never mind now," Edward said and snorted disgustedly.

James felt sorry for his older brother, even though Edward was a lazy sort, always looking to take the easy road. And a complainer of the first order, as Pa would say. Blowing up Pa's still had been an accident, but it could have gotten Pa thrown in jail. And Edward's one big idea, smuggling liquor into Texas, backfired something fierce, not to mention costing Captain Dorsett a pot full of money. Pa liked to say there were two constants in bad times: the good Lord and reasonable liquor. To find the downside constant in Edward's life all he had to do was look in a mirror.

173

Pulling the bayonet off the end of his Mexican musket, James checked its sharpness. Dissatisfied, he began to run the blade edge over his whetstone . . . and allowed himself to dream a little of being a Texas Ranger, hunting desperadoes and driving off Comanches.

Chapter Sixteen

His white-gloved hands clasped behind him, Morales stood by a campfire burning near a mud hut in La Villita, the old Indian village inside the Mexican lines. The smell of burned *frijoles* lingered in the air. He listened closely as Captain Reyes gave the thirty sharpshooters their orders for the attack on the wooden palisade. Reyes was specific about the duties of the men, making certain they understood the details of the plan. Morales was confident he had chosen the right officer to lead the initial assault.

Captains Escobar and Victoria were mustering the main body of the force on the other side of La Villita. Once all was in readiness, Morales would order the men up to the open flats of the Plaza de Valero.

At this moment, though, in the glow of the campfire light, he studied the faces of the sharpshooters. These were determined, unafraid, dependable men. Some had tasted combat fighting the Spanish for independence, as he had almost a decade ago. Others he recognized as brave men he had led in sorties against the Apache and the Comanche, as well as against the rebel troops at Zacatecas.

Each man was armed with a Baker rifle and bayonet. They wore the distinctive dark green cords and plumes of the *cazadores* on their tall, black Shako hats and green trim on their short, blue jackets, along with black cross-belts and white trousers. Morales nodded his approval. At least these were regular troops, not the convicts His Excellency had ordered conscripted from the prisons or the peons he'd pulled from their villages on the march north, to add numbers to his army. Those poor wretches were not trained *soldados,* in spite of the uniforms and old muskets they'd been handed. They'd been shown once, briefly, how to load and fire their muskets. Most acted like they were afraid of a firearm. Santa Anna's attack orders stated that those conscripts would not take part in this battle. Morales hoped that would be the case. Untrained, untested men were likely to panic in battle. And battles were confused affairs at best.

"*Coronel* Morales," Reyes said, inviting him to address the sharpshooters.

Morales stepped forward. "You men were chosen because you are the finest *cazadores* with the rifle. You will have a chance to prove it soon. You will do your duty. Rest now. You'll need it."

"*Sargento*," Reyes addressed the *cazador* at the end of the line, "dismiss the men."

The sergeant, his face partly concealed in shadow, snapped to attention.

Morales took Reyes aside. "If extra cartridges can be found, give them to your men," he told Reyes. "Providing covering fire while you and your men climb that wall will be no easy task."

"*Por supuesto.*"

"And you have assigned a reliable man to dispatch the forward sentry in front of the south wall, have you not?" Morales asked.

"It is taken care of."

"*Bueno.* Now, I did not see your second," Morales continued and asked Reyes why his lieutenants were not there.

"Both of my *tenientes* are bedridden, sick with the dysentery fever. *Teniente* Garcia came down with it just this afternoon."

"And no *medicos* worth a damn," Morales spat. There were a couple of so-called medical doctors that were forced to come with them, taken from villages they'd passed through when the army marched north. Morales wouldn't trust them to sew a button on a uniform, let alone sew up a wounded *soldado*. His Excellency's decision to undertake such a massive military operation without surgeons or medical supplies was disgraceful. "It will toughen the men," His Excellency had said. Appalling. *Bastardo.*

"Take a *teniente* from another company," Morales told Reyes.

"Entiendo," Reyes said. *"¡Sargento!"*

The *cazador* sergeant quickly appeared, and in the clear glow of the campfire, Morales recognized the old soldier's leathery features.

"I believe you know *Sargento* Ordaz," Reyes said.

"Of course," Morales said, glad to see him. "I would have lost more than my ear if he hadn't pulled me to safety at Zacatecas."

Sergeant Fermin Ordaz's smile cracked the creases of his face. "The *Coronel* is most kind."

"I thought your enlistment ended a few months ago. What are you doing here?"

"I went back home, but my wife, she was very angry to see me. She said I did not write her enough. I told her I would write more next time and rejoined the army."

"A true *cazador,*" Morales said and laughed. "How is your leg?"

"A few pieces of lead still there the *medicos* did not get out, but they are nothing, sir."

It had been hard for Morales to imagine that Ordaz had saved his life when he first saw him after he had awakened in the hospital. Ordaz was a slight man, and older with much graying hair. But he had the strength of a bull, and, though badly wounded with a leg full of buckshot, he had managed to carry Morales over his shoulder off the battlefield and back to the medical tent. Ordaz's leg wound kept him in the hospital for several days. He had not taken part in the rape of Zacatecas.

"The *sargento* volunteered for this mission," Reyes said. "With the *Coronel*'s permission, I believe he will make a fine second."

"Very well," Morales said, clapping Ordaz on the shoulder. He then asked Reyes about the spirit of the rest of the men.

"They will fight," Reyes said. "But you should know there was a rumor."

"What rumor, *Capitán*?"

Reyes looked at Ordaz. "Tell him, *Sargento.*"

"Some of the men," Ordaz said, sounding almost embarrassed, "they say the rebels have mined the walls and the inside of the fort with many barrels of gunpowder. They say once we are inside, the rebels will blow themselves up and us with them."

"And where did the men get this idea?"

"The sound of all the digging coming from the fort. Every day and every night we have heard it. And much swearing. Some say it's a bad omen. *Muy malo.*" Ordaz snorted dismissively. "I say it is soldier's superstition."

This was all because His Excellency had the men sitting around here waiting for too long, Morales thought disgustedly. And he'd heard the digging at times himself. He guessed the rebels were building earthworks. Or shoring up the walls. Perhaps both. But blowing up the fort? Not these rebels, not Travis. There was no glory in such an act. But rumors like these could become dangerous, spreading like a sickness.

"Is that what you told the men? Soldier's superstition?" Morales asked.

"No, sir. I told them the rebels were burying their money and valuables."

Morales liked that. Sergeant Ordaz was no fool. He knew how to talk to the men and, just as importantly, how to make them listen.

"And how did they take that, *Sargento*?" Morales asked.

"Gold and silver can make a man forget all his troubles."

"Indeed they can," Morales said.

"But the men know they are here to fight," Reyes said.

"We will not fail you, *Coronel*," the rugged little sergeant said.

CHAPTER SEVENTEEN

"How does it look to you?" Moses asked.

"Appears quiet enough to me," Crockett said.

"Perhaps it is time, then."

"Reckon so."

They stood at the palisade wall by the cannon emplacement and peered out into the darkness, broken only by a scattering of campfires inside the Mexican lines to the south. Crockett had mentioned earlier that it seemed to him fewer campfires were burning all around the Alamo tonight. Moses, wearing the brown serape over his buckskin shirt, the battered straw hat, and the old moccasins Sergeant Abamillo had given him, agreed.

After his little talk with Abamillo, Moses had decided on his route to the river. He had been at the palisade watching for close to an hour. So far, he hadn't seen any movement out there, but he'd heard much, like the tramping of feet, the scratch of metal against metal, a raised Mexican voice. Sound carried much further and keener at night. But then there had been little, if any, sounds for a while. That could mean the Mexicans had turned in or were lying there quiet and biding their time. Either way, Moses decided there was no reason to linger any longer.

"Well, *monsieur,*" Moses said offering his hand, "I bid you *adieu.*"

Crockett shifted his rifle to his left hand and shook Moses's hand. Crockett had a strong grip. An encouraging sign, Moses thought.

"Best of luck to you, Mose. You be careful." Crockett grunted. "I still can't figure you shaving off that long moustache of yours."

"Such is life," Moses said and silently asked for the emperor's forgiveness. Again. He vowed he would grow it back but knew it would not be the same.

"Kick out that fire," Crockett said, indicating the campfire close by. "Kill his silhouette."

Suddenly it was much darker by the single gun emplacement. Moses turned to the other men close by.

"Au revior, mes amis," he said to them and

pulled the straw hat down tighter on his head.

Someone said low, "I sure wouldn't be going out there without a rifle or something."

Moving around the cannon, Moses took hold of a coarse timber post to hoist himself up to climb through the embrasure when a big hand clasped his shoulder. He looked back and saw it was Crockett.

"You at least have a good knife, don't you?" Crockett asked.

"Oui. Absolument." Moses grinned and, using his thumb, pointed behind his back where he carried his hunting knife in a sheath stuck in his trousers.

Crockett nodded, looking reassured.

Slipping through the opening, Moses took a firm grip of the rough-hewn lower part of the embrasure and carefully lowered himself down against the wall. It was about an eight-foot drop from the bottom edge of the opening into the ditch below, and Moses, being just over six feet tall, landed easily with a soft thud in the hard ditch.

Crouching low, he followed the palisade ditch toward the stone south wall. He didn't want to give any Mexican sentry who might have spotted him an easy target.

There were voices above him.

"You think old Mose has lost his sand?"

someone said.

"Don't know," someone else said. "But if I was a betting man, I'd say he jest might be leaving the table with all his winnings this night."

Reaching the corner of the south wall, Moses peered around the edge and saw the earthen and timber lunette jutting out from the wall protecting the main gate. A campfire burning inside threw up a warm glow, and he saw the top of the head of a sentry. He was wearing a coonskin cap and faced south, looking out at the Mexican lines. Moses made a sharp, quick sound to draw the sentry's attention. That sentry jerked toward him, and another immediately popped his head over the lunette wall, his rifle aimed and ready to shoot.

"No, no. *Ne tirez pas.* Don't shoot. It is me, Moses," he whispered urgently.

"It's that French feller," the first sentry said.

"Damn, I like to come near to blowing your fool head off," the other sentry said irritably. "Get now," he said and mumbled something else Moses couldn't hear.

Moses raised his hand in thanks and scurried into the ditch surrounding the lunette. Keeping low, he moved around to where the ditch met the south wall again and quickly found the *acequia* bed running out from underneath the wall. Glancing up at the southwest corner, he saw a young sentry at the big eighteen-pounder nod down at him. The sentries in the lunette must have passed word up to the men on top of the wall, Moses thought. It would not do to be shot by a comrade. He was relieved that, after making up his mind about his route, he had found the men who were assigned as the forward sentries outside the south and west walls had been reminded he was going out.

Moses followed the *acequia* bed between the wall and the old stone house some yards away. The air was cold and still. There were a few dim lights he could make out in the town. Perhaps a small fireplace, or candles in windows, he guessed. In the trees directly ahead, he saw only five campfires burning. A few others burned further up on the right. They could all be seen from the west wall of the Alamo. But there were not nearly the number he had seen out this way from the fort last night — at least three times as many.

Peering hard into the darkness, he saw no Mexican sentry posted. And no sounds of any activity. Except for the campfires there was nothing to indicate any Mexican soldiers there. Were they asleep, as Abamillo said? Were they there at all? Maybe the campfires were left to burn as decoys to give the look of soldiers encamped.

To his left about one hundred or so yards he counted four torches burning on the bridge that crossed the river. Four sentries stood guard there, two at each end. He decided Abamillo was right; better to cross the river than to hazard an *affrontement* on the bridge.

It was getting colder. He crawled forward, stopped, and listened. Nothing. Moving forward again, he came upon the ford where the *acequia* met a small stream. That stream came down from the north, past the Alamo, turned, ran parallel to the west wall, and emptied into the river. *Move slowly,* he told himself. *Make no noise.*

Mon Dieu it was dark. He could barely see anything in front of him. But he had to keep moving and started crawling again. Thankfully the grasses, though dead and brown, were lying down underneath him, making no sound. The ground dipped. He remembered there was a gentle slope down toward the river.

He chanced rising up to a crouch, took a step, and stopped quick. Something tugged at his serape. Every muscle tensed. Wait. A soldier would have raised an alarm, or run him through with a bayonet. Carefully he reached back under his serape for his knife and slowly turned his head. A mesquite bush had snagged the serape. The thorns were long and sharp. He remembered there were thickets of mesquite scattered about. Pulling the serape free he crawled forward and could make out the sound of the river. A peaceful murmur. The lights in the town had disappeared, the cottonwood trees along the riverbank blocking his view.

He made his way closer to the river, his knife in his hand. It was fifty or sixty feet ahead. Perhaps more. Pausing by a large mesquite bush, he kept watch for any sentries and listened closely. There was only the murmur of the river. No! Something else! A whisper? A rustling?

A horse nickered.

Moses pressed himself down, the side of his face against the ground, and stayed very still.

The sound of hooves came closer. Leather squeaked. A bridle jingled. How many horses? One, two, more? No, two, he thought.

The horses halted. One was a grey that caught the light from a campfire. The other was dark and blew out a snort.

"Teniente," the grey rider called out in a loud whisper. It appeared to Moses that the grey rider wore a bicorn hat. An officer.

There was movement at the trees. The lieutenant came out quickly, a sword swung at his side.

Moses was certain the lieutenant was not out here alone.

"Sí, Capitán," he said.

The captain and the lieutenant spoke low. Moses cocked his ear toward them, trying to make out what they were saying. All he heard was *"el momento."*

Suddenly, the captain and the other rider spurred their horses toward Moses and the bush. Moses remained pressed to the ground as they rode past. While the lieutenant disappeared back into the dark, Moses heard him clearly this time.

"Arriba, soldados. Arriba," the lieutenant said low but urgently. *"Guardar silencio."*

Staying down, Moses raised his head slightly.

Merde! he thought and felt a cold sweat run down his back and race down his arms to his hands. He gripped his knife tighter as the trees before him seemed to come to life. Black shadows passed by the campfires. They wore tall Shako hats and carried rifles with bayonets. Dozens became a hundred.

And still more came! They hurried, with little sound or commotion, northward.

Do not move, Moses thought. *Don't make a sound. Don't even breathe.*

Chapter Eighteen

Drawing the razor across his wet chin, James scraped off the last of a three-day growth of whiskers. The razor, a straight blade with a tortoiseshell handle, belonged to Preacher, who had allowed James to borrow it when he said he wanted to scrub and clean his face. Needed to. Like something was making him do it.

James sat inside the little room at the northeast corner, the one where he and Moses and the others had slept. He watched his progress with the razor reflected in a broken piece of mirror glass. It was propped up on the table, and beside it burned a candle, casting its golden glow on his face. He rinsed the whiskers off the razor edge in a basin of water he'd set by the mirror. Satisfied with the job, he was about to step outside to toss the water when Georgie appeared at the doorway.

"Edward said you were in here," Georgie said.

"I'm here, but where have you been?" James asked. "You been gone over an hour."

Georgie came into the room and sat down at the table. "I was with Gertrudis."

James drew his head back. "For better than an hour?"

"Almost."

His little brother didn't appear much different. He wasn't grinning like a man with a big secret.

"Well, what happened?"

Now he saw the grin spread across Georgie's face.

"We talked," Georgie said.

James frowned. "You talked?"

"That's right. And I helped her fetch her small chest out of Colonel Bowie's quarters and take it to the old storeroom, their new quarters."

"You moved a small chest from one end of the fort to the other. And talked. All that took you a whole hour."

"Close to."

"Mind if I ask what you talked about?"

Georgie glanced down at the ground and chuckled. "That's the thing about it. I don't know, exactly."

James stared at Georgie for a moment.

"You don't know."

"Remember when we saw her and her sister moving their things?"

James nodded.

"Turns out that was Colonel Bowie's idea. Juana told me he claimed it would be safer for them to be away from him. You know, if the Mexicans come. I wasn't so certain about them being safer somewhere else, but she said the Colonel insisted."

He wants to try to protect them, is all, thought James.

"But it was Juana who said for me and Gertrudis to get that little chest they forgot," Georgie continued. "Colonel Bowie didn't even know we come in. He was mumbling to himself lying there in his bed. He's in real bad shape. But when we come back to the storeroom, Juana says she had some things she had to do for the colonel. I figured she was set to run me off, but she real quick picked up her baby, went out the door, and left us setting there all by ourselves."

So Juana had a heart after all, James thought. "She was giving you and her sister some time. She's seen how the two of you been looking at each other." *And she also knows what's coming,* but James saw no point to mention it.

"That's the way I figured, too," Georgie said.

"So what about all this no-talking talking you two did?"

Georgie smiled. "It was something, really. Gertrudis doesn't know much American. And I don't speak her language a whole lot. But she started talking to me, and, I don't know but it sure sounded pretty, the way she said it. She's got that smile of hers, and those big, dark eyes."

"And what did you say to her?"

"Oh. Well, I told her about you and me wanting to be rangers after this ruckus is finished. And that, well, she had right pretty eyes and all." Georgie laughed. "I know it sounds silly, us jabbering at each other, and neither knows what the other is saying, but it didn't seem to matter. It was just nice sitting there with her. If only for a little while."

Georgie was a sweet kid and a good brother, James thought. "I'm happy for you, Georgie."

"Did I tell you she let me hold her hand?"

James smiled and shook his head.

"It wasn't for long. Juana came back, and I snatched my hand away right quick." Georgie's smile faded into a frown, and he said, "I don't want to tell Edward about any of this. You know how he is. I don't care to hear him say anything bad about Gertrudis."

"I'll see to it he doesn't."

"I appreciate that, James."

"We best move along," James said as he tucked Preacher's razor blade inside the handle. "Must be near to eleven. Or is it later?"

Georgie wore a sheepish look. "I wouldn't know, exactly. I gave my watch to Gertrudis."

"That watch was a gift," James said, not unkindly. "What made you do that?"

"I guess I wanted her to have something of mine," Georgie said. "To remember me by." He shrugged. "Seemed like a good idea, I thought."

James considered his little brother a moment and said, "You're right. It was a fine idea."

CHAPTER NINETEEN

Susannah had left little Angelina with Ana while she went looking for the men who had given her clothes to wash but hadn't come to call for their things yet. She had decided not to wait for them. It gave her something to do, that restlessness still nagging her.

" 'Tis a great kindness you've done me, ma'am," Johnnie McGregor told her in his Scottish brogue when she handed him his black cap, what he called his bonnet. She had stitched up the toorie, the red feathery topknot, where it had torn loose from the cap. "I've felt nearly undressed wi'out me bonnet." He pronounced it "guid as new."

"That playing you did on your bagpipes did all of us good," she said.

"I thank ye, ma'am. An' I'd be most happy to play ye're daughter a tune on her weddin' day."

At the twin-cannon battery inside the compound facing the front gate, she found old Jacob Darst helping with stacking bags of grapeshot. She noticed something different about him, and realized he had washed the tobacco drippings out of his graying beard. He was grateful to have his socks darned. "It'll ease the pain of this blister on my foot."

Feeling thirsty, she went to the well nearby. As she dipped the bent ladle into the bucket and took a sip of cold water, she saw young Galba Fuqua coming toward her. He held a musket in his right hand. His left was bandaged.

"I've been looking for you," she said. "What happened to your hand?"

With his bandaged hand, he pointed at his post up on the south wall at the gun emplacement and said that bricks covering a window in the wall below the eighteen-pounder had fallen out. "Firing that big gun must of loosened them. Made a good-sized hole in that window," he said. "Captain told me to gather up bricks to fill it, and I cut my hand on a piece of wood. Sliced open my palm. Went to the hospital, and Doc sewed me up."

"Looks painful."

"Yes, ma'am. Ten stitches. Hurts like the devil, it does."

That explained why she couldn't find him.

197

"I have your washing," she said, reaching inside the sling tied over her shoulder and pulling out his light-yellow cravat.

"I was meaning to see you about that," he said, taking it from her hand. He sounded a little embarrassed. "Thank you. And you sewed up the hole, too."

"I wanted to be sure you had it back."

Susannah liked Galba. She'd had no opportunity to talk with him since he had ridden in two nights ago with the other thirty-one men from Gonzales. There'd been little time to talk with any of those men, really. A few of them, like Galba, were still only boys.

Galba and his father and uncle had been neighbors of her and Almeron. Galba's mother had passed away before the family made it to Texas, and not two years had passed since his father had died. The whole town came out to attend his funeral. He'd been in business with his brother, Benjamin, running the Luna, the "best grog shop west of the Mississippi," or so the sign over the bar had proclaimed. Galba had been working in the Luna since before his father passed away.

"Your Uncle Benjamin didn't come with you and the others," she said.

Galba sighed. "No, he said he would to stay in town, keep an eye on the Luna. He was afraid somebody might break in, steal all his liquor, and anything else in there."

"But he must be proud of you."

Galba shook his head. "He was a mite upset I left."

"What for?"

"Since I'm not there, he's having to sweep the place out, clean the tables, and water down the whiskey."

"He waters down the whiskey?"

"Had me pour out half the whiskey in every bottle and refill it with water. I know my father would never approve of that, but Uncle Benjamin, he figured to make every bottle pay for itself, twice."

She thought it was a wise thing Almeron and the other men in town hadn't known what Benjamin had been up to. They'd have tarred and feathered him and run him out.

"I don't mind telling you I'm glad to be shut of him," Galba continued. "He threatened to fire me when he caught me pitching pennies back in the storeroom with Bill King. You know Bill come in here with me. Him and Johnny Gaston."

Susannah knew those two boys. They hailed from decent, God-fearing families.

"I've got Johnny's shirt here," she said, reaching into the sling. "Can you see that he gets it?"

"I will, Mrs. Dickinson," Galba said, taking the rolled-up blue shirt.

"It's funny, I suppose," she said, "but talking about home and all, I couldn't help remembering that fancy dress ball Tommy Miller threw at his hotel."

"That was last summer." Galba smiled.

"That's right. Almeron and me saw you there. With Lucy Summers."

"Her folks invited me to come with them as their guest."

"You and Lucy danced quite a few reels together, as I recall."

"Johnny Gaston cut in on me once or twice."

"Tommy Miller's place was so small, and there was so many people they had to take the floor in shifts." Susannah laughed. "John Tinsley was one of the fiddlers. I forget the other one."

"I don't rightly remember him either, but I believe he came over from San Felipe. Mr. Tinsley was killed, you know."

"Oh, no."

"When those bandits came through."

"You mean the same ones that broke into my house?" she asked.

"We figured it had to be."

"Good Lord," she said, raising her hand to her brooch.

"Close as we could tell, Mr. Tinsley shot it out with them when they tried breaking into his house. Found blood around, so he must've hit a couple of them. We found him on his porch, shot in the head."

"So sad."

"They'd ransacked the place. Same as they did yours. Folks said it was scoundrels out of Louisiana, looking to take advantage of our miseries here."

"Worse than scoundrels." She shook her head ruefully.

"Father and Uncle Benjamin and me, we came through Louisiana on our way to Texas. Father called it a paradise for assassins, thieves, and politicians. I know if he was still alive, he'd be here." Galba shrugged. "Only me now."

"He'd be real proud of you."

"Staying here I figure I can stand as tall as any man."

She saw a trace of disquiet cross his face.

"Galba!" a fellow in a long coat hollered down from the gun emplacement. "Give us a hand up here."

"I'm coming."

He cast his eyes down at the cravat in his hand and said, "Lucy made this for me. She was crying when she gave it to me right before we all left town to come here. Crying hard, too. Like to hurt herself. I promised her we'd all be back."

Susannah's heart ached.

"You know," he said, smiling at her, "this Wednesday is my birthday. I'll be seventeen."

"Galba!" the man hollered again.

Galba cleared his throat and said, "Much obliged for the washing."

CHAPTER TWENTY

Moses's feet and legs had nearly gone numb. He was halfway across the river, waist high in the frigid water. Downriver to his left, the four sentries on the bridge leaned lazily against the railings, talking to each other. *Splendide!* They weren't paying attention to anything around them. And Moses did not want to give them a reason to look his way.

He had to be careful. The numbness in his feet made him wary of the smooth rocks in the riverbed he had to cross.

Crouching by that mesquite had been bad enough, holding quiet and still while it seemed like half of Santa Anna's army moved out of those trees. Then he'd waited to make sure no one remained behind. No campfires were lit, no sound of talk. All he could see looking into those trees was blackness.

Having started across the river, there was

no turning back.

Jésus-Christ the water was cold, he thought. *Keep moving. Another step. Don't hurry. You slip, you fall.*

He thought he could see the bank on the other side. Many trees there. He'd have to be careful.

Another step. His foot slid and wedged between two rocks. He tried to pull it free. Stuck! *Bon sang!*

He made a quick glance at the bridge sentries. They were laughing over something. Reaching into the water, he pulled on his leg. His foot would not budge. *Merde!* He felt like a damn fool recruit, the kind the sergeants in the *Grande Armée* said didn't know the difference between a whore's nook and a sow's ear.

At least the current was gentle. No sucking feeling trying to drag him under. But his foot was still stuck. He couldn't yank too hard on his foot. Splashing sounds would draw the Mexicans on the bridge. He tried again to loosen his foot. The numbness was spreading. Mixed with the cold, he worried he might lose his balance. This was no way to meet death. Freezing cold and stuck in a river. *Absurde. Grotesque.*

And suddenly his foot came free. He had

no idea how, but he did not care.

Moving forward, he sensed the bank sloping up, and he rose out of the river, his clothes dripping water. The dewy grass was slippery. He leaned against a tree and rubbed his legs and feet, trying to put the feeling back into them.

Peering toward town, he could make out a few flat-topped buildings. Hesitating, he listened for any sounds. Nothing. If he ran into any soldiers, he would explain his wet trousers by saying he'd had a little too much to drink and didn't know how he ended up all wet. He took a step and snapped a twig under his moccasin.

An owl trilled loudly.

Moses stood very still. A few feet ahead, he heard a rustling.

He reached for his knife. The blood raced through his feet and legs now. He held his breath.

The tall shape of a Shako hat rose up.

Moses clutched his knife, ready to strike. But there was something odd about the Shako hat. It should have been standing taller.

A small voice whispered, *"¿Quién es?"*

The Shako hat moved closer. The top of it was barely to Moses's chest.

"¿Que está allí?"

It was only a boy. Ten years of age maybe. Had he been left as a sentry in the town? Another step and he would be at Moses's feet.

Moses squatted down and grabbed him, clamping his big hand over the boy's mouth. *"Silencio,"* he whispered, putting his knife to the boy's throat. The boy stiffened, dropping his rifle on the grassy ground. He wore a Mexican army uniform that was baggy on him.

Moses didn't want to cut him. But what was he to do with him? He had to keep him quiet. And quickly. Moses saw no other choice. He raised his hand to give the boy a sharp blow to the head with the butt of the knife.

The little soldier stomped his heel hard on top of Moses's foot and slipped out of his grip!

"¡Guardia! ¡Guardia! ¡Ven aquí!" the boy shouted, running toward the bridge.

"Petit bâtard," Moses growled.

The guards on the bridge brought their rifles up.

Moses saw the boy clear the trees.

One of the guards took aim. Another guard said something, motioning with his hand. The first guard lowered his rifle.

Moses waited. He did not want to attract

them with a sudden movement.

The boy neared the bridge, his Shako hat bobbing on his head. It was hard to hear him now. He was pointing back at the trees. One of the guards shook his head wearily. The boy persisted and ran up onto the bridge. The guards listened. Two of them gave each other looks. Another appeared to scold the boy.

Moses saw his chance and moved, following the riverbank as it bent around to the right, keeping the bridge in sight.

The soldiers waved the boy away. The kid persisted. One of the guards went after him, using his bayonet. The boy soldier ran off into the woods on the other side of the bridge.

Moses quickly reached town. There'd been no soldiers along the riverbank. Not a soldier in sight. He stopped at the corner of a small house. Loud snoring inside.

Pulling his straw hat down and adjusting his serape, Moses quietly made his way along a hard dirt road, heading south. The town appeared quiet. Still no soldiers in sight. At the end of the road, he could hear the river close by.

And it suddenly struck him. He had brought no canteen of water.

Imbécile!

Well, he would follow the river for a few miles and then decide what to do. There were plenty of watering holes and streams to the east. He only had to reach them. And east was where he was headed. Gonzales lay due east. About seventy miles. Quite a bit further was Louisiana. American soil. It would be a long walk, but he would be alive.

Looking back toward the Alamo, beyond the trees, he could make out part of the south wall and the lunette at the main gate. And he had the strangest sensation. Everything appeared eerily quiet around him. Even the river seemed to have stilled.

Asking God to take *pitié* on his friends, Moses whispered *"adieu"* as he turned his back on the Alamo and made his way into the darkness of the trees.

CHAPTER TWENTY-ONE

Leaving Georgie and Preacher at their posts, James and Edward came down off the north wall for their turn to warm themselves at the campfire below. They joined Cleland and Hardin, who ate corn mush from a bowl he held in his hands. Sergeant Abamillo was there, too. James noticed Edward sat across the fire from Abamillo so to be as far away from the big Tejano as he could.

"Damn, Hardin," Edward said, "you still eating?"

Hardin, his spoon halfway to his mouth, paused and said in his squeaky voice, "I'm still hungry."

"I thought you were the one said you couldn't stand that stuff anymore," James said.

"I can't," Hardin said, his mouth full, "but there ain't nothing else to eat. Must need it, I reckon." He scooped another spoonful

209

into his mouth, his beard bobbing up and down as he chewed.

James figured Hardin was fighting his nervousness about the prospects of tomorrow. James wasn't hungry at all. But he made no mention of either.

"It sure turned dern cold all of a sudden," Cleland said as he added more wood to the fire and rubbed his hands together.

James had concluded Cleland had to have the thinnest blood of any man he knew, for, once the sun went down, Cleland would complain about the cold. And cold as it was this night, it wasn't near as cold as it had been.

"You all mind if an old Tennessean takes a spot to warm his bones?"

James didn't realize David Crockett was standing next to him until he spoke those words.

Crockett had come by about every other night since this fracas started. It was well known he liked making rounds of the fort, particularly at night, to stop and sit a spell with the men and talk a bit. He'd told all manner of tales. Like the time he lost both his grist mill and gunpowder mill in the same night when he was living on Shoal Creek and it flooded, adding that he was well acquainted with hard times, and plenty of them. And there was the time he was elected town commissioner of Lawrenceburg, even though he had no idea what he was supposed to do. But he said he must've done something right on account they didn't fire him, and that's when he realized how a fellow becomes a politician, by not confusing folks with facts once they've made up their minds. Never once did James hear Crockett repeat a single story.

As a matter of fact, James didn't know that Crockett had written his biography until the night he heard Captain Martin talking to Crockett, saying that he'd read it and hoped he'd made a profit from it. Crockett had half smiled at him and said that the last time he'd heard talk of profits was back home on a Sunday morning when the minister read from the Old Testament.

"Set yourself down," Edward said, making room for Crockett on the wooden bench he was sitting on.

"Much obliged," Crockett said as he sat and held his hands open to the fire. He was still wearing his coonskin cap from earlier that day. James had only seen him wearing it twice before. It had been bitter cold both those times. Much colder than this night. He must have his reason, James concluded.

For all he knew, Crockett was wearing it for luck.

"How are you boys this night?" Crockett asked.

"Doing our best to keep warm," Cleland said.

Crockett noticed Abamillo and said, *"Buenas noches, amigo."*

James noted a lot of Tennessee accent in Crockett's Spanish talk, and it did make a difference in how his Spanish sounded. After a moment, he saw a grin spread across Abamillo's hard face.

"Buenas noches, Señor Crockett," the big Tejano said with a nod of his head. "Your Spanish, it is much better."

"I didn't think I'd ever figure your lingo," Crockett said with a chuckle.

James noticed everyone enjoyed Crockett's comment, except Edward, who looked away. Even David Crockett wouldn't change Edward's mind about Mexicans.

"Now I must go back up on the wall," Abamillo said and rose and left.

"You want some corn stew, David?" Hardin asked, offering up his bowl.

"Not for me. You have it."

"I can't swoller no more," Hardin said, setting the bowl down.

James heard Edward grunt.

Crockett had placed the butt of his flint-lock rifle on top of his boot and rested the barrel against his shoulder. That rifle had a large silver band fitted around the breech that gleamed in the firelight. It wasn't Crockett's fancy prized rifle, "Pretty Betsy." This "Betsy," as Crockett called it, was plain except for that band holding it together. James had heard that it had somehow been damaged during Crockett's travel to Texas. The more he studied it, the more aroused his curiosity became to find out the story. He was about to ask about it when Crockett spoke.

"I recall a mighty cold winter when I was a boy, about eight or so. Back home we had a neighbor, Mr. Hudnall. He went out to kill a deer, and he brought it to our house. I thought it was for us, but turns out it was so cold that night he knew he wouldn't make it home. And it was just as well, because that deer had froze fast to his shoulder while he was carrying it. We had to build up the fire to thaw it before he could get away from it."

James and the others laughed.

"Terrible cold that night," Crockett said, staring into the fire.

It became quiet. Almost spooky quiet, James thought, like nobody wanted to talk anymore. And then Cleland spoke.

"You, ah, thinking about tomorrow, David?"

"No," Crockett said slowly, like he was pondering something important. "I was remembering about the time I come home after serving my first term in Congress. Listening to men jabbering and jawing all day long in Washington had left my ears ringing. After a couple of days spent with my wife, Elizabeth, and our children, three boys and three girls, mind you, I took my dogs and went out bear hunting.

"Pretty soon the dogs picked up the scent, and I come over a rise and see this big ol' grizzly bear setting in a tree. I move around careful, raised up ol' Betsy, and put a ball in his breast. That bear didn't budge. Dogs are still barking. I move a little closer and put another ball in him about where I put the first. Well, that griz shudders and falls out of the tree and takes off running.

"Me and the dogs, we chased him into a rocky crevice. I see him hunkered down in there, and I can't really get a shot at him. So I climb down, pull out my knife, and got it at the ready." He glanced at James. "I'm as near to him as I am to you, and he raises up that big brown head of his and takes a swipe at me with his paw. I feel the wind rush by my face as I then stuck him with my knife and killed him."

"Lord," Cleland whispered.

"Well," Crockett continued, "it takes me the rest of the day and half the night to haul him up out of there. Must've weighed close to four hundred pounds. After skinning and butchering him, I headed back home with enough bear bacon to last us quite a spell."

"Must've been frightening," Cleland said.

"Oh, no," Crockett said. "That was the easy part. Facing Elizabeth empty-handed was what had me scared."

They all laughed as Crockett stood up to leave.

"Is that a true story, David?" James asked.

James watched as Crockett glanced around at each of them, then said, "Sounds true, don't it?"

"But weren't you scared of that bear?" Edward asked.

"Hell, yes," Crockett said. "But I didn't let him know it."

CHAPTER TWENTY-TWO

Standing by the twin-cannon battery at the Plaza de Valero, Morales pulled out the gold pocket watch he had purchased years ago in Mexico City and opened it. It was nearing half past eleven.

His three light companies of *cazadores* had earlier moved into position on the right flank of the cannon battery that faced the south wall of the Alamo. The thirty *cazadores* under *Capítan* Reyes were on the left. A few scattered campfires crackled. They were *Capítan* Reyes's idea. "No point letting the rebels think we have departed the field," he'd suggested.

Some two hundred yards away stood the Alamo chapel and the wooden palisade. It seemed that only a single campfire burned behind the palisade wall now. Many of the defenders inside were likely asleep by this time, or nearly so, as His Excellency had predicted. Glancing to the left, Morales saw that a campfire behind the lunette at the main gate still burned steadily. He thought he spied a hat appear above the lunette wall. A sentry having a look. He counted three sentries standing guard on top of the south wall. And two posted atop the chapel at the rear battery. There was also the lone sentry in a small trench about fifty yards outside the wall. He could not be allowed to alert the rebels.

After moving into position, Morales had passed the order for the men to eat and try to sleep. They would need all they could get before the battle. The meal had consisted only of hardtack. About the size of the palm of a hand, those tough, flat squares of cooked flour and salt were the only food His Excellency had seen fit to provide for the men. The rains had ruined half of the stores of hardtack, because they'd been poorly packed. Of those that remained, Morales had often witnessed the men trying to soften them up using the butt of their rifles to break them apart and then sloshing the pieces in a tin of river water. Sometimes it worked. The soupy mush was better than nothing at all.

While making his rounds, Morales had seen many of the men lying close together on the ground, trying to keep warm on this cold night. How ridiculous His Excellency's order that the men carry no blankets, Morales thought. Fortunately, all was quiet at the moment.

And Morales was fully awake. He doubted he would sleep at all. Running his plan of attack over in his mind, he was searching for any item he might have miscalculated, any risk overlooked. A sharp-eyed sentry might detect the thirty *cazadores* moving into position. The ditch in front of the palisade wall may be deeper than expected, leaving the men stuck there. An ill-timed cough could give away the whole attack.

He heard someone approach. It was Sergeant Ordaz.

"Con perdón del Coronel," he said.

"Of course, *Sergento,"* Morales said. "But what are you doing up? You should be sleeping."

"I am too restless, sir. I could not sleep, even if I wanted to. I was seeing to the men, that they are resting."

"And are they?"

"Sí, Coronel. As best as can be expected."

Morales turned back to observe the Alamo. Ordaz stood a step behind him to his right.

"How are the spirits of the men? Any

more soldier's superstitions?" Morales asked.

"No, sir. They know a battle is coming."

Morales nodded.

Ordaz stood by, silent.

Morales sensed Ordaz had something more on his mind. "What about you? Speak freely."

"I am ready for a good fight."

Morales waited.

"That fight," Ordaz said, pausing for a moment, "I believe it would still be good a day from now, if *General* Santa Anna waited for the big cannons."

Perhaps His Excellency would have waited, Morales thought bitterly, if *la mujer* had not cut short his bedchamber privileges.

"Your concerns and those of the men are noted," Morales said.

"*Por supuesto, Coronel.* As I said before, we will not fail."

They heard whispering behind them, near a campfire.

"*¿Quien es?*" Ordaz asked sternly. "*Respóndeme.*"

A *cazador* stood up at attention. "Forgive me, *Coronel,*" he said. "I did not mean to disturb you."

Morales noticed the *cazador* held something in his hand. "What do you have there?"

"*Mi Biblio, Coronel.* I could not sleep. I was reading a passage from it."

There could be nothing wrong with that, Morales thought. "Which passage?"

"The letter of Paul to the Romans."

"Read it," Morales said. "Out loud."

"*Sí, Coronel.*" The *cazador* opened his Bible and tilted the page toward the campfire to see it better. He began reading.

" 'If God is for us, who can be against us?' "

CHAPTER TWENTY-THREE

Weary, Susannah fixed herself another cup of tea. She had pushed herself for hours. Though she wanted to sleep, she could not. She needed Almeron. The last she had seen of him since supper was when he'd rushed in to tell her Lieutenant Zanco needed him at the corral. Some kind of problem with the cannon there, and Zanco wanted Almeron's help. That was over two hours ago. And there was much she wanted to say to her husband before this night was out.

Thankfully, Angelina was asleep on the bed. Susannah was about to sit down with her baby when Anthony Wolf appeared in the doorway with his two boys, Nathan and Aleck. They stood in front of their gangly father, one of his big hands on the shoulder of each boy. Both youngsters held a rolled-up blanket in their hands. Younger Aleck's eyes were red, as though he'd been crying.

"Excuse me, ma'am," Wolf said, removing his hat.

"Mr. Wolf," she said, "is everything all right?"

"Yes, ma'am," he said. "Forgive my coming here at this late hour."

"No. It's fine. Come in, please."

"You heard Missus Dickinson, boys," he said and followed them inside. "I spoke with your husband, and he said to come and ask you."

Aleck lowered his head and wiped his nose across his sleeve.

"It's a favor I need," Wolf said. "Can my boys stay in here, with you?"

"Of course," she said. She'd half expected this as Wolf had kept his boys with him every night inside the chapel. But this night was different. Everyone knew it.

"They both got blankets," he said. "They won't be no trouble."

"You're welcome here, boys," Susannah said.

She saw Nathan glance up at her, his face the picture of fret.

"Thank you, ma'am," Wolf said. Then he squatted down so he could look at the faces of both boys.

Susannah saw Aleck's eyes brim with tears.

"Now you stay in here with Missus Dickinson," he said. "No matter what happens, no matter what you hear, do not leave this room. You understand?"

"But I want to help you," Nathan said.

"I know, son."

"Me, too," Aleck said, the tears beginning to fall.

"You are good boys," Wolf said, "and I'm right proud of you both. You been helping me right along. But I need to know you're safe."

"But we can do more," Nathan said.

"We can load your rifles for you like you showed us, and . . . and lots of things," Aleck said, trying to hold back tears.

"You taught us how to shoot. We can help you kill them Mexican soldiers," Nathan said.

"I know you can," Wolf said, swallowing hard. "But I want you two to grow up and make Texas a place folks will be proud to call home. A real home. Like your ma and me always wanted you to have."

As he stood up and came toward her, Susannah saw the face of a man who was giving up everything in his life.

"There's an aunt, my departed wife's sister, name of Miriam Cates," he said, keeping his voice low. "She and her husband live in Nacogdoches. When this business is all settled, could you see to setting them on their way to their aunt for me? I got nowhere else to turn. I'd . . . I'd surely rest easier knowing they were in your hands."

Might she be spared when the attack came? Susannah wondered. Would they all be killed? How could anyone know? She looked from the pleading in his eyes to the worried faces of his boys.

"I'll see to it, Mr. Wolf," she said.

"Thank you, ma'am," he said and let out a heavy sigh. "Everything will be fine, then."

Susannah, feeling like her heart was rising into her throat, reached up and put her hand to her mouth as Wolf turned to Nathan and Aleck.

"You mind Missus Dickinson. Do what she tells you." He squatted down again, put his arms around both boys and held them close. "And remember something else. You don't never start a fight. But if one comes, you be sure and finish it."

Wolf stood up, and Susannah saw his eyes fighting tears. He walked quickly out the doorway. He did not look back.

Taking some of the hay from her bedding, Susannah placed it in a corner of the room and said the boys should try to sleep.

Aleck cried softly as he lay down and

curled into a ball.

Susannah covered Aleck with his blanket and stroked his shoulder. Nathan unrolled his blanket and covered himself. She wanted to tell them both it would be all right, but Nathan spoke.

"We won't be seeing our Pa again, will we?"

Susannah did not know how to answer him. She wished Almeron would hurry back. "Go to sleep now," she finally said.

CHAPTER TWENTY-FOUR

On the north wall, James pulled his blanket closer around his shoulders and blew out a long sigh. God, he was tired, but sleep refused to come. Must be near midnight, he guessed.

Twisting around, he saw Captain Martin and his gun crew asleep at their cannon. A yawning sentry was standing his watch. The torch stood burning by the cannon, ready to put the touchhole to fire. Keeping that torch lit was as important as keeping the gunpowder dry.

He heard Edward snoring. His older brother sat a few feet away, arms around his tucked-up legs, head down and hat pulled low. Edward sputtered, and then silence. Further on, Abamillo, his Tejanos, and the other men assigned this section were sleeping by their rifles. Beyond them at the center gun battery, where three torches burned, a sentry leaned on his rifle.

James couldn't blame the sentries. Everyone was bone tired. But the sentries outside the fort were the ones who truly needed to stay awake. James had that duty one time, posted outside the north wall. It was miserable cold that night, sitting in a little trench fifty yards out. You didn't dare sleep in case the Mexicans came. James never said it to his brothers, but he was so scared sitting out there. If the Mexicans attacked, you were to signal with a shot and run back to the walls, where they threw down a rope, and you climbed up quick as hell. Nobody volunteered for that duty.

Below him, inside the courtyard, Hardin and Cleland had not moved from the base of the wall. They slept down there because of Edward's snoring. But if an alarm were raised, they would be at their posts in an instant. Everybody's rifles and shotguns were primed and ready.

Across the compound, James saw Georgie and Preacher at the campfire, warming themselves. A few other campfires burned. Men huddled around them, sleeping.

And though James could barely make it out, Travis's independence flag hung from the pole over the hospital. He smiled and thought: *Kiss my ass, Santa Anna, and go to hell.*

Reaching into his shirt pocket, James pulled out the piece of red cloth with the medal inside that Moses had given him. Unfolding the cloth, he looked at the five-pointed cross and ran his thumb over the engraving of Napoleon on the gold piece in the center. "The Legion of Honor," Moses called it. It was a handsome thing. Awarded for bravery. James still didn't understand why Moses had given it to him. James knew he had done nothing to earn it, surely nothing to call brave, in spite of Moses telling him he would. Holding off Santa Anna's men one more time was the best James could see happening at this point. And, without reinforcements, that didn't appear too promising.

James looked at the medal again. Awarded for bravery . . .

Georgie came up and sat down next to him, pulling his blanket close.

James glanced about. "Where's Preacher?"

"He'll be along," Georgie said and gestured to the medal. "What do you have there?"

"Moses gave it to me. Got it for bravery, he said, beating the Russian army in a battle."

"How come he give it to you?"

"Don't know exactly," James said.

"Kind of pretty," Georgie said.

James folded the medal up in the red cloth and put it in his shirt pocket. He noticed Georgie leaning over and looking down at the storeroom in the corner, the one where Gertrudis and her sister were, and where a flicker of candlelight could be seen through the crack of one of the window shutters.

"You all right?" James asked.

Georgie nodded and leaned back. "Like to see her again, is all."

James said nothing. He would have liked to see that cousin of the Dorsetts again, Charlotte Booth. And those green wildcat eyes of hers. What a time they'd had.

"James?" Georgie whispered.

"What is it?" he said, low.

"I need to talk to you."

"Go ahead."

"It's, well, it's about what's coming."

James turned his head toward him.

"I heard some of the men talking, down by the fire." Georgie glanced around to check if anyone was listening. Edward had not moved, his head still down. "Well," Georgie continued, "they were saying it don't hurt much."

"What doesn't hurt?"

Georgie looked worried. "The bayonet.

When it, you know. They said it's over real fast."

"Don't pay them any mind, you hear me? Think about something else. Like winning this fight."

"I know," Georgie said. "I reckon I'm still kind of . . . it's just I never been in a scrape like this before."

None of us been in a scrape like this before, James thought.

"You remember Jed Meeker's place over in Anuhuac?" James asked.

Georgie said he did.

"I was in there one day picking up supplies, and this fellow come at me."

"Who? Did you know him?"

"Lukas Skinner."

"Oh, that nasty cuss."

"That he was. Claimed I cheated him on some furs or some such thing. To this day I think that son of a bitch Chambers put him up to it. Skinner come swinging a piece of wood, calling me everything but a white man."

"What did you do?"

"I wasn't about to take a whipping from the likes of Skinner, or show Chambers he could scare me off. Made me mad. Skinner got in a lick, but I bloodied him good and blackened his eye. Took that piece of wood away from him and busted it over his head. Probably still can't wear his hat right."

Georgie smiled.

"That's what you're going to do," James continued. "You going to get mean. Mad dog rabid mean. Because these Mexican boys, they're coming for blood."

"I just don't want to let you down."

"Don't worry about turning rabbit," Edward suddenly said, startling both of them. "No place to run anyhow."

"How long you been listening?" Georgie asked, perturbed.

"Long enough," he said. "I'll tell you something else, too. Running from a fight is —"

"Nobody said anything about running!" Georgie said, an edge in his voice.

Edward sniffed, looked away, and put his head back down, mumbling.

James leaned close to Georgie. "Don't worry about what he said. When those Mexicans come, you have at them 'til they're down and dead."

Georgie nodded. "I will."

"Stay close to me. You'll do fine."

Georgie pulled his blanket up and lay down next to James.

A moment passed. Georgie said, "I wish we could've gotten Thomas Jefferson Chambers. For what he done to Pa."

"Me, too, Georgie," James said.

He glanced at Edward. His head was still down. He didn't say anything. Maybe he'd gone back to sleep.

There was movement on the hospital roof. James squinted to see it better. Travis's independence flag was being lowered. One man was handling the rope. Another stood by. He untied the independence flag and tied another in its place. They raised it up the flagpole. It looked like that blue one, the one the New Orleans Grey fellows brought with them. James was too tired to try and figure out why they were swapping flags. Hell, it didn't matter anyway, so long as Santa Anna could see it.

Settling back, James let Charlotte Booth into his head again. Her bewitching smile. That voice, full of invitation. He thought about the spot on the riverbank where they'd sat and had a picnic one Sunday afternoon in the shade of a big tree. He remembered a warm breeze coming up and the way the long grass laid over in waves. Charlotte had leaned forward and touched his face and kissed him. God, she was beautiful.

CHAPTER TWENTY-FIVE

Inside the sacristy, Susannah waited for Almeron. She sat at the table in the glow of a candle flame, the front of her skirt pulled up on the tabletop. The inside hem, torn open, faced her as she whipstitched it back together. Her dingy-colored petticoat covered her legs. Working the needle and thread kept her hands busy and her mind off the terrible thoughts of what might come tomorrow. No. What would come. *Stop thinking that,* she told herself and pulled the needle through the hem too hard and broke the thread.

Blowing out an exasperated breath, she quickly rethreaded the needle and heard the sound of approaching boot steps on the flagstone.

Almeron came in through the doorway, weary and worn.

"Everything took so long. Forgive me," he said, keeping his voice low. Then he saw what she was doing. "Did you rip your dress?"

"No," she said and tied off the knot of thread, then bit the excess free with her teeth. "I sewed my brooch into the hem."

"What'd you do that for?"

She said that Ana Esparza had told her that if the soldiers got inside the fort, they would take valuables. "I don't want them putting their hands on it."

She saw the concern on his face, though she knew he was trying hard not to let his worry show.

"I sewed Will Travis's ring inside the hem, too," Susannah said and told Almeron about his request. "He was determined that Angelina have it. In spite of my feelings about him, I couldn't say no. It would have been cruel."

"He sets a lot of store in that ring. You did right." Almeron smiled and looked over at Angelina asleep on the bed, swaddled in the oniony smelling blanket. "How's our little girl?" he asked and leaned down and kissed her.

"Been asleep for the last few hours. Some water?" she asked, reaching for a clay jar she'd brought in earlier. Her hand began to shake, and she grabbed it with her other hand to make it stop.

"I could use some," he said and sat down hard in the chair. He pulled his flintlock pistol from inside his belt and laid it on the table as a sound and movement in the corner drew his attention.

"Oh, that's right. Anthony's boys," he said. "They haven't been any trouble?"

With a quick, nervous smile, Susannah placed a cup and the jar on the table, then sat on the edge of the bed, hands clasped tightly together in her lap. "They want to be with their father. Finally went to sleep here not long ago. How are your men?"

He nodded that they were fine and poured himself some water. "But Wild Ned McCafferty broke his leg."

She knew the name. During the fight for San Antonio, McCafferty, a short-tempered fellow, had led an attack on a house full of Mexican soldiers by hacking holes through the rooftop while other Texians fired on the house from the street. McCafferty was the first one to drop through the ceiling, a flintlock pistol in one hand and a sword in the other. His men told how he shot a Mexican sergeant, tossed away his pistol, pried the bayonet loose from the sergeant's musket and, using it and his sword, commenced slashing and stabbing every soldier he could find, like he'd gone crazy. Scared the sin out of the Mexicans, some throwing their rifles down and running out of the house. Like Almeron, McCafferty had served earlier in the army as an artilleryman. A lieutenant. Travis had assigned him the nine-pounder battery on the east wall at the cattle pens.

"How did he manage to break his leg?" she asked.

"Worst case of bad luck, I guess." Almeron explained that Travis had ordered him and Lieutenant Zanco to go to every battery and personally see to it each gun was in fit working order and had enough powder and shot and such. "Wild Ned was coming down the gun ramp to us and somehow caught his foot on one of the support posts. Fell right over the ramp. Came down on his right leg. I heard it snap. Broke just above his ankle. Got him to the hospital, and that ankle had swelled up like a ripe watermelon. He was cussing something fierce."

"I am sorry about his mishap," she said, relaxing her hands, feeling a little less fretful.

"Had to commend young Zanco, though," Almeron said and drained his cup.

"Why's that?"

"He volunteered to take Ned's post commanding the cannon. Travis gave it to him."

"I'd say Lieutenant Zanco is a good man," she said. "A little more water?"

"Please. That he is. James Bonham said he would stay on duty at the chapel battery tonight. He's a good man, too."

Susannah's hand began to tremble as she finished pouring and set the jar down. Dispirited, she sat in the hay and clasped her hands together again to make the shaking stop.

"I don't want to worry you," she said. "There's so much you already have to . . . I'm sorry." Lord, she hated feeling scared.

Almeron sat down next to her and put his hand over hers. "Sue, you and Angelina are all I have. I . . . I only wanted the best for us. I'm the one who should be sorry."

She looked into his kind eyes. "No regrets," she said and kissed him.

He sat back against the wall, and she took hold of his arm with both her hands, laid her head against his chest, and fought back the tears. She did not want to cry, not this night. She wanted to feel his arms, those strong loving arms, around her.

Looking up through the open roof of the sacristy into the black night sky where clouds covered the moon and stars, she prayed. *Dear God, I beg you, please, please, no matter what happens to us, spare our daughter. Somehow let her survive the coming storm and be allowed to live a full life. Protect her. Please.*

She lowered her eyes and watched the flame burning in the candle on the table. A few more hours of wax was left still to melt. That single small flame seemed to be the only light in the world this night.

And then the words came out. She hadn't even thought about them. She couldn't stop them. "I wish Santa Anna would show his face, because I would walk right up to him and kill him for you."

"I know you would, Sue. I always said you got more gumption than anybody I ever knew. I love you."

"I love you, sweetheart."

She felt him pull her closer. There was comfort in the steady rise and fall of his chest, the gentle sound of his breathing, the warmth of him.

She wanted to hold on to Almeron through the night.

She hoped for one more day with him.

She hoped.

CHAPTER TWENTY-SIX

Morales opened his pocket watch. It was half past three.

From the south side of the Plaza de Valero, he watched Reyes, Ordaz, and the advance skirmishers move out over the open ground toward the wooden palisade. They crouched low, rifles at the ready, moving slowly to avoid unnecessary noise. They also carried the two scaling ladders His Excellency had allotted Morales's men. Better Reyes's skirmishers have them, Morales decided. Give them every opportunity to breech the wall, gain a foothold inside the fort and bring this thing to an end.

The Alamo sat quietly in the distance. A couple of campfires still burned behind the palisade, as did the torches at each of the cannon emplacements along the south wall: the southeast corner, the lunette at the main gate, and at the center of the wooden palisade. Reyes and his men had less than thirty minutes to reach the palisade two hundred yards away before the attack began at four. Chances of being discovered increased the longer they had to wait down in the ditch in front of the wall.

"Twenty-five years ago, my father fought the Spanish at the battle of Monte de las Crucas," Morales recalled Reyes telling him earlier that night. "He said that before a battle, the blood pumps faster, the stomach turns tighter, and the mind, it worries more. But once the fighting begins, there is no more time for worry. There's only the fight. Winning the battle is all that matters."

Only if the battle is worth fighting, Morales had thought. But he replied, "That is certain, *Capitán*. And return with as many of your men as you can."

The clouds still covered the moon, and, within minutes, Morales lost sight of Reyes and his men in the darkness.

Behind him, Escobar and Victoria waited with the main force of nearly one hundred *cazadores*. Their blood pumping, stomachs tightening, and trying to ward off their worries, too, no doubt, the same as Morales was doing.

Ten minutes passed. Fifteen. Twenty.

There had been no shouts. No shots fired. The rebel sentry in the trench outside the south wall must have been killed. Ordaz had said he would see to it personally.

Surprise is still on our side, Morales thought with some relief.

Two minutes to five. Controlling his anger, Morales closed his pocket watch and shoved it back inside his pocket.

What was His Excellency waiting for? The attack was to begin an hour ago. No bugle had sounded. No message delivered about the delay. What in God's name was he thinking?

Morales could do nothing for Reyes or Ordaz or their men, hunkered down in the ditch at the palisade. He could not see them. He could not send them relief. Remain calm and quiet. That was all they could do. That was all Morales could do. *¡Mierda!*

He had not slept all night. There was no point.

Escobar and Victoria had reported that most of the men had managed some sleep before being roused shortly before two this morning. The companies had been formed into ranks of two long tandem lines, and then they waited, bellies down on the ground, rifles beside them.

And three hours later, here they still were,

belly down. It was so cold. Men were shivering. No blankets or coats, by order of His Excellency. And all they could do was wait.

Sergeants moved up and down the lines, kicking at the men's feet and prodding them with their wooden staffs to keep them alert. Morales had heard some of their "encouraging" whispers to the men. "Stay awake! You wouldn't want to miss the fight." "No, you can't smoke! *Idiota.* Might as well send up a flare telling the rebels we're coming." "Tighten those chin straps. Your Shako hat might save your damn heads from getting caved in."

Thankfully, Escobar and Victoria were good officers. They did not panic or pester with questions. They understood that battle plans could change. They also knew, as Morales did, that His Excellency would sound the attack when he was ready, despite any previous orders. Or good sense.

Morales glanced at his watch again. Eight minutes past five. *¡Jesús Cristo!*

Clouds were breaking up. Moonlight bathed the Alamo! Morales tried to see through that damn abatis to find Reyes and his men. Was a rebel sentry awake? Would he see the skirmishers there, crouched and waiting? And as quickly as they opened, the clouds closed back over the moon, cloaking the Alamo again in near darkness.

"Madre de Dios," he whispered.

A few long moments passed. To his right, he heard a squeak of leather, the jingle of a bridle. *That must be General Ramírez y Sesma's cavalry, or part of it,* Morales thought. He recalled His Excellency's order to the general that no rebels or *soldados* "escape" the battle.

Almost a quarter past five.

The horizon to the east was still black.

Morales could picture His Excellency at the northern battery, in safety, sitting, like a proud peacock, on his silver-studded saddle astride his big, black horse. His uniform was brushed and clean with all that silver filigree hanging from his neck to his sleeves. But His Excellency would not dirty his uniform this day. It disgusted Morales. Santa Anna was the most vain man he had ever known, and many of Morales's fellow officers agreed, though none would ever say it out loud.

Twenty-three minutes past five.

Soon the advantage would be lost. The difference between a hundred *soldados* killed or a thousand.

Morales could not see Reyes's men. Surprise was still with them. Yet, all they could do was wait there beneath the palisade, silent and unmoving. Reyes and Ordaz would not lose their heads, and they would not allow the men to lose theirs, either. Good men all.

No sign of rebel sentries on the walls, on top of the chapel, or at the main gate. They *had* to be sleeping. No alarm from inside the Alamo anywhere. *Perhaps God truly is on our side,* Morales thought.

A *cazador* behind him sneezed. A sergeant whispered a harsh warning.

There was a faint shout. It came from far off. Morales couldn't make out.

And then the harsh flinty bugle call sounding the charge. At last!

Morales drew his sword with his right hand and made the sign of the cross with his left as Escobar and Victoria, drawing their swords, ordered the men to their feet.

Chapter Twenty-Seven

"¡Viva Santa Anna!"

James's eyes snapped open, and he sprang to his feet, pulling on his hat and bringing his rifle up with him.

A bugle sounded out in the darkness, and the thunder of hundreds of feet pounded the ground.

"To your guns, boys! Here they come!" Captain Jameson shouted from the center battery.

"¡Viva la república!"

"¡No tomar prisioneros!"

James cocked his rifle, watching for Mexican soldiers. He could hear them coming fast, but he couldn't see them yet. No damn moonlight.

Captain Martin's gun crew on the eight-pounder to his left readied a charge of canister, and a wild-whiskered crewman grabbed the torch.

"Get up here!" Edward hollered down at

245

Hardin and Cleland, who'd been sleeping at the base of the wall.

"Damn thing!" Hardin swore, kicking his blanket free from his feet as he and Cleland clambered up to their posts.

Lowering his rifle, Georgie wiped sleep from his eyes and raised his rifle again.

"*¡Matarlos a todos, muchachos!*" Abamillo bellowed at his men.

Shooting a glance to his right past his brothers and friends, James saw Abamillo and his Tejanos with rifles ready. The big Tejano threw the front of his serape back over his shoulder revealing the Comanche war hawk club he kept in his belt, like he wanted to make it easy to get at.

"Steady!" someone shouted. "Pick your target!"

"Can't see nothin'!"

"*¡Muerte a los rebeldes!*"

James caught sight of Travis, rifle in hand, running up the ramp to the center battery, shouting something James couldn't make out, what with all the hollering. His slave Joe was right behind him with a shotgun.

"*¡Viva Santa Anna!*"

"Prepare to fire!" Captain Martin shouted.

James heard drums and bugles. The Mexicans were playing that damn "Degüello."

"Good God," Preacher cried.

246

"What's wrong?" James asked.

"Can't find my bifocals," he said.

"Forget 'em," Cleland said.

"I need them to see," Preacher said irritably, searching his pockets.

"*¡Arriba!*"

A high whistling sound made James look up. Rockets — five, six, more — arched overhead trailing bright, white light, revealing hundreds of Mexican soldiers, three lines deep. No, four lines! Charging from the northwest. About a hundred yards distant and coming fast. Captain Martin's cannon was looking right down at them. They were near shoulder to shoulder. Blue uniforms. White pants. Black Shako hats. Every man armed with a rifle, bayonets gleaming in that eerie light.

"James?" Georgie said urgently.

Looking his way, Georgie pointed straight ahead. In the dimming trails of the rockets, James saw hundreds more soldiers, line after line, at a full run, approaching the *acequia,* coming straight for them.

Goddamn! Not even sixty men defended the north wall. Something tugged deep in James's gut, pulling at him, hard. Is that what scared felt like? His hands were suddenly clammy. But there was no place to go. He would be no coward. *God help me not to run,* he thought. He glanced at Georgie, who was looking past him down at the storeroom where Gertrudis and her sister were. The burning candle could still be seen through the cracks in the door.

"Don't you worry about her," James told his little brother. "You do like I said and wade into them 'til they're dead."

Georgie nodded once.

"Shit Miss Agnes!" Preacher swore. He'd not found his bifocals. "How many you see?"

"All of them!" Edward shouted.

CHAPTER TWENTY-EIGHT

Susannah felt Almeron's hand slip suddenly from her fingers as he leapt up and grabbed his flintlock pistol from the table.

"To your guns!" he shouted as he ran out into the chapel nave where torchlight glowed on the walls.

Dear God, Susannah prayed, *please keep him safe.*

Shouts and orders echoed.

"Hurry! To your posts!"

"Give the bastards hell!"

"Check your powder!"

"Prepare to fire on my command!"

As Susannah scooped Angelina, swaddled in her blanket, into her arms, she saw men run past the sacristy doorway, their footfalls pounding up the ramp to the guns. Her heart raced. Holding her daughter was all that kept her hands still.

Nathan and Aleck sat up straight, twisting their heads, following the sounds, scared looks on their faces.

"Come here, boys," Susannah called to them.

They scrambled over, clutching their blankets. Trembling, Aleck threw his arms around her waist.

The candle had nearly melted down on the table. The flame had grown small.

Then a strange, bright light filled the room, throwing shadows across the walls from side to side, followed by a shrill whooshing sound. Susannah looked up through the open roof and saw several glowing, white trails of light streaming overhead. Like angels in flight.

Chapter Twenty-Nine

"*¡Adelante!*" Morales shouted, raising his sword.

He and his *cazadores* charged across the hard, grassless ground of the Plaza de Velero toward the wooden palisade.

Behind him, his men shouted their battle cry.

Rockets arched across the sky, trailing white, throwing light down below. They were coming from positions across the river. More streaks of white light soared over the Alamo.

In that bright light, Morales saw through an open tangle of branches in the abatis. Reyes was pulling himself up to the embrasure cut into the wooden wall where the rebel cannon stood. He knew it was Reyes by his white-plumed bicorn hat. Below him, a skirmisher pushed him up, his hand under Reyes's boot.

He heard the "Degüello," and musket fire.

Cós and Duque must already be at the north wall, he thought.

Reyes suddenly slipped, losing his footing, but raised himself back up just as fire and smoke shot out from the cannon. Reyes's hat pinwheeled away wildly, its plume on fire. His head disappeared in a spray of flame, grapeshot, and gore. His lifeless body fell back and out of sight into the ditch.

"*¡Rapido!*" Morales shouted and ran faster.

Rebels appeared at the top of the palisade. They leaned over and fired down into the thirty skirmishers. Yellow flashes of fire shot out of the ends of the muskets. Morales couldn't see his men there, the ditch and abatis blocking his view. But the yellow and red flashes answering from below told him they were putting up the fight he had intended.

"*¡Arriba!*" Morales heard Victoria shouting.

Another round of rockets lit up the Alamo, the hard ground of Plaza de Valero, the blackened squares where the *jacales* once stood, and Morales and his men.

A rebel sentry on top of the south wall shouted, pointing frantically, warning the men down in the lunette. That cursed lunette.

A ladder went up against the palisade wall. A skirmisher climbed.

Two rebels, leaning over the wall, one on either side of that ladder, swung around, took aim, and blasted that skirmisher off the ladder.

"¡*Vamos!*" Morales shouted. Keep moving!

CHAPTER THIRTY

James heard the boom of a cannon and rifle fire coming from the south wall and the corral pens on the east.

"Bastards are coming from all sides!" Edward shouted.

Looking down the barrel of his best rifle, the gift from Captain and Mrs. Dorsett, James had both his eyes open as he kept a Mexican soldier in his sights. Aim for the center, Pa had taught him, and it's a strong chance you'll hit something. That soldier was hollering, his mouth open wide as he ran forward. The lines of soldiers were closing fast. Sixty yards. Fifty yards. Plenty close enough to hit now. Suddenly, the soldier fired his musket from the hip and bright flashes from other Mexicans firing their muskets lit up the line of them — for an instant. James heard the sound of lead balls striking the wall. Someone howled in pain.

One of Abamillo's men was hit and went down.

More rockets flew over.

James fired at the Mexican soldier he held a bead on and saw him fall in that bright light as rifle and musket fire exploded all along the north wall. Damn it was loud.

"All batteries! Fire!" Captain Jameson commanded.

The three cannons at the center of the wall thundered, spewing flame and canister shot, dozens and dozens of lead balls, flying fast, spreading out.

"Fire!" Captain Martin yelled. His gunner put the torch to the touchhole of the eight-pounder. It jumped as canister flew into the oncoming Mexican lines.

That first whiff of pungent black powder stung James's nose. But it was nothing to the sound of the screaming he heard. In the light from the rockets, he saw what looked like the whole front line of Mexicans had been brought down, some missing arms and legs, some cut right in half and still screaming.

"Goddamn!" Edward shouted excitedly.

"Reload!" Captain Martin hollered. "Grapeshot!"

James stood, startled. He'd never seen such before. But the other lines of Mexican soldiers kept coming, jumping over the bodies, the limbs. They were yelling. No words that he could make out. Just hollering. Probably for blood. But they would not have his blood!

"Pour it into them!" James shouted.

Long rifles and shotguns flashed fire and lead balls and buckshot. James reached down for another of his rifles and nearly butted heads with Georgie doing the same. Georgie looked scared, that was sure, but he snatched up a rifle and brought it to his cheek and fired down into the Mexicans, as did James.

"Tell me where to shoot!" Preacher cried.

"Just aim for the sound of 'em, Preacher," Hardin said. "You'll hit one, sure!"

Preacher leaned forward and fired.

A rocket arched through the sky, shedding white light.

James reached down and picked up one of his Mexican muskets, cocked it, aimed, and fired. He saw the Mexican he hit drop his rifle and grab his head, like he was trying to hold in his brains.

The light dimmed. Mexicans stopped and raised their rifles. Flashes of red and yellow spit from their guns in the quickening darkness.

James heard a yelp, and the wild-whiskered man holding the torch spun around and fell, a bloody hole in his chest, the torch still clutched in his hand.

Another gun crewman snatched it up.

"Fire!" Captain Martin yelled.

The cannon unleashed its load of grapeshot in a loud, fiery blast. Mexicans fell screaming in pain. The hot iron chunks of the grapeshot put holes in them, big and small, their uniforms smoking. Some didn't move after they hit the ground.

But they kept coming. There were still so many of the bastards.

James fired again. More rockets. Good God, the Mexicans were almost to the wall!

"Fire!" Captain Jameson shouted. Two cannons in his battery unleashed hot iron.

One of Abamillo's Tejanos leaned over and fired into the Mexicans, and James realized two Tejanos lay at Abamillo's feet, dead.

Cleland threw a smoking rifle down. "We need more men here, damn it!" he cursed and snatched up another.

James grabbed the musket Moses had left him and saw Preacher sitting down, angry, holding a wadded kerchief against his ear. Copious blood ran down the side of Preacher's face as Hardin tied a bandana around his head.

"Get to the hospital!" James said.

"Won't do it," Hardin said.

"I can fight!" Preacher hollered. "How close now?"

"They're at the wall!" Edward shouted and cocked Pa's rifle and fired.

"Take my shotgun, Preacher," Hardin said, pressing it into Preacher's hands. "You won't miss them with this."

Preacher leapt up, leaned over, and fired into the enemy below. "Mighty is the hand of the Lord!" he shouted.

James aimed the musket and fired into the soldiers, too, and quickly pulled back from the edge of the wall.

"You holding up?" he said to Georgie, who tossed down a Mexican musket and picked up his long rifle, the one Captain Dorsett had given him. There was black powder smudged on Georgie's face, and he was spitting over and over. "What's the matter?"

"Got powder in my mouth tearing open a cartridge."

"Ladders!" Cleland shouted.

CHAPTER THIRTY-ONE

"¡*Miren! ¡Más soldados!* At the cattle pen!" Susannah heard Gregorio Esparza shout from Almeron's battery at the top of the nave.

"Swing batteries two and three around!" Almeron shouted. "Let's give Lieutenant Zanco and those men on the pen walls some help."

Oh, my good Lord, please help us! Susannah prayed. The cattle pen was on the east side of the fort, next to the chapel.

"Battery one! Fire!" Almeron shouted. The roar of the cannon shook dust from the walls. Angelina squalled louder, and Susannah held her closer. Aleck and Nathan covered their ears with their hands.

"Battery two! Fire!" Bonham shouted.

Chunks of white plaster fell from the wall and hit the flagstone floor, shattering into pieces. Susannah hunched forward to protect Angelina from the falling debris.

"¡Niños prisa!" Susannah heard Ana saying, and, a moment later, Ana, holding a burning candle in her hand, stood in the sacristy doorway with her children, blankets about their shoulders. Susannah saw the scared faces of Ana's children, especially little Maria. But Ana wore a grim look. The one Susannah had seen for so many days.

"We should all be together," Ana said. "¿Sí?"

Susannah motioned quickly with her hand. "Come in. Come in."

"Battery three! Fire!"

Ana hurried her children inside, pointed them toward the corner where Susannah sat, set the candle on the table, and sat down on the floor with Susannah and Wolf's boys. Susannah heard Ana tell her children something in Spanish, and they put their hands together and lowered their heads in prayer while Ana held her arms around them.

Susannah and Ana's eyes met, and Ana whispered bitterly, "Santa Anna is the devil."

"Hurry up with that next load!" Bonham shouted.

"Send the bastards to hell!" Almeron shouted.

Aleck whimpered, and Susannah pulled his head close to her.

"You scared?" she heard Nathan whisper.

Looking over at him, she saw he was talking to Ana's oldest boy, eight-year-old Enrique, his eyes darting from the walls to the doorway, like he was searching for something.

Ana whispered to him, and Enrique looked at Nathan and nodded and said something in Spanish.

Ana said, "He says he wants to help his *papá.*"

"Me, too," Nathan said.

"Fire!" Almeron shouted.

The walls shook and plaster fell.

"Fire!" shouted Bonham.

CHAPTER THIRTY-TWO

"*¡Asalto!*" Morales shouted. "*¡Asalto!*"

The sound of cannon fire erupted to the north and east as Morales and his men were nearly to the abatis. The cannons on top of the mission roared, briefly lighting up the sky over the chapel, firing death toward his friend Romero. From the sound of gunfire ahead, the fight at the palisade wall was fierce.

Morales waved his sword, and the ranks divided, Victoria's company rounding the abatis to the right, and Escobar and his company on the left with Morales. They made for the palisade, as he had planned. And he saw the lunette looming. Morales could have avoided the damn thing by staying with Victoria's company. He abhorred the thought of being struck again by a load of deadly grapeshot, but he was the commander. The example. That didn't mean he wasn't scared.

He ran faster. The cannon at the lunette could fire at any moment. Hurry! Outrun the grapeshot!

More rebels clustered on top of the south wall where it met the palisade, firing down into Reyes's men, others shooting toward Morales and Escobar's men.

"Stay with me!" Morales shouted, waving his sword.

The cannon at the lunette fired. Morales's hat flew off his head, and something hot nicked his chin. Men behind him screamed in agony.

He did not look back but put his white-gloved hand to his chin. There was blood. Damn!

"*¡Asalto!*" he shouted and ran faster.

Escobar's men took up the cry.

"*¡Muerte a los Tejanos!*"

"*¡Viva Santa Anna!*"

More rebels on top of the south wall swung their fire at him and his men. Morales saw that after firing, the rebels dropped their rifles, reached down, brought another up, and fired again. But, exposed as Morales's men were, those rebels had to stand and lean over the wall to shoot at them, offering themselves as tall targets. Reyes's sharpshooters had silenced some of them.

Clearing the abatis, Morales charged into

the ditch at the base of the palisade. At least half of Reyes's men were already cut down. Ordaz directed the fire of those remaining. Pressed against the wall, the sharpshooters, rifles raised, took aim at the rebels and fired. Some scrambled for the cartridges on the belts of the dead.

One ladder was up against the palisade to the left of the embrasure, and a *cazador* was climbing. A rebel in a tall hat appeared over the palisade, shot him off the ladder, and pushed it back off the wall. Two more of Reyes's men braced the second ladder against the other side of the embrasure. Both were shot down before they could start climbing.

Victoria and his men swarmed into the ditch. Musket and rifle fire rose to an almost deafening pitch. Black powder smoke filled the air. More rockets lit up the fight. Morales shouted at the men, urging them on. More than one hundred *cazadores* jostled for room to fire, to climb two ladders, to fight rebels who fired rapidly and mercilessly down into them.

"Over the wall!" Morales shouted, stepping over bodies, making his way to the nearest ladder. Sword in hand, he took hold of a rung and started climbing when a burly *cazador,* shot in the chest, fell dead against him, knocking him off the ladder and onto the ground.

Scrambling to his feet, Morales swore and saw a skinny *cazador* scurrying up the ladder. Suddenly shot in the face, he fell backward, his leg tangled in the ladder, leaving him hanging upside down. A big rebel pushed the ladder away. Looking up, Morales saw the rebel wore a toothy grin and a coonskin cap. Was that Crockett? The big rebel brought another rifle up to his cheek, aimed down at him, and pulled the trigger. *Click!* Misfire! The big rebel's grin disappeared as he uttered an oath.

A *cazador* sharpshooter stepped in front of Morales, his rifle raised, and fired. The ball struck the big rebel in the eye, snapping his head back. He spun around and collapsed, hanging over the wall. The coonskin cap fell off his head, landing on a dead body sprawled in the ditch.

Morales ordered some of the men out of the ditch and up into the abatis, where they fired on the rebels as they showed themselves over the palisade and at those firing from the top of the south wall. That murderous rebel fire had to be quelled.

Ordaz shouted to the men to follow him as he raised a ladder and quickly climbed.

A rebel leaned over the palisade, holding

the barrel of his musket in both hands, and swung it down, catching the top of Ordaz's Shako hat with the musket butt, knocking him off the ladder. Ordaz picked himself up off the ground, dazed but unhurt, the side of his hat caved in.

"Fire!"

Hot yellow flame lit up the ditch as grape-shot tore into the men firing from the abatis.

Morales stumbled backward over a dead *cazador*. The blast cut a bloody swath, leaving bodies, smoking, blackened, missing faces, hands, arms.

Smoke hung like a shroud. Cries and moans rose along with the sound of more musket fire.

Morales felt someone take his arm. It was Victoria trying to help him to his feet.

"Where's *Capitán* Escobar?" Morales asked.

"No sé." Victoria shook his head. "Are you hit, *Coronel*? Your chin. It's bleeding."

"It's nothing," Morales said and saw his white trousers were smeared with blood. The blood of his men.

Time to take those still alive out of this slaughter pen. His attack had failed. Crockett's men fought like devils.

A few rockets soared overhead. And he saw it. Salvation. Not ten yards from the southwest corner of the fort. The old stone house. Shelter. Reassemble. Plan a new attack.

"*¡Capitán! ¡Sergento!* Take cover behind the stone house!"

Victoria and Ordaz shouted orders to the men.

"To the stone house!"

"Take the ladders!"

Morales led the retreat, charging out of the bloody ditch and around the lunette as the rebels there and on top of the south wall continued to shoot at them.

"Ready!" he heard a rebel shout from inside the lunette. "Fire!"

The second cannon there thundered. Jagged grapeshot cut through his men.

Morales looked back. There was smoke and screams, men dead and dying. A *cazador* took a few wobbly steps. He held part of his Brown Bess in his hand, and he fell screaming. Morales realized the grapeshot had torn the man's arm off at the shoulder. Another *cazador* rolled on the ground, his leg ripped off above the knee. Blood spurted. Some of the men stopped to carry the wounded.

"Leave them!" Morales shouted. "Get to cover!" He knew they couldn't care for the wounded. But how many were left alive?

That was all that mattered at this moment. Maimed men couldn't fight.

Coming through the pall of smoke, Ordaz urged the men with him on to the stone house.

Morales thanked God that no more rockets had launched again, making them easier targets for the rebels to see. They were easily in range of the rebel muskets and rifles. And the sun seemed so slow to rise this day.

Up on the southwest corner of the wall, the gun crew on the eighteen-pounder had not fired. More good luck! If the rebels could have fired on them with the big cannon, they would have. Perhaps they couldn't lower the elevation of the gun. No matter. He and his men were safe for the moment behind the stone house.

"Where is *Capitán* Escobar?" Morales said.

A corporal answered. *"El Capitán está muerto."*

"Dead? Did you see him?" Morales asked.

"I saw him fall, *Coronel.* At the abatis, when the *rebeldes* fired their cannon."

"And *Capitán* Victoria?"

Ordaz, his face splattered with blood, reported Victoria killed at the palisade wall. "He was ordering the men out. A rebel ball hit him in the throat."

268

Reyes, Escobar, Victoria. Three fine officers, all dead. Morales said nothing. There was still a battle to fight. His Excellency's orders.

"How many men are left?" Morales asked.

Ordaz answered, "I count sixty-eight, *Coronel.*"

Cut down by half, Morales thought bitterly. Crockett's men were truly devils. *Muy cierto. Diablos.*

CHAPTER THIRTY-THREE

James fired and saw the Mexican carrying the ladder fall.

Georgie dropped onto one knee and yanked a lead ball from his shot pouch to reload his smoking rifle.

James took a bead on another Mexican carrying a ladder, pushing his way through the mob of soldiers trying to reach the wall. James fired, hitting him in the head. The Mexican went down, his ladder disappearing in the confusion of bodies. They were screaming and yelling and dying. And James didn't care.

Pouring powder from his horn, James primed and loaded his Dorsett rifle. All the guns he'd primed and loaded before the battle were spent. The same for his brothers. Likely all the other men on the north wall, too. They'd given Santa Anna's men every kind of hell. But now they had to reload and fast. James would depend on the rifle he knew best. He rose up, aimed, and fired, flame and lead blasting out the end of the muzzle. Through the smoke he saw a soldier fall, his face bloody. *Keep firing,* he told himself. *Shoot them down!*

Edward was crouched low, holding Pa's rifle, "My Lizzie," his back to the fight. What was he waiting for? Then Edward looked his way, and James met his eyes. Edward muttered something and rose to his feet, aimed over the wall, fired, and ducked down to reload.

"Looks like they're running!" Captain Martin shouted. "Keep after them!"

A Mexican officer was holding up his sword and hollering at his men. Sounded like he was saying "poor a key, poor a key." A whole slew of soldiers who'd been clustered around the northwest corner had turned and were running west toward the river, away from the Alamo!

Bringing his rifle up, James took aim at the officer and fired. God must've been watching over that fancy-dressed Mexican because James hit a soldier who went rushing by in front of him.

Captain Martin's gun crew and the few defenders posted on that end of the west wall fired after those retreating Mexicans.

But there were still hundreds of them at

the foot of the north wall, jammed there. James saw them every time he leaned over to fire, and plenty of them shot back.

James rammed another ball down the barrel of his rifle, glanced over, and saw Georgie fire into the Mexicans.

"Why don't the rest of them run?" Georgie asked, wiping the sweat off his brow.

Close by, Preacher fired another load from his double-barreled shotgun.

"More buckshot!" he hollered, and Hardin handed him a fistful of rounds. Preacher shoved them into his pocket, then opened the breech and loaded each barrel.

James cocked his rifle and leaned over the wall. A Mexican was looking up at him over the barrel of his own musket. James pulled his trigger first, his lead ball finding its mark. The Mexican crumpled down against the wall.

Preacher leaned over the wall and squeezed both triggers of the shotgun, firing a deadly spread of buckshot. Suddenly, he staggered back, blood and bone flying up in a sickly red spray out of his back.

"Preacher!" Hardin shouted.

Preacher stumbled, that big body of his trying to stay upright. The shotgun dropped from his hands, and he fell forward over the wall into the Mexicans below.

Without a word, James rammed another ball down the barrel. Pour it into the bastards!

Hardin snatched up the shotgun and loaded it with two rounds of buckshot. "Sons of bitches!" he shouted as he fired into the soldiers.

A few more rockets whooshed overhead, their white trails lighting up the sky.

Abamillo gave a fierce cry and fired down into the mass of men.

James realized he'd heard no cannon fire from Captain Jameson's battery. Glancing that way, he saw Jameson and his men using rifles. The Mexicans must be too close to the wall for the cannons to be of any use. He also saw that the men on the wall were already thinned out.

But where was Travis? Or his slave, Joe? There was a body lying at the bottom of Captain Jameson's gun ramp. James couldn't make out the face, but the scabbard of a sword was at his side and a red sash around his waist. Aw, shit!

Cannons at the chapel boomed, firing at the east side. James saw flashes of rifle fire on top of the hospital roof. The men there were shooting down at the corral. Holy Christ!

James heard the whirl of a musket ball fly

past his head as he reloaded. Sweat dripped into one of his eyes. The smell of burnt gunpowder was thick in the air amid the cries of the dying and the clamoring of the living.

"Roof's burning!" someone shouted.

Part way down the west wall, the thatched roof of the long house next to Travis's headquarters had caught fire, likely from a rocket. Almost instantly the roof was engulfed in bright orange flames. It lit up half the courtyard of the fort.

CHAPTER THIRTY-FOUR

The rumble of the cannons above thundered in Susannah's ears. Rifle fire cracked sharply. Relentlessly. The men shouted and swore.

Angelina cried, and Susannah could do nothing to calm her. There was only noise and shrieks and the walls shaking. She wanted to cry, too. But she refused to allow herself.

Ana and her children prayed.

"Drive them back!" Susannah heard Almeron shout. "We'll show these bastards!"

"Fire!" It was Bonham. A cannon roared. A big chunk of plaster fell and struck a barrel.

Aleck let out a yowl. Nathan scurried over to him. He whispered in his brother's ear. Susannah couldn't hear what he said. Aleck shook his head and quieted down, but she still felt his trembling.

"*¡La muerte de Santa Anna!*" Ana's husband

Gregorio shouted.

Enrique looked up. Susannah couldn't tell if it was worry or anger on his face. She saw her candle flame disappear in a wisp of smoke. But Ana's candle burned brightly. Plaster dust swirled in its glow.

At the front doors of the chapel, men called for more shot and powder and cartridges.

"Take what you need, lads!" Susannah heard Major Evans say.

God, please help us, Susannah prayed, watching the candle flame. *God, help us.*

"Fire!" Bonham yelled and a cannon boomed.

"Some of them, they are running!" Ana's husband shouted.

"They're almost out of range of our guns!" Almeron shouted.

Were the Mexicans retreating? Susannah wondered. She heard scuffling.

"Enrique! No!" Ana said harshly.

Susannah saw Enrique dart out of the sacristy and into the torch lit nave. Nathan jumped up.

"Nathan!" Susannah shouted, grabbing his shirtsleeve, but he yanked himself free and bolted out through the doorway.

"¡Ven aquí!" Ana shouted, up on her feet and starting after them.

"Here, where are you off to, lads?" It was Major Evans's voice.

"Let me go!" Nathan yelled.

"¡Mí papá! Papá!" Enrique cried.

Evans's tall shape appeared in the doorway, carrying each struggling boy under an arm like sacks of grain.

"Mrs. Esparza, you in here?"

"Sí," she answered.

He set the boys down, saying, "Stay in here, now."

"Gracias," Ana said, taking Enrique in her arms, a quiver in her voice.

"They will," Susannah said to Evans, who ran back out into the nave.

Nathan sat next to his brother, pulled his legs up to his chest, wrapped his arms around them, and dropped his head down on his knees.

Enrique cried and struggled, but Ana held on to him, talking to him in Spanish, trying to calm him down.

Susannah knew little Spanish, but she did understand one thing Ana said. *"Muy valiente."* It meant very brave.

Susannah wanted to scold Nathan, tell him he'd scared the life out of her. But when she leaned over, close to his ear, she said, not unkindly, "Your brother needs you. And you need him."

"We run them off! Look there!"

Nathan jerked his head up and wiped away a tear at the sound of his father's voice, coming from the battery at the top of the chapel.

"No!" Almeron shouted. "They're attacking the northwest corner!"

CHAPTER THIRTY-FIVE

Morales peered around the side of the abandoned stone house. A roof fire had broken out inside the fort on the west side. It threw enough light that he counted maybe thirty men, maybe less, on top of the south wall, including the gun crew on the eighteen-pounder. By his calculation, more than half of the rebels had left their positions on the south wall. Probably fewer than ten were still inside the lunette. And perhaps Crockett's devils were no longer at the palisade. From what he could hear, it sounded as though all the fighting was concentrated at the north wall.

His men were tired, he knew. But they were anxious to continue the battle. They still had the two scaling ladders. And the cannon inside the lunette faced only east and south, not west, toward what was left of his command.

Morales quickly calculated a plan. Time

was critical. It could work. It would have to.

He turned to Sergeant Ordaz and explained his plan of attack. It was simple. Direct.

When he finished, he peered out again at the south wall. Still only a few men remained on it. A rocket plunged down! Another roof caught fire on the west wall. Then he heard them. The anguished cries for water, the calls for help of his *cazadores.* Those brave ones lying maimed and bleeding — arms and legs torn off, holes in their stomachs, insides spilling out, faces shredded — on the Plaza de Valero, at the palisade wall, and in front of the lunette. The ones he had to order left behind. The unfortunate ones. Because His Excellency let his little *verga* do his thinking.

"*Sergento* Ordaz," he said, keeping his voice steady and his eyes on the south wall. "Prepare the men."

CHAPTER THIRTY-SIX

"You hear that?" Hardin called out.

"What?" James couldn't hear anything but gunfire and shouting.

"Swear it sounded like a bugle!"

James didn't hear any bugle. But that damn "Degüello" had stopped. What did that mean?

More rockets flew across the sky.

"Sweet Mary!" Cleland cried.

James saw them. Mexican soldiers! Hundreds more! Four lines deep! Charging straight for the wall. Drums and horns started up the "Degüello" again.

"¡Viva Santa Anna!"

"Goddamn Santa Anna!" Hardin hollered at the Mexicans crowded below at the foot of the wall. He cocked both barrels and gave them a double blast from his shotgun.

"Put it into them!" James yelled and fired.

"James! Your leg!" Georgie shouted.

James glanced down. The bottom of his

pant leg had caught on fire. Burning paper wadding from his rifle barrel must have drifted down. He quickly patted it out with his hand.

A hail of gunfire erupted from the charging Mexicans.

Abamillo was hit, bleeding from his chest, but the big Tejano stood there, firing like he didn't even feel it. He was the only Tejano left standing.

"They're climbing the damn posts!" Edward shouted, holding Pa's rifle.

Shit! Those timber posts ran the full length of the outside of the north wall!

James reloaded, cocked his rifle, leaned over to fire, and his hat flew off. A musket ball had taken it right off his head but had missed him. Leaning over the wall he shot a Mexican soldier, hoping it was the son of a bitch who'd shot off his hat.

"Shoot them down!" Cleland hollered.

Pulling back to reload, James saw Georgie and Cleland fire down the wall. And Edward was — Hell, where did he go? Glancing into the courtyard, James couldn't see his older brother anywhere.

There was a sickening sound, and Cleland dropped to his knees, shot through the mouth. He fell to the side. His eyes rolled back into his head, and blood and pieces of teeth gushed out of his mouth.

Preacher and Cleland shot dead! Edward, too, for all James knew.

"Damn you bastards!" James pulled out another patch and ball. He was running low on both. If they got over the wall, there wouldn't be time to reload anything, his rifle, a Mexican musket, nothing!

"They're coming!" Hardin shouted, reloading his shotgun.

Georgie slammed the butt of his rifle into a soldier's face as another soldier coming up next to him reached across and grabbed Georgie's coat. Jerking away, Georgie fell backwards over Cleland's body.

The Mexican pulled himself up, his musket slung over his shoulder.

James plunged the patch and ball down the barrel with his ramrod.

The Mexican had both feet on top of the wall.

James yanked the ramrod out.

The Mexican pulled his musket from around his shoulder. The bayonet flashed.

James cocked his rifle. No time to aim!

The bayonet lowered.

James pulled the trigger, firing at the same instant Hardin cut loose with both barrels of his shotgun, blasting that Mexican off the wall, a big bloody hole in his chest.

Breathing hard, James nodded his thanks to Hardin, who helped Georgie to his feet.

Behind James a voice called out, "Let's get to it!"

James turned. A bunch of men were climbing up to him from the courtyard.

"Huzzah for Tennessee!" Captain Martin shouted.

Crockett's men! Maybe a dozen, maybe more. They commenced shooting the Mexican soldiers climbing the timber posts.

Fire had spread to two more rooftops on the west wall. From the light of those fires, James could see there was no attack at the main gate or anywhere on the south wall. All the fighting was right here!

"We run the Mexicans off at the south wall and come to give you boys some help," a Tennessean wearing a blue cap standing just ahead of James said as he primed his rifle pan. Blue cap's body jerked oddly, startling James, and blue cap fell dead.

"¡Arriba!" A Mexican officer shouted as he came over the wall, sword glinting from the firelight.

James threw his rifle down and grabbed his Mexican musket, the one with the bayonet. He lunged at the officer, ramming the bayonet through his chest, almost to the hilt. The officer's eyes grew wide, bulging out, his mouth trying to form a word. The sword came up and then dropped from his hand. James yanked the bayonet free.

"James!" Georgie shouted. "Look!"

Mexicans swarmed over Captain Jameson's battery! Men on the hospital roof hollered and fired at the northeast end of the north wall. The Mexicans had breeched the wall there, too!

Hardin leapt off the wall and into the courtyard. What was he doing? "Hardin!" James shouted.

"*¡Hijos de putas!*" Abamillo shouted, swinging his war hawk club, bashing in the head of Mexican at the top of the timber post in front of him.

"Look out!" James shouted but too late.

A Mexican charged across from Jameson's battery and stuck Abamillo in the side with his bayonet. The Mexican yanked it out, but the big Tejano grabbed him by the throat, swung his other arm, and drove that pointed stone club deep into the Mexican's head as two more Mexican soldiers stabbed Abamillo in the back with their bayonets. His knees buckled, his hand still clenched around the dead Mexican's throat.

"Fall back!" someone cried. "Fall back!"

Then James heard Captain Martin shouting.

CHAPTER THIRTY-SEVEN

Morales signaled Ordaz.

"*¡Fuego!*" the sergeant shouted, and half the remaining *cazadores* began firing from the cover of the old stone house at the rebels all along the top of the south wall, at the eighteen-pounder and those behind the lunette. There were no parapets or rooftops between the southwest corner and the main gate. No men there. Any attackers going after that stretch of wall would be caught in a rebel crossfire between the corner and the building rooftop over the gate.

Rebel gunfire answered Ordaz's sharp-shooters.

Morales heard the rebels shouting. "Put it to them!" "Fire the eighteen-pounder!" "They're too close! Can't lower the gun elevation!"

Three thatched roofs along the west wall burned; their flames threw those rebels manning the southwest corner into dark relief, making them better targets for Ordaz and his men. Morales counted about a dozen rebels on the wide platform where the eighteen-pounder stood.

With thirty *cazadores* and the two ladders, Morales moved swiftly across those few open yards toward the southwest corner of the Alamo. No rebels fired on them. Morales guessed they simply didn't see them. He was certain, though, that the dark eastern sky, with barely a tinge of red against the clouds low on the horizon, was to his advantage.

Reaching the west side of the corner, Morales motioned to the men with the ladders, and they raised them up against the wall. His sword at the ready, Morales climbed. His men followed, scaling the ladders, one hand grasping the rungs, the other holding their muskets. Every musket was loaded. The men would have time for one shot. After that, bayonets.

Sounds of battle coming from the north wall had grown louder, fiercer. Ordaz and his men kept up their firing, concentrating on the rebels manning the lunette.

"Look here!" a rebel cried. "They're setting up to attack the main gate!"

Reaching the top of the wall, Morales peered over. A torch burned by the cannon.

Ten rebels there fired down on Ordaz's men. Some standing, others kneeling. A few rebels lay on the platform, dead or wounded. Two stood on the side of the cannon closest to Morales. One wore a long coat. The other had red whiskers and was hurriedly trying to reload his shotgun, and shouting curses.

Morales pulled himself over the wall. The man behind him followed quickly. The *cazador* from the second ladder was on the platform, rifle ready.

"*¡Arriba!*" Morales shouted.

The rebels turned. In the torchlight, Morales saw horrified surprise on some faces, dark determination on others. "They're coming over the wall!" "Take 'em!" Rebels came at them. One swung around and fired, hitting that first *cazador* and knocking him backward, a bloody, smoking hole in his chest.

More *cazadores* gained the platform. "*¡Viva Santa Anna!*"

"Mex bastards!" red whiskers shouted. He didn't reload his shotgun. Holding it across his chest with both hands, he charged Morales to shove him back off the wall.

Morales bent low and drove his sword through the rebel to the hilt. There was hate in red whiskers' eyes. "Damn you," Morales heard him say, and red whiskers wheezed out his last breath.

Morales waded into the rebels, slashing, cutting. A piece of the cannon wheel in front of him splintered from a rebel ball striking it. Men screamed. Rebels and *cazadores* had no time to reload. Rifles became clubs. Bayonets drew blood.

A rebel on top of the roof over the main gate pointed and shouted, "West wall!"

One of Ordaz's men shot him down.

No reinforcements rushed forward. No Crockett, or his men.

"Spike the cannon!"

Long coat grabbed a mallet and a barbed spike from a box by the gun. Morales slashed him deep across the face with his sword before he could drive the spike into the touchhole of the barrel. Long coat slumped over the cannon, dead.

"Retreat!" a rebel cried.

A handful of them jumped into the courtyard. Others ran down the earthen ramp.

Morales saw some rebels climbing off the south wall and rushing across the courtyard. The gun crews at the twin-cannon battery facing the main gate were turning their cannons toward him and his men!

"*¡Adelante!*" he shouted. "*¡A los cañones!*"

Waving his sword, he and his *cazadores* charged down the long ramp.

CHAPTER THIRTY-EIGHT

"Great God, Sue, the Mexicans are inside our walls!" Almeron shouted from the doorway of the sacristy.

Susannah saw his face smeared with dirt and sweat. And fear was in his eyes! She had never seen it before in all their years together. Her stomach tightened. He crossed to her.

"Dios mío," Ana whispered.

Susannah felt his face brush hers and then his brief kiss on her lips. He kissed Angelina. His face was next to hers again, and he whispered in her ear, something about saving his daughter.

Before she could ask, he pulled away and ran back out the doorway, nearly knocking someone down.

She called out his name, but it was too late. He was gone.

CHAPTER THIRTY-NINE

"They're breaking through the wall!" Captain Martin shouted. "Christ, we need more men here!"

Rushing past James, Georgie darted across the platform to the west wall where the captain, what remained of his gun crew, and the few defenders still there fired down into the Mexicans.

The Dorsett rifle in his hands, James reached the edge of the west wall as Georgie shot a brawny looking soldier wielding a big axe, battering at the bricked-up window below, a window James had helped seal shut. Gertrudis and Juana were in the room on the other side of that window.

Shoving his hand inside his shot pouch, James realized it was empty. And where was his powder horn? Had it come loose? Fallen off? Hell!

Another Mexican picked up the axe and swung it against the crumbling adobe bricks and mortar. Other Mexicans armed with axes and crowbars rushed down the wall, finding other bricked up openings and pounding at them!

The burning roofs threw light everywhere. One of the roofs suddenly collapsed. Sparks and flame shot into the sky.

The men on the cannon at the embrasure on the west wall fired as Mexicans tried to storm through it. James saw bodies shredded in the fiery spray.

"¡Matarlos!" a Mexican officer shouted.

Captain Martin, standing by James, shot the officer dead.

A Mexican soldier fired.

Captain Martin groaned, clutching his stomach. Blood covered his hands, and he fell in front of his cannon.

James saw the Mexicans had broken through the bricked-up window below and were climbing through into where Juana and Gertrudis were!

"No!" Georgie yelled and spun around.

"Wait!" James shouted. He grabbed at Georgie's coat, but his brother jerked away and leapt down into the courtyard. James jumped off the platform after him, landed on a dead body, lost his balance, and hit the ground rolling, his rifle flying out of his hands.

Getting to his feet, he saw the door of the storeroom burst open and a Mexican run out. Georgie shot him down. James didn't hear the women screaming. But he heard Georgie's long, loud, savage cry, something he'd never heard out of his brother before.

Snatching the dead soldier's musket and using the bayonet, Georgie attacked and stabbed the next Mexican coming through the doorway.

As James picked up a musket with a bayonet attached, he saw an officer rush out the door. The officer carried a sword. Georgie yanked his bayonet out of the dead soldier's gut. The officer ran his sword into Georgie. Georgie's mouth hung open, silent. The officer pulled his sword out, and Georgie fell dead.

"No!" James screamed and lunged at the Mexican officer, ramming the bayonet deep into him. The officer doubled over and dropped to the ground. The bayonet was stuck! James couldn't pull it free!

"There's too many! Retreat! Retreat!" he heard someone holler.

A Mexican soldier charged, bayonet forward.

His foot on the officer's chest, James yanked the bayonet out. The soldier was nearly on him.

A rifle cracked, and the Mexican spun around, hit in the side. Howling, he rolled on the ground.

The face of one of the Tennesseans appeared. He wore a tall hat with a single feather sticking out of the band. A streak of blood ran from his wild crop of hair down the front of his face. "Come on, son!" he said.

CHAPTER FORTY

"*¡Tomar los cañónes!*" Morales shouted, charging the two cannons in the courtyard.

The rebel gun crew had swung one cannon around at Morales and his men. The other one was stuck, as men, shouting and howling, tried to move it.

Morales ran straight at the black round hole facing him at the end of the cannon barrel. Straight at death. He did not waver. It was his duty.

"*¡Tamarlo!*" he shouted. Take it! Take the cannon!

He saw a rebel drive a spike into the barrel of the second cannon. It was useless now.

His *cazadores* spread out behind him, bayonets ready. Some veered to the right, engaging the rebels coming off the south wall.

Holding a torch, an old rebel with a graying beard brought it down to the touchhole of the cannon.

Almost on top of the cannon, Morales opened his mouth wide in a ferocious, defiant scream!

A Mexican lead ball struck the old rebel, knocking him back, the torch dropping from his hand.

Morales and his men charged into the rebels, slashing and stabbing and cursing, driving them back from the cannons.

On the right, *cazadores* sent rebels running. Others lay dead.

A feral shout.

Morales turned. A young rebel raised a knife over his head, ready to plunge it down. Morales had no time to bring up his sword. He would die at the hands of this boy.

The rifle butt of a *cazador* caught the boy hard against his face, so hard, Morales heard the crack of bone. The boy hit the ground, his knife skittering away. Blood ran out of his mouth onto the light-colored cravat tied around his neck. His eyes fluttered. The boy's face was broken, his jaw crooked. Morales knew this rebel was of no more consequence.

Most of the rebels retreated inside the long stone building and a squat adobe, connected to the long stone one, forming an L shape. A few had taken cover behind sandbags stacked underneath the archway of the main gate, and they fired at Morales's men. Others at the main gate were firing through the loopholes cut in the heavy gate doors into the lunette on the other side. It was as Morales had planned. They had driven the rebels off the south wall and now Ordaz and his men were assaulting the lunette.

"To the gate!" Morales shouted, rallying his men. *Cazadores* ran past him. Something made him look back. He saw the rebel with the crooked jaw was gone.

CHAPTER FORTY-ONE

Cradling Angelina, Susannah heard little Maria Esparza shriek.

Galba Fuqua leaned against the doorway. Ashen. Gaunt. Both hands cupped his jaw. Blood covered his chin and had dripped onto his cravat and shirt and down his forearms.

Nathan gasped.

Ana pulled her children close, protecting them. Whispering something.

On her feet, Susannah hurried to Galba. His hands still held his jaw. He opened his mouth a little, squeezed his eyes shut. He was trying to speak, to form words, but they came out like low, mushy notes. She saw one side of his face was red and purple and swelling.

"What is it?" she said. "Tell me."

He tried to speak again, and more blood suddenly bubbled out of his mouth and dripped down his chin and onto his hands and arms.

"Oh, my Lord," she said, reaching her hand out toward him.

He shook his head, his eyes watery, and hurried away. His blood had smeared on the stones of the doorway.

What had been so important he wanted to tell her? She had tried to make out what he had tried to say but failed. Helpless, the tears came.

Chapter Forty-Two

Carrying his musket, James followed the feather hat Tennessean. Keeping low, they hurried past the burning barracks. Flames leapt out of the windows, licking up the walls. The heat was fierce.

The sounds of the flames and battle mixed in James's ears as he and feather cap moved past Travis's quarters and ducked into the open section between it and the house beyond. On the other side of that house was the west wall battery, but James couldn't see it to tell if there was anybody still on it. But it looked like the roof fire at the small storage house to the far side of the battery was about burned out.

Feather hat aimed and fired at Mexicans coming down along the west wall buildings. "Cock that musket and shoot something!"

"I got no powder or shot," James said.

Feather hat cursed and pulled a flintlock pistol from his belt and held it out to James, butt first. "Use this. They get close, it'll put them down."

The big pistol felt strange and awkward in James's hand, but he was happy to have it.

The north wall was clearly lost, and the fight had moved into the courtyard. James saw the fellows on top of the hospital roof firing down into the Mexicans, but there weren't many left up there. Men were shooting from the windows of the granary and the hospital. James saw flashes of gunfire from both floors. *Put it into the Mexicans!* Georgie surely had done so, by damn.

Maybe Edward had sought cover in the hospital. Or maybe he —

"Damnation!" feather hat said. "Look there!"

The Mexicans had broken through the main gate! They were pouring in! An officer there was waving his sword. Men were taking cover inside the low barracks, but there were so few of them. And the Mexicans kept coming!

The cannon on the raised west wall platform suddenly fired. Mexicans at the main gate fell! That puny New Orleans Grey fellow in charge of the west battery had turned his gun on them! *Give them another round!* James wanted to yell. Then a bunch of Mexicans broke away from the main gate, fired a volley at the battery, and charged toward it.

"Let's give those men some help and —" James stopped. He saw him. Edward. His rifle in his hands. Running. At least a couple dozen men followed him. Maybe more. It was hard to tell through all the smoke.

"Edward!" James shouted.

His brother kept running. Hardin was with him! Where were they going? They had to be headed for the south wall! Or maybe the chapel was under fire. Damn smoke from the fires stung James's eyes.

Feather hat waved his arm. "David!"

James saw Crockett through the grey haze. It appeared he was coming from the direction of the granary. He had seven or eight men with him, firing at Mexicans as they moved across the courtyard.

"Micajah," Crockett said to feather hat and nodded toward the west wall battery. "I think that cannon there'll make a fine spot for us to give them some hell."

James realized there was no more shooting at the Grey fellow's battery. He saw the Mexicans running back to the south wall. They must've killed every man.

He followed Crockett and Micajah and the others. The fellow in front of him was bowlegged and carried a shotgun.

Chunks of adobe rained down on James, and he ducked his head. He couldn't tell where the shots had come from. The bow-legged fellow suddenly dropped to the ground, howling in pain. His leg below the knee hung twisted and bloody.

Some of Crockett's men returned fire.

"Pick Daniel up," Crockett said, and two Tennesseans put Daniel's arms over their shoulders and ran with him. Daniel was cursing a streak.

A Mexican came running, hollering in Spanish, bayonet ready.

Turning fast, James quickly brought the pistol up and fired, feeling the kick in his hand.

The Mexican fell forward, rolling over and over, Shako hat askew, shrieking, both his hands holding the bloody crotch of his white pants.

"Come on!" Micajah shouted.

At the west wall battery, a gunner lay sprawled over wooden pillars on one side of the ramp. James saw the little New Orleans Grey fellow on his belly, his head and arm hanging limply over the edge of the platform.

The two Tennesseans rushed up the earthen ramp. They set Daniel down against one of the cannon wheels. James was right behind them. The rest of the gun crew lay dead — shot, bayoneted. Grabbing the rifle and powder and shot pouch of one of the dead men, James quickly reloaded.

"Look there, David!" one of the Tennesseans said in a raspy voice.

James saw it, too. The Mexicans had hauled the cannon from the northeast corner emplacement and two of Captain Jameson's cannons from the north wall down into the courtyard. They were lining them up. An officer was shouting orders.

"They're preparing to fire on the hospital!" Micajah exclaimed.

"Sons of bitches!" Crockett said. "Let's swing this gun around. Give them a taste of Tennessee!"

Gunfire sounded!

Micajah fell next to James. Daniel's body slid away from the wagon wheel, shot through the chest. James heard a moan. Crockett lay on his back, blood running out of three holes in his chest. He raised his arm up, like he was reaching for something, like he saw something above him. A ragged breath, and Crockett's arm dropped heavily at his side.

"Damn you!" another Tennessean shouted.

James and the others fired at the Mexicans

running toward them.

Four Mexicans fell. The other five kept coming. Yelling and hollering, James and the remaining Tennesseans ran down the ramp and waded into them. Using his bayonet, James stabbed one of the Mexicans, and then a sharp searing pain cut him across the side of his ribs. A bayonet had sliced him! James saw the Mexican's sweaty face beneath his Shako hat as he yanked the bayonet free. It tore through meat, and James felt blood running.

Dropping the musket, he took hold of the Mexican's blue jacket with one hand and, with the other, pulled out his tomahawk, swung it hard, and drove it into the Mexican's face.

"Come along," the raspy voiced Tennessean said, pulling James to his feet.

James snatched up the musket. Mexicans lay bleeding. One of the Tennesseans was holding his head. He spit blood as he leaned over and picked up his rifle. The stock was broken, split in three places. Staring at his busted rifle, the Tennessean chuckled, then keeled over, blood running out of his ear. A runty fellow with stringy hair and sharp features rushed to his side and checked to see if he was breathing. He turned to the others and shook his head.

"I'm real sorry," the runty fellow said, closing the dead man's eyes with his hand.

"Let's move, double quick," raspy voice said.

Raspy voice helped a fellow with black side-whiskers up the ramp to the gun. He limped badly. A Mexican had stabbed him through his foot. His moccasin was all bloody and squished when he walked on it. Going up with them, James noticed the runty Tennessean carried a big hunting knife tucked in his belt. The blade was red with blood. Some of that red had rubbed off on the man's buckskin shirt and pants. James also heard black side-whiskers saying he could still fight, damn it!

Cannons roared! James turned. The Mexicans fired on the granary and the hospital. Doors turned to splinters. Mexican soldiers charged in. James heard shouts and cries and gunfire. James knew those poor men inside had no chance. No chance.

A couple of windows on the first floor of the hospital burst open. Were those pieces of white cloth waving? A few men crawled out, tossing down their rifles, throwing their hands up, some even kneeling and shouting, "Surrender! I surrender!" But then fiery bursts erupted from the upper windows, firing on the Mexicans below.

"¡Matar a los bastardos!" "¡Muerte a los banditos!"

More Mexicans raced up the stone stairs to the second floor of the hospital, while other soldiers charged the men with their hands up, stabbing them over and over with their bayonets. No mercy. No quarter. The screaming and wailing and yelling James heard sounded like something out of a nightmare. Blood for blood.

"Load this cannon. We'll show these Mexican butchers," raspy voice said.

James picked up a bag of grapeshot. All he knew right now was that if it was his time to die, he vowed to die on his feet. "Bend your knee to no man," Pa had said.

CHAPTER FORTY-THREE

"What in the name of all that's holy do you think you're doing?"

Susannah's head snapped up. That was Major Evans shouting.

"It's clear country on the other side of that wall!" another voice cried.

"The Mexicans are out there!" Evans shouted.

More voices. "I don't see any!" "Me neither. We'll take our chances."

Oh, my Lord, she thought darkly. They're leaving! They musn't. She heard the sound of men running down the earthen ramp.

Aleck drew closer to her. She looked down. He had peed his pants.

"We need every man!" Almeron shouted. "You can't go."

"Not me! I'm getting out of here!"

Susannah glanced at Ana, who shook her head.

"You're damn cowards! Deserters!" Bonham shouted. "The whole miserable lot of you!"

"You stay then. I'm being smart!" a different voice shouted. "Come on, Hardin. Let's get while we still can."

She bowed her head. Tears ran down the side of her nose and dripped onto Angelina's hair.

Damn you Santa Anna, this is all because of you. Men killed and dying, Susannah thought. *Please God, in your infinite mercy, strike that man down and cast him into the terrible and everlasting fires of hell.*

Chapter Forty-Four

"No!" the rebel screamed, raising his arms to block Morales's sword.

Morales ran him through.

Slashing with bayonets, his men killed all the rebels inside the archway of the gate. Morales nearly lost his footing in the blood soaking into the ground.

Ordaz reported, "The rebels at the west-wall cannon are dead."

"Very good," Morales said.

Rebel rifle fire erupted from the loopholes cut in the shutters of the windows of the long stone building and the adobe.

Morales ordered men to swing the still operational eight-pounder cannon they had just taken in the courtyard around and train it on the door of the long building first. Less than twenty rebels would not keep his men pinned down. There were cannonballs stacked, along with bags of grapeshot. "Use the solid shot," Morales told his men. They would blast open the doors.

"Look out!" a rebel cried from inside.

The cannon roared. A solid ball slammed into the side of the doorway at the long building, tearing out a large chunk of the wall and shattering the door into pieces.

"Reload!" Morales shouted. "The other building next!"

The cannon fired again. The door on the adobe was blasted apart. Morales heard rebels inside screaming in agony.

Morales charged the adobe with half the *cazadores.* Ordaz took the others and stormed into the long building.

Inside the adobe, the rebels had overturned tables, firing from behind them. A lead ball whirled past Morales's ear as he came through the doorway. Big kettles stood in cold fireplaces. This was the garrison's kitchen. Morales and his men attacked.

A big rebel held a knife in one hand and a meat clever in the other, slashing wildly with both. Morales and a *cazador* came at him from different sides. The big rebel knocked the *cazador*'s bayonet away with the cleaver. Morales got in close and stabbed the rebel through his belly. The rebel cried out, dropped his knife, grabbed Morales's sleeve, and raised the cleaver to strike. Two *cazadores* ran the big rebel through, one bayonet in the chest, the other in the gut. Morales saw the life go out of the rebel's eyes.

A panicked rebel threw a pot, dropped to his knees, and begged, "*¡Clemencia! ¡Clemencia!* Don't kill me!" Four *cazadores* descended on him, stabbing him over and over. A wooden spoon struck Morales in the face. Within minutes, the rebels all lay bleeding. Morales had lost five *cazadores,* dead, and nine were wounded.

He left the adobe while his men searched for any rebels that might be hiding, or any pretending to be dead. A corporal with a cut across his cheek reported that *cazadores* were doing the same in the long stone building.

"*Bueno,*" Morales said as he saw Ordaz running toward him. He was glad to see the sergeant.

His Brown Bess musket in hand, Ordaz said, "We searched for rebels inside the house there." He pointed at the small place beside the main gate. "We found only one rebel inside. A big man. He was in his bed. He killed two *cazadores.* One with his flintlock pistol and one with this."

He pulled a knife from his belt and handed it to Morales. It was large and heavy and glinted in the firelight. The blade was wide like a cleaver. Like nothing Morales had ever seen before. A beautiful thing. And savage. He had heard of a man named James Bowie and the formidable knife he carried. This Bowie was also known to be inside the Alamo. Morales decided it must be his knife.

"This big man," Ordaz said with a smirk. "He is not so big any more."

Ordaz's bayonet, Morales noticed, was red with blood.

Morales considered the knife in his hand. "Spoils of war, *Sergento?*"

"A soldier's right, *Coronel.*"

Indeed it was. Morales handed the knife back to Ordaz.

"Prepare to assault the chapel," Morales said.

"Cannons, *Coronel?*"

Morales nodded. "Bring the eighteen-pounder down here. Use it and the eight-pounder." He pointed at the smaller cannon they had captured earlier. "Do you know about the Franciscan monks, *Sergento?*"

He said he did not.

"They built the mission churches all over Mexico. Those Franciscan monks, they liked heavy doors."

Gray smoke cloaked the fort. The façade of the chapel was hard to make out through the haze, but Morales was certain he saw figures of men clustered at those big doors. There were also flashes of rifle fire all along the north end of the courtyard, up along the west wall where the big fire still burned, and in the fight for the old convent. The smoke did nothing to muffle the screams and cries and swearing. It was clear to him the rebels weren't giving up.

CHAPTER FORTY-FIVE

"Hurry now!" raspy voice said, the torch in his hand.

The runty fellow was shoving the load of grapeshot down the cannon barrel with the ramrod.

Standing beside the cannon, James cocked his musket. He'd loaded it, knowing there'd only be time for one shot, and then he'd use the bayonet or bust the musket barrel over a Mexican's head. And he still had his tomahawk. Damn, his side where that bayonet had sliced his ribs was burning with shrill pain. He'd taken a bandana off the Grey fellow and tucked it inside his shirt over the wound. It was already soaked with blood.

The runty Tennessean pulled the ramrod out of the cannon barrel and picked up his rifle.

James wiped a sweaty hand on his pant leg. All the smoke made it difficult to see, but it sounded to him like the fight at the hospital was drawing down. Those other two building fires were about burned out, too.

The Mexicans would be coming soon enough. James held tight to the musket, feeling awful scared. He glanced at the others. Suddenly, there was something he wanted, no, *needed* to know.

"My name's James. James Taylor," he said.

Raspy voice blinked and glanced at him. "Francis Reddin," he said. "Proud to know you."

"Caleb Hughes." He had the black sidewhiskers and leaned against the cannon wheel on the other side.

The runt put out his hand. "I'm Augustus Kinloch," he said and shook James's hand. "They call me Little Gus."

Caleb slumped over on the other side of the cannon. Grabbing hold to the wheel, he straightened up. "I'm all right," he said, taking a firmer grip on his rifle.

Light to the east drew James's eye. Some of the smoke had parted. The light was reddish-yellow, just beyond the chapel. Dawn was breaking.

"¡El cañón! ¡El cañón!"

James could make out Mexicans charging across the courtyard. How many? Ten? Fifteen? Hell, it didn't matter anymore, he thought grimly. Bringing his musket up to his shoulder, he took a bead on the Mexican at the front of the attackers. He wished it was that damn Santa Anna.

Reddin raised his torch.

The Mexicans fired.

Two Mexican lead balls struck Reddin, and he stumbled, falling back on the platform, the burning torch landing beside a keg of gunpowder.

"Damn you bastards!" Little Gus shouted, grabbing the torch.

"*¡Muerte a los americanos!*"

"Go to hell!" Augustus put the torch to the touchhole. The cannon jumped. A blast of red fire shot out the end of the barrel. Pieces of hot iron ripped through the Mexicans.

James saw more than a dozen men blown backwards and torn up. Part of a leg spun wildly away. The Mexicans still alive howled horribly, clutching for missing limbs or at their bloodied faces. God! Awful!

But James was still alive. He and Caleb fired, each dropping a soldier. The other Mexicans rushed forward, their bayonets gleaming deadly in the breaking light.

"*¡Muerte a los banditos!*" "*¡Matar a los americanos!*"

James saw Death coming. "You Mexican

318

sons of bitches want my life, you'll pay a dear cost for it!" he shouted.

"Wade into them, boys!" Little Gus shouted.

Summoning a vicious yell, James charged down the gun ramp. Little Gus, holding his torch in one hand and his hunting knife in the other, and Caleb, even with his bloody foot, were right there alongside him, hollering their own hellish war cries.

James ran straight at the Mexican at the front. Knocking the Mexican's bayonet aside with his bayonet, James slammed into the soldier. Tumbling over the edge of the ramp, they hit the ground hard. Dazed, James managed to pull out his tomahawk and sink it into the Mexican's chest.

Rolling off the soldier, James heard Caleb cry out. Above him on the ramp, he saw Caleb drop his rifle, his face a mask of pain. A husky Mexican had stuck his bayonet in Caleb's back. The husky Mexican yanked the bayonet out, and the whiskered Tennessean fell face first into the dirt. Little Gus jumped on the Mexican and rammed his hunting knife deep into his gut. Still stunned, James tried scrambling out of the way, but the husky Mexican let out a bellow and landed hard on top of him. God, he was heavy! Blood spilled from the Mexican's belly wound in a sickening warmth. Trying to squeeze out from under the body, James cursed. Soldiers ran by. His head snapped to one side. Like a mule had kicked him.

Dazed . . . on his back . . . the big Mexican, sprawled dead on top of him . . . James touched his face . . . sticky blood on his fingers . . . trying to focus . . . saw Little Gus on the ground, Mexicans stabbing him with their bayonets. Gus was already dead, but they kept stabbing, over and over, his eyes open . . . dead eyes . . . Little Gus's face blurred.

Blackness swept over James.

Chapter Forty-Six

"*¡Fuego!*" Ordaz shouted.

The eighteen-pounder cannon and the eight-pounder spit solid shot at the thick wooden doors.

Morales nodded. "Again."

Inside the courtyard, the fight for the old convent appeared finished. Exhausted *soldados* leaned against the walls or dropped to the ground, others on their knees. It was as if a fever had broken. Their officers and sergeants prodded them up, but the battle — the bloodlust — had taken its toll on the men. Soldiers knew it well.

There was still random firing as *soldados* cleared out rooms and huts along the west and east walls, looking for rebels who might be hiding.

Ordaz pointed at the roof of the hospital. The rebel flag was gone. The Mexican colors flew from the wooden pole. Morales watched as a breeze ruffled the red, white, and green stripes. And the eagle in the center of the flag devoured the snake.

Morales dropped his gaze. There was no pride in this day.

"*¡Fuego!*"

The heavy iron cannonballs slammed into the big doors, then thudded to the ground.

"Shore it up!" Morales heard rebels shouting inside the chapel. "More sandbags! Anything! Keep the bastards out!"

Behind Morales the *cazadores* waited. They were exhausted, but they were prepared to assault the chapel once the doors were breached.

Morales did not know how many rebels were left inside, how many had retreated to find protection there. He simply wanted this battle to end. He'd lost enough men, though he knew more would die before the chapel would be taken.

Turning to Ordaz, he said, "You reminded the men about any women who may be in the chapel?"

"*Sí, Coronel.*"

"*Bueno,*" Morales said sharply. "We do not molest women. We are not animals."

"*¡Fuego!*"

Battered with large round indentations, one of the great doors groaned, wood splintering.

"¡Fuego!"

"Hold, men! Hold!" a rebel shouted.

"¡Fuego!"

"The brace! It's giving way!"

Morales signaled Ordaz.

"¡Prepararse!" the sergeant shouted.

The *cazadores* brought their rifles up, bayonets forward.

"¡Fuego!"

Blasted off its hinges, one door collapsed backward, tearing the other door down with it!

Morales raised his sword. *"¡Assalto!"*

Chapter Forty-Seven

"Thy kingdom come, thy will be done. Thy kingdom come, thy will be done. Thy kingdom come, thy will be done." Susannah whispered her prayer over and over inside the sacristy. She held Angelina with one hand and covered an ear with the other, trying to keep out the sound of the cannons and the pounding and the yelling and —

"Look out!" Evans shouted.

She heard a loud and terrible crash. Wood groaned and snapped. Men cursed God himself!

"They're coming!" she heard Almeron shout from up on the top of the ramp. "Prepare to fire!"

Ana's candle still burned on the table, and there was some light crossing the sky.

Ana held her children. Her boys, Enrique, Francisco, and Manuel, whispered prayers with her in Spanish. Little Maria cried.

In the corner, Nathan pulled his blanket

up over him and his little brother.

Shouting outside. *"¡Muerte a los rebeldes!"*

Guns fired! Men screamed!

"Give it to them!" Almeron shouted.

More shooting!

The bitter smell of gunpowder filled the air in the sacristy. Like the smell of death.

Figures, shadows rushed by the doorway.

"Thy kingdom come, thy will be done. Thy kingdom come, thy will be done. Thy kingdom —"

"Major," she heard someone cry out and then a sickening groan.

"Fire!" Bonham shouted.

Many guns fired! Agonized cries followed! Susannah wanted to shout for Almeron. Was he killed? Was he wounded? Bonham? Ana's husband? The rest of the men? More gunfire echoed through the nave.

Please God! Please! Spare my little girl, Susannah prayed.

A man ran through the doorway. Tylee! He held his rifle and looked scared as anything she'd seen. His eyes darted about the room. Then he turned, facing the doorway.

Mexican soldiers rushed in. Susannah saw their bayonets red with blood.

Swinging his rifle at them, Tylee charged, knocking one in the head. The other Mexican soldiers ran their bayonets into him, driving him back against the wall, knocking over the table. The candle went out, casting the room into shadows.

Susannah hid her face. Her stomach turned as she heard Tylee's pitiful dying moans.

Ana cried out, *"¡No más! ¡No más!"*

Susannah looked up as a soldier snatched the blanket off Nathan and Aleck with his bayonet.

"No!" Susannah screamed.

Three soldiers drove their bayonets into the boys.

"Stop it! They're children!" Susannah cried out. "Oh, God!"

A soldier seized Susannah by shoulder and shouted, but his words made no sense to her.

Ana pulled at the soldier's arm, screaming at him to stop.

The soldier spun around, his hand raised to slap Ana's face.

From the doorway a voice bellowed.

Susannah turned and saw an angry Mexican. A big knife, like Jim Bowie's, was stuck in his belt.

One of the soldiers began to speak, but the angry Mexican cut him off with a word and a sharp jerk of his head.

"Sí, sergento," the soldier said, and he and the other soldiers hurried out.

The sergeant spoke to Ana in Spanish as Susannah crawled over to Nathan and Aleck. Both boys were dead. She wept, covering them with their blankets, and looked back at the sergeant. She wanted to tell him that he and all the rest of his men should burn in hell. But she could not stop the tears flowing down her cheeks to the corners of her mouth. She tasted salty tears.

The sergeant turned and left.

"What did he say?" Susannah asked, wiping the tears from her face.

"He says we are to stay here."

Frightened, Susannah covered her mouth with her hand, then pulled it away. "Do you . . . will they execute us?"

"I don't know. Santa Anna is not one to have his honor insulted."

Susannah let out a shallow breath and kissed Angelina. A ball of fret grew in her belly. Tylee lay dead across the room. Little Nathan and Aleck next to her. Stupid, senseless brutes killed them. They were only boys. Oh, God, there were so many boys here. And Almeron? What of him? God, help us, please. Looking up, she saw the gold dawn giving way to a blue sky.

"I am glad you sewed Travis's ring into

your dress," Ana said.

Susannah looked at her strangely. Why bring that up now?

"That one *soldado* told the *sergento* they were looking for any valuables. I told them we had none."

Before Susannah could speak, a gunshot startled her. It came from out in the nave. A moment later, two more shots followed.

"They are searching for any of our men still alive," Ana said.

"Animals," Susannah whispered, holding Angelina close. And she could not stop herself. "Goddamn animals."

A Mexican officer appeared in the doorway. He wore no hat, but his uniform collar and the epaulets on his shoulders had much silver filigree. Part of his face was scarred with old wounds.

"*Señora* Dickinson?"

How did the man know her name, she wondered. Summoning all the strength she could muster, she said, "I am Mrs. Dickinson."

The officer spoke quickly in Spanish.

Ana said, "*Coronel* Morales says if you wish to save your life, you must follow him."

"What about my friend?" Susannah said to the officer, nodding at Ana.

"We are coming, too," Ana said, tears well-ing in her eyes as she helped her boys and little girl up. "He has orders to take us to a house in town," Ana said. "You and Angelina. You will be safe there."

"*Es cierto,*" Ana's son, Enrique, said, and smiled at Susannah.

Ana said, "The *Coronel* says that Santa Anna does not make war on women and children."

Susannah ignored Colonel Morales's arm when he offered it to her as he led them out into the nave. In spite of the killing of the two Wolf boys and Tylee, what she saw inside the chapel made her shudder. Blood splattered the walls. The floor was smeared red with it. She stepped carefully. It was like walking through a slaughterhouse. And that raw iron smell of blood pervaded the very air, making it bitter and foul.

Bodies lay dead, many tangled together. She saw Rutherford, one of Almeron's men who'd sat at her table having tea the night before. He sat on the floor, his back against the ramp, like a rag doll thrown there. Shot in the face and bayoneted. Four Mexicans lay dead around him. She guessed he'd killed them before he was killed. She looked for Almeron. Some men were on their bellies. She couldn't see their faces, but one was missing a hand, like it had been shot off. Her shoes sloshed in the blood. Anthony Wolf still gripped the knife he'd plunged into the Mexican beside him. Blood glistened on the Mexican's face. James Bonham lay at the foot of the ramp. He'd been stabbed so many times in the chest it was a gaping, bloody hole. Susannah covered her mouth and held Angelina closer, as though to shield her innocent eyes from the gore. Stepping over Bonham, her foot slipped in the blood pooled around him. She let out a cry and felt herself steadied as the colonel caught her by the arm. Though grateful, she said nothing in thanks.

Glancing behind her, she saw Ana being helped along by Enrique. His brothers, Manuel and Francisco, and sister, Maria, clutched Ana's skirts in their hands.

The colonel pulled Susannah to one side. Turning, she realized she would have stepped on the body of Major Evans. He held a blackened torch in his hand. She did not see Almeron anywhere. Or Ana's husband.

Approaching what was left of the chapel entrance, Susannah gasped at seeing young Galba, pinned underneath one of the big doors. His jaw hung broken. Around his neck, the cravat Lucy Summers had given him was soaked red with blood.

Outside, the colonel escorted her toward the main gate. Bodies were strewn everywhere. And so much more blood. Crockett's body lay by the wall near the hospital, his white shirt so red now. Soldiers carrying bodies between them dropped them by him. Good Lord, was that Travis? She could barely breathe. This was no nightmare. It was horror, stark and real and frightening and sickening.

Soldiers prodded bodies with their feet, or with the point of their bayonets. Some collected rifles and stacked them in piles. Susannah saw others carrying their wounded out the main gate.

"There he is," Ana called to her. "Santa Anna himself."

Susannah saw a tall man at the main gate. He wore a bicorn hat with a big white plume, and he had a sword at his side. He appeared to be dressed all in black, until he turned. She'd never seen so much silver filigree. It covered the front of his jacket, his shoulders, and down his sleeves. Joe, Travis's Negro slave, stood near him. Three other men approached them. They wore fancy hats and a lot of filigree, too. Joe said something and nodded as a couple of soldiers dragged out a body from Colonel Bowie's quarters.

No, please, God, she thought.

The head on the body lolled to one side. Oh, Lord, it was Bowie.

Santa Anna glanced at the others with him, said something, and laughed; then they moved toward the west wall, Santa Anna motioning at Joe to follow.

Weren't there any survivors? Susannah wondered. Were they all dead? All butchered? Her stomach churned, and she swallowed her horror.

Susannah felt the colonel pull her along toward the gate past the long stone building. Soldiers came out of it, carrying more bodies and guns.

A musket cracked! Susannah stumbled. The pain in her right leg was fierce, like something had taken a bite out of it. Someone had shot her! The ball had passed through her dress and deeply grazed the back of her calf. She clutched Angelina close as the colonel helped her stay on her feet.

There was all manner of hollering.

"*¿Quien fue?*" the colonel shouted.

Outside the hospital, a soldier with a heavy moustache reluctantly raised his musket.

The colonel shouted, and immediately the sergeant with the big knife appeared. The colonel snapped words at him and then led her toward the gate.

Blood ran down her leg. Lord, it hurt! She could hear the sergeant shouting at the soldier as the colonel turned and spoke to Ana.

"He says you will be taken to town immediately, and a doctor will be summoned to treat your wound," Ana said.

"How did he know my name?"

Ana asked the colonel, then she told Susannah that a woman in town had gone to Santa Anna last night. "She pleaded with him to spare the lives of you and me and all the other women in the fort. The *Coronel* says he received the message only a short time ago. This woman mentioned you by name, he says."

Francisca Músquiz. It had to be, Susannah thought. Almeron and some others from Gonzales had stayed in her home after they took San Antonio from the Mexicans. When Susannah had arrived, Mrs. Músquiz insisted she stay there, too, saying that little Angelina needed a proper roof over her head. God bless that woman.

The colonel helped Susannah climb into a black buggy waiting outside the gates. Ana and her children quickly followed, and the colonel ordered the driver to hurry.

They headed for the bridge. The soldiers Susannah had seen carrying their wounded out the main gate were taking them to the river. All along the riverbank lay bleeding Mexican soldiers. Women from town moved among them, bandaging their wounds. But they could not stop the soldiers' terrible cries.

CHAPTER FORTY-EIGHT

James only saw blackness. His head throbbed, like someone was using it for an anvil. There were sounds, far off at first. After a few moments, he heard voices, Mexican voices, but didn't understand what they were saying.

James felt hands on him and was rolled onto his belly. His face in the dirt, he coughed and tasted grit in his mouth. Rough rope tied his wrists fast. Then his elbows were pulled in close and tied. He was too weak to resist. Coughing again, he opened his eyes. Dusty, scuffed, black brogans were inches from his face.

Hands took hold under his arms and hauled him to his feet. The sun was up. He squeezed his eyes shut at the brightness. His arms hurt, pinioned behind his back.

Opening his eyes, he saw a blurry figure in front of him. All in black. There was a big, frilly plume in his hat and shiny silver hanging off his shoulders.

The hands gripping him under his arms pushed him forward.

The blurriness faded. James saw Mexicans looking at him. Hundreds and hundreds of them filled the courtyard. Hate and blood in their eyes. Words flew at him. Curses.

Bodies lay everywhere. Naked. His fellow Texians! The Mexican bastards had stripped them bare. Blood caked dry around their wounds. God, it was pitiful. Three Mexicans were laughing, tossing something in the air, catching it on their bayonets. Johnnie McGregor's bagpipes, or what was left of them. The bag was shredded, the wooden pipes smashed. Jesus!

James glanced at the two guards on either side of him. One wore a coonskin cap, like the one Crockett had worn. The other looked at him and grinned menacingly. He had a broken front tooth.

The guard in the coonskin cap whispered something, and James turned his head toward him.

The guard pointed at the cap. James saw the medal Moses had given him pinned to the front of it. The damn thief! Straining at his bonds, he wanted to grab it back, but it was useless. *I'm sorry, Moses,* he thought.

James and his guards followed the Mexican officer to the chapel. One door lay battered on the ground, blasted off its hinges. The other crookedly sagged backwards. More naked bodies lay about. And more Mexican soldiers were gathered there.

Squinting up at the morning sun, James guessed it must be around eight, maybe nine o'clock. Then he saw the flag — that damn, stinking Mexican flag — flying from the flagpole on top of the hospital. He spit out a bloody wad.

His Mexican guards pushed him to the front of the chapel. Four dead Texians lay there, chests bloody from stabbings. Their arms tied behind their backs, like his. Executed. He recognized one man. He'd been on the north wall, but James didn't know his name. How had these poor wretches been taken prisoner? No matter. No man deserved to die like that. Not fighting men, anyway.

They spun him around roughly, so he was facing the courtyard. Something hard whacked the back of his leg, forcing him to his knees. He struggled to get up on his feet, but his guards held him down. A tall Mexican wore the fanciest uniform James had ever seen, with silver all over his chest, and a big hat. He didn't look too happy. Sounded to James like he was giving the general seven kinds of hell. He heard the general say something that sounded like "excellency." That had to be Santa Anna, the big son-of-a-whore himself.

There were other officers standing there, those frilly hats on their heads. Stone-faced. All of them.

Torn up blue rags lay at Santa Anna's feet. Something familiar about them. James could swear it was Travis's independence flag. That damn Santa Anna had ripped it to shreds!

The general nodded smartly at Santa Anna and stepped aside. The look on the general's face told James he'd been scolded, like some misbehaving child.

Santa Anna motioned with his hand, and James saw this other officer, who had a thin face and big eyes that bulged out like a bug's, come walking toward him. The two guards removed their hands from his shoulders and moved away.

James spit out a wad of blood and grit, barely missing bug-eye's black boots.

Bug-eye slapped him with his white-gloved hand.

The blood rushed to James's stung face; anger raced through his body.

"Your other rebel friends knew how to die with honor," bug-eye said in fair enough

English.

Looking from one end of the Mexicans there in front of him to the other, James said, "Nothing I see deserves honor. Just a bunch of damn Mex—"

Bug-eye slapped him again.

"Bastard!" James cursed, his face hot.

Turning to Santa Anna, bug-eye spoke to him in Spanish. Santa Anna narrowed his eyes and said something in an even tone.

With a smug smile, bug-eye raised his head and said, "His Excellency says that it will be his pleasure to watch you beg for your worthless life."

"Beg for my life before he kills me, you mean." James snorted. "You tell that miserable son of a whore when he dies, he'll be shaking like a shitting dog. And when this ruckus is over and Texas is free, his life won't be worth a gob of spit."

The smug smile gone, bug-eye stared at him.

"You afraid to tell him?" James said.

Bug-eye brought his gloved hand up and slapped James hard, then backhanded him, harder.

James jerked his head up, face twisted, teeth bared. "You're going to die, you bastard!"

Bug-eye stepped aside. Santa Anna signaled a group of six soldiers. They raised their rifles, the sun catching the steel of the bayonets, and charged.

Screaming his war cry, James struggled to his feet, got one knee up when the bayonets plunged into his chest and belly. His eyes squeezed shut. Horrid pain raced through him, like cold fire. He felt every blade, felt the blood gushing. Falling backward onto the ground, his eyes opened. He saw the ugly faces, the stabbing. But the awful pain was nearly gone. They were shouting at him, yet he heard nothing. His eyes closed again and opened. The sky had never looked so blue.

CHAPTER FORTY-NINE

It was past midday as Morales made his way out the main gate and turned toward the Alameda. His Excellency had given him the order earlier. It was time to see it carried out. The thought of it turned his stomach.

Outside the wooden palisade, *soldados* loaded the last of the naked bodies into wagons. These were the rebels who had tried to run from the battle, climbing over the wall to find safety. They didn't get far. General Ramírez y Sesma's cavalry had done their duty, just as His Excellency had ordered, and used their lances to cut down these miserable wretches.

Morales passed through the blood-soaked ground. Pieces of clothing lay scattered about. Other *soldados* collected the rifles and shotguns the rebels had carried and threw them into an oxcart.

A broken rifle stock rested in a dried pool of blood. Morales saw something was carved in the wood. "My Lizzie." It was excellent workmanship. Not that it mattered now.

Trees along the Alameda had been cut down, Morales noted, as Ordaz had seen to the construction of the two immense wooden pyres to burn the bodies.

Carts and buckboards had brought out nearly two hundred rebel bodies from the garrison already. Ordaz had seen to the stacking of the bodies on each pyre. Human pyramids, Morales thought. Disgraceful.

Two more wagons rolled up, and Ordaz ordered the *soldados* to unload them and be quick about it.

"How many more, *Sergento?*" Morales asked.

"These wagons should be the last, *Coronel.* The stink is already —"

Morales cut him off. "Finish it."

"*Sí, Coronel,*" Ordaz said, then shouted to his men, "*¡Rapido! ¡Rapido!*"

After the last bodies were stacked, Ordaz had the pyres doused with coal oil. He signaled the *soldados* holding unlit torches. They lowered them into the campfires. The torches blazed.

Morales gave the order.

The torchbearers set about their work igniting the pyres. Flames rose swiftly. Black smoke billowed into the blue, windless sky.

The pyres would burn through the night. Morales would never forget the stench.

CHAPTER FIFTY

Late that afternoon, Susannah woke from a fitful sleep in her room at Mrs. Músquiz's house. Her eyes were red from crying. The pain in her belly had not diminished. Almeron was dead, and she would never see him again. What would she and Angelina do now?

The frail Mrs. Músquiz knocked on the door and asked Susannah if she would like some tea. "I already have it made," Mrs. Músquiz said. "I'll join you, if you'd like."

A few minutes later, sitting up in her bed with her cup in hand, Susannah took a sip, its warmth comforting. Mrs. Músquiz sat on a chair near the open window. Angelina napped peacefully in the cradle Mrs. Músquiz had placed beside the bed.

Susannah took another sip of tea.

"I have received word," Mrs. Músquiz said. "Santa Anna will send for you tomorrow morning."

"What does he want with me?"

"I do not know."

Susannah closed her eyes. She did not want to see that butcher. Mrs. Músquiz was saying something about Ana and the other women being summoned, too, but Susannah paid it no mind. The thought of facing Santa Anna was too bitter, too foul to consider.

Opening her eyes, she turned her face toward the window and asked her friend about the thick black pillars of smoke to the east.

Mrs. Músquiz set down her cup of tea and said reluctantly, "They are burning the bodies."

Susannah snapped her head toward her. "My husband? Our friends?"

"It is Santa Anna's orders."

Susannah closed her red eyes. Not even allowed to bury her beloved. She had no more tears left to shed.

"*Señora* Dickinson?" asked the Mexican officer, standing outside the doorway of Mrs. Músquiz's house. He had very dark eyes and held his big hat under his arm.

"Yes," Susannah said.

"I am *Coronel* Juan Almonte. His Excellency, *General* Antonio López de Santa

Anna, requests your presence at his head-quarters. I am to escort you."

It was half past ten. Susannah, with Angelina in her arms, limped as she crossed the Main Plaza to the headquarters of Santa Anna. In spite of the discomfort she felt from her leg wound, she refused the offer of a cane, believing it would somehow show weakness. That would not do. Not this day.

She wore the same dress she'd worn through the siege. Mrs. Músquiz had washed it and stitched up the musket ball hole, but not before Susannah had opened the hem and retrieved her brooch and Travis's ring. This morning, she pinned the brooch on her collar and draped the ring and twine around Angelina's neck, then wrapped her in a blanket. Susannah also thought about what she had told her husband, that if she saw Santa Anna, she'd walk right up and kill him.

Almonte spoke excellent English, though she had nothing to say to him. She covered her nose at the stench of burning flesh. Two gray pillars of smoke could be seen to the east. And that ugly red flag no longer flew from the top of the church.

Almonte informed her that since she spoke no Spanish and His Excellency did not speak English, he would act as translator.

She followed Almonte into the house to a big room. The butcher sat in a large chair near the fireplace. He wore that fancy uniform. There was a small, black, cloth bag on the table beside him. And a flintlock pistol with gold inlaid on the butt and stock. Likely loaded, she expected.

Walk right up and kill him, she thought. Snatch that pistol and shoot him through the heart. But Angelina moved in her arms, and Susannah knew she could not kill him. Almeron's last words came to her. Save their child.

Almonte spoke, and Susannah heard him say her name.

The butcher said something. He smiled as he spoke. Susannah's skin crawled. But a curious feeling came over her. As though Almeron were there at her side, reminding her that she had more gumption than anyone he'd ever known.

Almonte said, "His Excellency says he is pleased to make your acquaintance. He says the circumstances are most unfortunate."

She said nothing but kept her eyes on the butcher, choosing not to allow him to try to beguile or cow her.

A look passed between the butcher and

Almonte, and the butcher said something else.

Almonte nodded and turned to Susannah. "His Excellency says you have a beautiful child. He would like to know her name."

"Angelina," Susannah said.

"His Excellency says it is a perfect name for such an angel," Almonte translated.

She wanted to tell Almonte to tell him to not even look at her daughter but instead said, "Thank you."

The butcher smiled and spoke.

"This is most generous, *Señora* Dickinson," Almonte said.

"What is?"

"His Excellency says it would be his honor to invite you and your daughter to be his guests at his estate in Jalapa."

"Guests?"

"*Sí.* He says he will provide you with transportation and that you may stay for as long as you wish."

"No."

The butcher spoke, moving his hands around this time.

Again Almonte translated. "His Excellency says perhaps you would reconsider. He says he is willing to adopt the child, to raise her and see to her education. His Excellency also wishes to remind you that

348

you have no husband, no money, and no provision to care for your daughter. He offers her every advantage that money could procure."

The words tumbled out of Susannah's mouth. "I would rather see my daughter starve than hand her over to him. He killed my husband. He burned my husband's body. My friends are dead. I've been shot. And now he wants to take my daughter from me? You tell him he can go to hell for all I care. My daughter and I will stay in Texas."

The butcher was frowning.

Almonte smiled, turned to the butcher, and spoke his Spanish quickly.

She saw the frown on the butcher's face disappear, replaced with a kind smile that left her confused. He continued to speak, but his tone became stern.

"His Excellency says you may go whenever you wish, with his blessing," Almonte translated.

Now Susannah was even more confounded.

"He assures you safe passage with your daughter and will provide you with blankets, food, and a good *burro.* Also, a fine horse for you to ride. Better for you because of your wound. In return, he asks only that you try to find Sam Houston and deliver a message to him."

"What message?"

Almonte took a small piece of parchment from a table. Folding it in half, he handed it to her.

"He asks you to tell Sam Houston what happened here. Leave nothing out. This letter tells Sam Houston that Texas belongs to Mexico and that all pirates will meet the same fate. The good, His Excellency says, have nothing to fear."

Susannah saw the butcher reach into the cloth bag. She heard the sound of coins clinking. He pulled out his hand, and Almonte took what was in it.

"Please," he said to her, and she held out her hand. He placed two coins in it. "His Excellency wishes you to have this money for your journey." He went on to tell her that Joe, the free Negro formerly owned by the pirate Travis, would be her escort to find Houston. "You may leave as soon as you wish."

The butcher rose from his chair and nodded to her courteously.

She said nothing, trying to sort this whole business. Almonte ushered her out. Once outside, she asked, "What did you tell him I said in there?"

Almonte smiled. "Exactly as you said. '*Se-ñora* Dickinson thanks Your Excellency for his very kind and generous offer but asks, with your permission, to remain in Texas with her daughter at this time.' "

She hated to admit it, but he was a sly one.

An hour later, she had said her good-byes to Ana and her family, grateful that the butcher had told them they would not be harmed and could remain in San Antonio, their home.

Joe rode the mule, while Susannah, holding Angelina, sat astride her horse and set out on the Gonzales Road heading east to find Houston and his army.

At the charred, smoldering pyres, Susannah stopped, placed her hand on the brooch at her neck and said good-bye to Almeron. Then, her lip trembling, she said a prayer for all of them. Good men. Husbands, fathers, brothers, sons.

She bent her head down and kissed Angelina.

"Let's get moving, Joe," she said and clicked at her horse.

She would find Houston and deliver the butcher's letter. He had much blood on his hands, and he'd have to answer for it. She'd tell them all what had happened at the Alamo so they could set things aright. There'd be more pain. More blood. More loss.

Looking back, she saw the walls of the Alamo, battered and red with blood.

Her chest heaved as she recalled Almeron's words: "There are things worth living for, and worth dying for."

EPILOGUE

Susannah Dickinson

Susannah reached General Sam Houston near Gonzales a few days later. "All killed, all killed," were her first words. Handing Houston the message from Santa Anna, she told him of the burning of the bodies. With tears in his eyes, Houston assured her that her husband and the others had not died in vain. "The Alamo will not be forgotten," he promised her.

Many wives and children of the defenders beseeched her for any details, any last words from their loved ones. When Lucy Summers asked about Galba Fuqua, Susannah told her that Galba's thoughts were of her the night before the battle and that he wore the cravat she'd given him in the fight and had died bravely. Lucy fell into her arms and wept.

Along with the other citizens of Gonzales, Susannah and Angelina fled in the exodus that became known as the Runaway Scrape to East Texas and remained there in what became the city of Houston.

Following the war, Susannah, along with many veterans and widows, applied to the Congress of the Republic of Texas for aid, back pay, and promised tracts of land. The Congress denied her appeal, claiming the new republic had limited means. However, she still owned the league of land she and Almeron had lived on near Gonzales, though she eventually sold it.

Living in Houston, Susannah reportedly found work as a laundress in a brothel.

Several marriages followed. In 1837 she married John Williams. The next year, she divorced him, alleging physical abuse. Later that year, she married Francis Herring, a man who liked his liquor — so much so that one night he took her brooch from her dresser top while she slept, hurried out to a tavern, and traded it to a whiskey drummer on his way to St. Louis for a bottle of rye. The drummer wasn't interested at first but changed his mind when Herring told him that the brooch had belonged to Jim Bowie's wife and that Bowie was holding it in his hand when he died at the Alamo. "My wife was there," Herring said. "She swears it's God's honest truth."

Susannah didn't speak to her husband for two weeks after he told her he'd sold it to the drummer, and, after that, it was only when she decided she had to. Herring died a few months later. The doctor listed the cause as digestive failure, but folks who knew him agreed it was due to excessive drinking.

Susannah opened a boarding house and, in 1847, married Peter Bellows, a ne'er-do-well, according to some reports. A few years later, he accused her of operating a "house of ill fame." Because of this scandal, certain congregants of the First Baptist Church in Houston, which Susannah had joined, voiced their "disapproval" of her membership. She not only withdrew from the church, she left Houston and moved to the town of Lockhart, almost two hundred miles away. When Susannah did not appear at the court proceedings, the judge ruled the allegations true and granted Bellows his divorce.

In Lockhart Susannah opened another boarding house in 1857. It was in Lockhart that Providence finally smiled on her, and she married Joseph Hannig, a prosperous man and loving husband.

Susannah was often asked to relate her experiences in the Alamo, though with the passing of time, her memory began to fade.

She died in 1883 and was buried in Austin. The marble marker on her grave reads, "Mother of the Babe of the Alamo."

Angelina Dickinson

Known as "The Babe of the Alamo," Angelina lived with her mother in Houston until, at age seventeen, she married a farmer named John Maynard Griffith, who was apparently handpicked by her mother. Angelina and her husband lived on his farm in Montgomery County, Texas. Over the next five years, they had three children: Almeron, Susannah, and Joseph.

However, Angelina found farm life dull and her husband duller, and they divorced. After shipping the oldest boy off to an uncle and the youngest children to their grandmother Susannah, Angelina followed the siren call of big-city excitement to New Orleans. Stories circulated that she quickly fell into prostitution there.

Possibly around 1864, she married Oscar Holmes, had another daughter, Sallie, abandoned both in New Orleans, and drifted back to Texas.

Sometime after 1865, she ended up in Galveston where it was reported she "embraced the life of a courtesan."

It may have been there that she met Jim Britton, a former Confederate officer. She gave him Travis's ring. (It is now part of the collection at the Alamo museum in San Antonio.)

While it is uncertain if she married Britton, she died in Galveston of a uterine hemorrhage. She was thirty-seven years old.

General Antonio López de Santa Anna

Emboldened by his victory at the Alamo, Santa Anna made plans to pursue Houston and the rest of his pirates. He vowed to destroy them and any hopes of Texas independence.

Having received word that Houston had only five hundred men at best, Santa Anna decided seven hundred *soldados* and fifty mounted lancers would be sufficient.

In making preparations to pursue Houston, Santa Anna sent *"La mujer"* and her mother in his personal carriage south across the Rio Bravo. "To safety," he told them. It is unclear if he ever saw his new young "bride" again.

Torrential rains slowed Santa Anna in his pursuit, but he finally caught up with Houston and his ragtag army several weeks later on a high grass plain near a bend of the San Jacinto River. General Cós joined

Santa Anna with five hundred reinforcements.

Overconfident, Santa Anna chose not to post sentries around his camp, and Houston attacked during the Mexican army's afternoon *siesta* on April 21.

Routed and in disarray, the Mexican soldiers fled. Texians, shouting, "Remember the Alamo," shot many of them down. The battle was over in eighteen minutes.

Santa Anna had run, shedding his ornate uniform for the blue jacket of a common *soldado.* He was rounded up and brought in, but his ruse was discovered when other prisoners stood and saluted, addressing him as *"El Presidente."*

He signed the Treaties of Velasco, in which he gave up all rights to Texas. In return, Houston promised him safe conduct back to Mexico. Defeated and discredited, Santa Anna retired to his home in Jalapa.

A few years later, the French attempted an invasion at Veracruz. To halt the French advance, the Mexican government appointed Santa Anna commander of the army. He drove the invaders back, in spite of having three horses shot from under him and losing half of his left leg to a cannonball. He had the amputated leg buried with full military honors.

Though he lost the leg, he regained his popularity and became acting president in 1839. He had a prosthetic leg of cork made. Two years later, he took over Mexico as dictator. Ordering his amputated leg dug up, he paraded with it through Mexico City in an elaborate ceremony and then had it placed on a special monument for all to see.

During the Mexican-American War, American soldiers captured his cork leg. (It remains on display at the Illinois State Military Museum in Springfield.) A replacement was quickly made, a peg leg. It, too, was captured. Personal excesses and defeat in the Mexican-American War led to his exile in Cuba.

For years he schemed and connived to return to Mexico but finally abandoned his efforts and wrote his memoirs.

When Mexico declared a general amnesty in 1874, Santa Anna returned to his native country. Crippled and nearly blind, he died there in obscurity on June 21, 1876.

Colonel Juan Morales

Of his 125 *cazadores*, thirty-seven men were killed and fifty-eight wounded during the attack on the Alamo. Many of those wounded were maimed for life. Morales always maintained the battle was a mistake to fight and never forgave Santa Anna for the loss of every man.

After the fall of the Alamo, Santa Anna sent several battalions to Goliad to reinforce General Urrea's men against rebel forces under Colonel James Fannin. Morales commanded one of those units and defeated the Texians at Coleto Creek on March 19. Fannin and three hundred rebels were taken prisoner.

A week later, after Urrea, Morales and other Mexican officers failed to convince Santa Anna to spare the lives of Fannin and his men, Santa Anna had Fannin and his rebels executed. Just as at the Alamo, Morales believed Santa Anna had blundered.

After the loss of Texas, Mexico was ravaged by internal strife. In the ensuing years, Morales helped put down a number of revolts, becoming a favorite of Santa Anna, who promoted him to brigadier general.

Then in 1847, after the United States had declared war on Mexico, Morales was made commander of the Mexican defenses at the port of Veracruz.

On March 9, General Winfield Scott's forces laid siege to the city, surrounding it by land and sea. Scott demanded surrender. Morales refused.

Naval batteries began pounding the city

walls. Reinforcements never came. And then on March 25, under cover of darkness, Morales climbed into a small boat and fled the city. His second in command, General José Juan de Landero, surrendered three days later.

Furious, Santa Anna ordered Morales imprisoned and tried for treason. But for reasons unknown, no trial was held, and Morales was released.

Disgraced, Morales believed the time had come to overthrow His Excellency and began planning a coup.

A few weeks later, in a house he was staying in at the town of Atlixco, south of Mexico City, he was found dead. The doctor who examined the body said the circumstances were quite strange. Morales's lungs were filled with water. He had died, apparently in his bed, from drowning.

Sergeant Fermin Ordaz

Sergeant Ordaz survived the battle of San Jacinto. On his return to Mexico, he was posted to the garrison at Matamoros at the mouth of the Rio Bravo. Drunk in a cantina one night, he wagered the big knife he'd taken from Jim Bowie on a gambling bet and lost it to the owner of a riverfront whorehouse.

Colonel Jose Romero

Colonel Romero fled his command at the battle of San Jacinto. He was apprehended by a Texian patrol four days later and returned to Mexico with the remnants of Santa Anna's army.

There is no record of Colonel Romero after this. It is as though he vanished. However, legend has it that in 1845, a Corporal Vicente Ruiz, said to bear a striking resemblance to Romero, was part of a punitive expedition against a band of Chiricahua Apaches in northern Mexico. The forty soldiers left the Presidio San Augustín del Tucsón in September. They were never heard from again.

Gertrudis Navarro

When the Mexican soldiers began battering through the bricked-up window of their quarters, Gertrudis blew out the candles, and she and her sister, Juana, and the baby hid behind Juana's large wooden trunk that had been brought in the night before.

They could still hear some random firing an hour later. Cautiously, they stepped out into the courtyard.

A couple of soldiers immediately descended on them. They screamed. One pawed at Gertrudis's dress searching for any valuables. The other tore Juana's *rebozo* off her shoulders as she attempted to protect her baby.

A Texian named Mitchell appeared seemingly from nowhere and stabbed the soldier assaulting Gertrudis. Another defender, dried blood streaking his face, tried to shield Juana. Other soldiers ran up and bayoneted both men to death.

Juana cried at them to stop. Gertrudis saw Georgie's body a few feet away and covered her mouth.

The soldiers pushed the women aside and ransacked their room, breaking open the trunk and taking coins, rings, and other valuables they found.

A lieutenant ordered the soldiers out. Turning to Gertrudis, he demanded to know who they were.

She told him their father was Angel Navarro, the *"jefe politico"* of San Antonio. He ordered them to wait and instructed a sergeant to see to their safety.

Shortly, Gertrudis and her sister were escorted out of the Alamo and over to their father's house in town.

Gertrudis had sewn the watch Georgie had given her into the folds of her dress. Once inside her room, she tore open the seam, clutched the watch in her hands, and sobbed.

A few years later, she married a local merchant, José Cantú. They had eight children. She spent all her life in San Antonio.

When she died, she was buried with a rosary wrapped around her hands placed over her chest. And, as she requested, inside her right hand was Georgie's watch.

Juana Alsbury

Juana spent most of her life in San Antonio.

Her husband, H. A. Alsbury, was often away. Being something of an adventurer, he involved himself not only in the Texas fight for independence but also in the Mexican-American War. He was captured in 1842 and sent to Perote Prison in the Mexican state of Veracruz.

Juana and her son followed him as far as the town of Candela in Mexico. She waited for him there until his release after serving two years.

They returned to San Antonio, where he died a few years later. Juana then married her first husband's cousin.

In 1857, she petitioned the Texas state legislature and received a pension for the belongings she lost at the Alamo.

She died in July 1888.

Ana Esparza

Shortly after arriving at the Músquiz house with her children, Ana's husband's brother, the *soldado,* came to see her. He told her that he had requested permission from Santa Anna to find Gregorio's body. "I asked that I be allowed to take it and give it a proper burial," he said. "I did not wish to see it turned to ashes with the others." Santa Anna granted his request.

The following day at the Campo Santo cemetery, Ana and her children stood at the graveside of Gregorio while Padre Linares read a Bible passage over him.

Ana did not remarry. She died in 1847 on a ranch the family owned near San Antonio.

Thomas Jefferson Chambers

The man James Taylor held personally responsible for the murder of his father and the "legal" stealing of the family land was a supporter of Santa Anna, until the Texian victory at Gonzales. After that, it appeared evident to Chambers that the rebels might just gain independence.

He asked the Texas provisional government to appoint him a major general. In return he would raise 1,145 volunteers in the United States and return, ready to fight, by May. He used ten thousand dollars of his own money to finance his venture, to be reimbursed by the Texas government.

He did not return to Texas until June. While he did send some troops who fought at San Jacinto, they were less than half the number of volunteers he promised. He also submitted an account for $23,621. Texas approved the amount but had no money to pay him. Instead, he received 1,280 acres of land.

In 1838, he ran for the Texas senate and lost.

Though he owned much of the land in and around the town of Anuhuac on Trinity Bay, he lived in Round Point, in the very house that had belonged to the Taylor family.

Deciding to embark on a new financial scheme, he changed the name of Anuhuac to Chambersea and proceeded to sell much of his property there. Old residents of the town were not pleased.

A dispute over a three-thousand-dollar debt to one John O'Brian resulted in O'Brian obtaining a judgment against Chambers, with O'Brian receiving portions of Chambers's land on Trinity Bay, including the old Taylor place. Believing he'd been defrauded, Chambers took O'Brian to court. Losing the case, Chambers decided to act on his own, declaring, "If I cannot hold the land I claim by law, I will hold it by my rifle."

Hiding in the bushes behind a fence forty paces from the Taylor house, where O'Brian had taken up residence, Chambers ambushed him, firing both barrels of a shotgun when he came out the door. O'Brian fell dead, and a friend with him named Ferguson was grievously wounded but recovered. He identified Chambers as the assassin.

Astonishingly, Chambers was not indicted. He also regained his property. O'Brian's widow, Mary, pursued legal action against Chambers for years, but he always managed to secure continuances from the court.

After Texas was annexed in 1845, Chambers attempted to re-enter Texas politics. He was defeated for the legislature in 1849, and for the governorship in 1851 and 1853.

However, he was able to have Chambers County created in 1858. His nephew was named a county judge. The two represented the county at the Succession Convention in 1861. That same year, he lost his third try for the governorship.

When Confederate forces arrived, he allowed them to place gun batteries on his property to guard the mouth of the Trinity River, as well as his own wharf.

In 1862, he went to Richmond to request a military command. As he was unable to raise the required number of men, he was refused.

Returning to Texas, he again ran for governor. He lost.

On the night of March 15, 1865, Chambers sat with his wife and two teenage daughters in the parlor of the fine house he had built on a bluff in Anuhuac. A shotgun blast through an open window ended his life.

No arrests were made.

Moses Rose

Wanting to get far away from Santa Anna's army and avoid any Mexican patrols, Moses walked east all night. Without benefit of moonlight or torch, he encountered a massive thicket of prickly pear cactus. Numerous thorns pierced his legs and feet. But he kept walking.

Some weeks later, having walked nearly two hundred miles, Moses stumbled — lame, exhausted, and in terrible pain — into the home of old friends Mary Ann and Abraham Zuber. They spent days pulling thorns from his swollen legs and feet and treating them with salves. He related his story of leaving the Alamo to them many times, worried they might call him a coward. They did not.

Moses continued east to Nacogdoches, where he found work in a butcher shop.

Heirs of Alamo defenders sought him out for word on their loved ones as well as to appear as a witness for them before the Texas Congress in their attempts to secure land due them for their relative's service.

In 1842, he moved to Logansport, Louisiana, and died there in 1851. He never did grow back his long moustache.

Often asked why he left the Alamo, he invariably answered, "By God, I wasn't going to die!"

Questioned as to how he felt about leaving, he would say he was "the coward of the Alamo."

One time, though, a newspaper reporter asked what he thought of the men who stayed behind to fight. A sad smile crossed his face. "Ah, *oui,*" he said wistfully. "If only the emperor had had a thousand like them."

AUTHOR'S NOTE

The Alamo stands as a symbol of bravery, an icon for heroism, a salute to courage. It has also been derided as a mark of Manifest Destiny, a representation of empire building.

Over a dozen films have been made about the battle, creating myths that have, over time, become facts in the minds of many. Authors have studied the story of the Alamo — events precipitating the siege, the battle itself, and the aftermath — examining every lead, every scrap of information they could find. And the legends, tales, truths, and fictions persist. Eyewitnesses have told their sides. But, memories fade. Embellishments are added. Facts get mixed up.

And still there are questions. Did William Barrett Travis draw a line in the sand with his sword? Was David Crockett taken prisoner and executed in front of the Alamo chapel? Or was he killed during the battle at the outer west wall lunette? What happened to Jim Bowie's famous knife? How true and accurate is the diary written by Lieutenant José Enrique de la Peña, who served with General Santa Anna in Texas? How many flags flew over the fort? Which flags? Where was the flagpole located?

These questions, and more, may never be answered.

But one thing I believe is certain. Valor, blood, fear, and gumption all played significant roles on both sides in the battle.

Fact and lore abound about the Alamo. I have taken the liberty of incorporating both into this work of fiction, while trying to remain truthful to the events. David Crockett, James Bowie, and William Barrett Travis are not inventions. Neither are the three Taylor brothers, Edward, James, and George. Nor are Susannah Dickinson, her husband, Almeron Dickinson, and their daughter, Angelina; Louis "Moses" Rose; or Colonel Juan Morales. Each of them was present at the Alamo and plays a significant part in this novel.

With only a handful of exceptions, I have used actual persons who were at the Alamo during the battle. They are Gertrudis Navarro and her sister Juana Alsbury; Major Robert Evans; Lieutenant Charles Zanco;

Captain Albert Martin; James Tylee; Lieutenant James Butler Bonham; Anthony Wolf and his two sons, Nathan and Aleck; Juan Abamillo; Ana Esparza, her husband, Gregorio, and their children, Enrique, Manuel, Francisco, and Maria; Galba Fuqua; and John MacGregor. On the Mexican side of the battle were General Antonio López de Santa Anna, General Don Martín Perfecto de Cós, Colonel José Romero, Colonel Juan Almonte, Colonel José Miñon, and the brother of Gregorio Esparza, a *soldado* whose name was Francisco.

Others mentioned in this novel who actually existed, though they are peripheral to this story, are Sam Houston; Captain Theodore Dorsett, his wife, Mary, and their daughter, Amanda; Lieutenant Edward McCafferty; Amos Pollard; Tapley Holland; Major Robert Williamson; General Manuel Fernández Castrillón; General Joaquin Ramirez y Sesma; Colonel Francisco Duque; Lieutenant Colonel Ygnacio de Labastida; Joe, Travis's black slave; Anson and Elizabeth Taylor; and Thomas Jefferson Chambers.

In all cases, however, their words are mine.

The following individuals were exceedingly gracious and generous, and I am sincerely grateful, as their assistance was invaluable: Leslie Stapleton, Director, The Daughters of the Republic of Texas Library at the Alamo, San Antonio, Texas; Jackie Brookshire, Museum Assistant, Chambers County Historical Museum/Archives, Anahuac, Texas; Aquilia De La Cruz, Branch Librarian, Chambers County Library, Anahuac, Texas; and Kevin Ladd, Director, Wallisville Heritage Park, Wallisville, Texas.

The array of books and various other sources about the battle at the Alamo and those who fought there, as well as about Texas and its war for independence, is truly staggering. The sources I consulted are: *Santa Anna's Mexican Army 1821-48,* Rene Chartrand (Osprey Publishing, 2004); *A Narrative of the Life of David Crockett Written by Himself,* David Crockett (Carey, Hart & Company, 1834); *The Blood of Heroes,* James Donovan (Back Bay Books, 2012); *The Alamo Story,* J. R. Edmondson (Republic of Texas Press, 2009); *Historical Vignettes of Galveston Bay,* Jean L. Epperson (Dogwood Press, 1995); *Santa Anna of Mexico,* Will Fowler (University of Nebraska Press, 2007); *Alamo Defenders, A Genealogy: The People and Their Words,* William Groneman III (Eakin Press, 1990); *David Crockett, Hero of the Common Man,* William Groneman III

(Forge, 2005); *Eyewitness to the Alamo,* William Groneman III (Republic of Texas Press, 2001); *Texian Iliad: A Military History of the Texas Revolution, 1835–36,* Stephen L. Hardin (University of Texas Press, 1994); *The Alamo 1836: Santa Anna's Texas Campaign,* Stephen L. Hardin (Osprey Publishing 2001); *Chambers County: A Pictorial History,* Margaret S. Henson and Kevin Ladd (Donning Company, 1988); *Forging Napoleon's Grande Armée: Motivation, Military Culture, and Masculinity in the French Army, 1800–1808,* Michael J. Hughes (NYU Press, 2012); *A Time to Stand,* Walter Lord (University of Nebraska Press, 1961); *The Alamo: An Illustrated History,* George Nelson (Aldine Press, 1998); *The Alamo and the Texas War for Independence,* Albert A. Nofi (Da Capo Press, 2001); *A Line in the Sand: The Alamo in Blood and Memory,* Randy Roberts and James S. Olson (The Free Press, 2001); *Early Settlers and Indian Fighters of Southwest Texas,* Andrew Jackson Sowell (Ben C. Jones & Company, 1900); *Rangers and Pioneers of Texas,* Andrew Jackson Sowell (Shepard Bros & Company, 1884); *13 Days to Glory,* Lon Tinkle (Texas A&M University Press, 2005); *The Encyclopedia of the Mexican-American War: A Political, Social and*

Military History, Spencer C. Tucker, Editor (ABC-CLIO, 2012); "Myth and the History of the Hispanic Southwest," David J. Weber (University of New Mexico, 1988); and *The Alamo Defenders: A Critical Study of the Siege of the Alamo & the Personnel of Its Defenders,* Amelia W. Williams (Copano Bay Press, 2010).

I'm most grateful to Tiffany Schofield, senior editor at Five Star, and her splendid team for all of their tireless work. I'm also indebted to the copy editors and proofreaders for their superb expertise; in this case, Deni Dietz, Erin Bealmear, and Cathy Kulka, respectively.

I'm also very grateful to Shannon Hensley at Abrams Garfinkel Margolis Bergson, LLP, for her help and guidance.

And I thank my wife, Marilyn. Being married to a writer, she lives with the stories I tell as much as I do. As my first reader, she gives me her support and advice. I'm thankful every day for her love, understanding, patience, and humor.

Thomas D. Clagett
Santa Fe, New Mexico

ABOUT THE AUTHOR

Thomas D. Clagett spent nearly twenty years working as an assistant film editor in Hollywood. His credits include *The Two Jakes*, Jack Nicholson's sequel to *Chinatown*, and the MTM TV series *St. Elsewhere*.

His first novel, *The Pursuit of Murieta*, is a Will Rogers Medallion Award Honorable Mention winner. *Booklist* called it "A well-told, disquieting story."

West of Penance, Clagett's second novel, won the New Mexico–Arizona Book Award for best historical fiction, and the Will Rogers Medallion Award first place gold medal for inspirational fiction. He is also the author of *William Friedkin: Films of Aberration, Obsession and Reality*, about the Academy Award-winning director of *The French Connection* and *The Exorcist*.

A member of the Western Writers of

America, Clagett lives with his wife, Marilyn, and their cat, Cody, in Santa Fe, New Mexico. His website is www.thomasdclagett.com.

The employees of Thorndike Press hope you have enjoyed this Large Print book. All our Thorndike, Wheeler, and Kennebec Large Print titles are designed for easy reading, and all our books are made to last. Other Thorndike Press Large Print books are available at your library, through selected bookstores, or directly from us.

For information about titles, please call:
  (800) 223-1244

or visit our Web site at:
  http://gale.cengage.com/thorndike

To share your comments, please write:
  Publisher
  Thorndike Press
  10 Water St., Suite 310
  Waterville, ME 04901